PRAISE F(

"G.M. Ford is must reading."

—Harlan Coben

"Ford is a witty and spunky writer who not only knows his terrain but how to bring it vividly to the printed page."

—*West Coast Review of Books*

"G.M. Ford is a born storyteller."

—J.A. Jance

"He's well on his way to becoming the Raymond Chandler of Seattle."

—*Kirkus Reviews*

"G.M. Ford is, hands down, one of my favorite contemporary crime writers. Hilarious, provocative, and cool as a March night in Seattle, he may be the best-kept secret in mystery novels."

—Dennis Lehane

"G.M. Ford has a supercharged V-12 under the hood."

—Lee Child

"G.M. Ford writes the pants off most of his contemporaries."

—*Independent on Sunday*

FAMILY VALUES

OTHER TITLES BY G.M. FORD

Nameless Night

Threshold

Leo Waterman Series

Who in Hell Is Wanda Fuca?

Cast in Stone

The Bum's Rush

Slow Burn

Last Ditch

The Deader the Better

Thicker Than Water

Chump Change

Salvation Lake

Frank Corso Series

Fury

Black River

A Blind Eye

Red Tide

No Man's Land

Blown Away

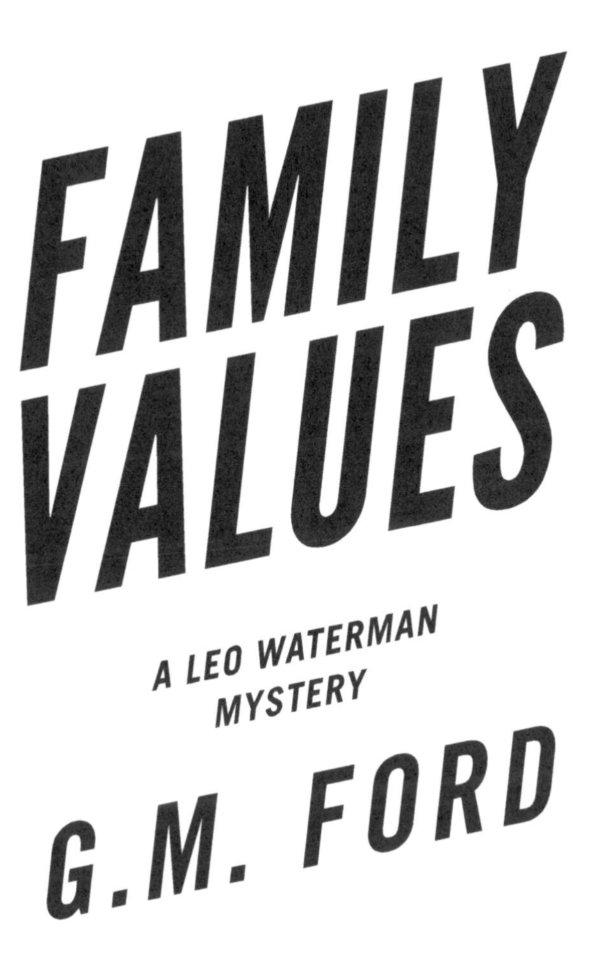

THOMAS & MERCER

This is a work of fiction. Names, characters, organizations, places, events, and incidents are either products of the author's imagination or are used fictitiously. Any resemblance to actual persons, living or dead, or actual events is purely coincidental.

Published by Thomas & Mercer, Seattle

www.apub.com

ISBN-10: 1477808973
ISBN-13: 9781477808979

Cover design by Cyanotype Book Architects

Printed in the United States of America

To A.J. Forever my friend.

Chapter 1

I hate surprises. People in party hats jumping out of closets give me the urge to smack 'em in the lip. But tonight was special, and I was making an exception to the rule. It was Valentine's Day, and I was back in Seattle a day early, so surprising Rebecca with a fistful of flowers and a box of Fran's Chocolates seemed like a nice, romantic thing to do.

I'd spent the past three days down in Mesa, Arizona, lounging around the hotel pool and selling off a couple of parcels of land I'd inherited as part of my father's estate. When things finished up a day ahead of schedule, I'd hopped the 1:25 back to Seattle, rounded up the flowers and candy, and was fighting my way through the afternoon rush hour when the steel-wool skies suddenly remembered it was February.

At first, it was a few big, sloppy drops sputtering down from the sky, clanging onto the hood of the car, splashing craters in the parking garage dust as I wheeled up Madison Street. By the time I'd crested the hill, the drops were the size of wharf rats and coming down hard enough to render my wipers spastic.

Took me twenty nervous minutes to cover the three-plus miles to Madison Park. The drumming of the rain was deafening as I pulled into the Lakefront Village parking lot. I turned off the car, cracked the window, and peeped out. It wasn't good. Along the street, the huge old rhododendron bushes cowered from the onslaught. I winced as I watched ranks of suicide raindrops spend themselves onto the shimmering asphalt.

I looked around. The only other car in the visitor's lot was a murdered-out Dodge van. Flat black everything, from roof to tires. Up where the residents parked, Rebecca's Beamer was nosed into her parking spot. I estimated I had about twenty yards to negotiate before I reached the covered walkway that shielded the condo owners and their cars from the nasty Northwest elements.

I gathered the flowers and candy, took a deep breath, and stepped out into the maelstrom. The rain was charging across the pavement in silver sheets; overhead, the wind roared through the treetops like a bullet train. I sucked air and made a dash for it.

I was making good time too, splashing along like Seabiscuit, until I dropped the damn flowers. By the time I'd retrieved the posies and waded under cover, my jacket was soaked through, and a thick rivulet of rain was rolling down my spine like a frozen ball bearing. I shuddered hard, stifled a curse, and then shuddered again.

I shook myself like a dog, made sure I had a firm grip on my romantic tribute, and started off again. Halfway down the covered walkway, I caught the silhouettes of two guys ahead in the gloom, moving my way. Another ten yards and I could make out their brown UPS uniforms, replete with those precious little shorts they wear rain or shine.

I treated them to a wry smile and a manly nod as we passed shoulder to shoulder on the walkway. Something about delivering flowers and candy in a typhoon made me feel vaguely foolish, but I shook it off and kept walking. I mean, what could those two guys say, wearing those friggin' shorts?

The far shore of Lake Washington was little more than a smear of lights. To my left, the sinuous curves of the 520 Bridge flickered through the veil of falling water. I turned right and walked three condos down. I straightened my shoulders inside my jacket, put on my best "eager young fella" look, and knocked on Rebecca's door.

Waited. Nothing. Knocked again. Nothing again. I scowled and looked to my left. The drapes were drawn. The lights were on. I knocked again. Not a peep.

I put my ear up to the door. I was listening hard when a faint whiff of something curled into my nostrils. I pulled my head back and knocked again, harder this time.

I stepped down into the shrubbery, put my face to the window, and peered between the drapes. The only things visible were a section of carpet and the back side of the kitchen island. I knocked hard on the glass and waited. Nothing moved.

I stepped back up onto the front porch and pounded on the door. Once again, no response. I pulled out my phone and dialed Rebecca's number, then leaned against the door and listened. And there it was—that song she used for a ringtone, some Patti Smith thing I hated. She had it set up to ring a couple of thousand times before it went to voicemail. I gritted my teeth and listened until it stopped.

That was the moment when the hairs on the back of my neck began to rise. As King County's medical examiner, Rebecca was perpetually on call. She went nowhere without her phone. Ever. We made jokes about how she took the damn thing to the john with her and what it was like to have to talk to other people under those unseemly circumstances. My chest began to tighten.

I set the flowers and candy on the porch, stepped back for leverage, and raised my foot. Then put it back down. I stomped around in a frustrated circle. Spent a few minutes lecturing myself. What if she was . . . ? What if . . . ? When I couldn't come up with another "what if" that made any sense at all, I reared back and gave the door all I had.

The door burst open and banged against the wall, telling me right away that the deadbolt hadn't been set—a security precaution I'd never known Rebecca to forget. Before I could move forward, a great burst of air came rushing from the interior. Cold air . . . chemical air. Bright, burning ice that bit my nostrils and gashed at my throat in the second before my screaming lungs puked it back out. Gas. Holy shit . . . gas.

I dropped to one knee. The air was better down lower but not much. "Rebecca," I croaked. "Rebecca."

And then I was moving forward: on my hands and knees for the first ten feet and then all the way down onto my belly, slithering across the carpet like a cockroach, my lungs on fire, my nose and eyes pouring down my face.

On the far side of the living room, I pushed myself to my feet, reached for the light switch, and then stopped my hand in midair as I had a sudden vision of the whole place erupting in a great ball of blue flame. I groaned and flopped back down onto the floor, where I vomited a couple of bags of airline peanuts onto the carpet and began crabbing forward on my elbows, swiveling my head as I moved along, trying to find her with eyes that felt like they were filled with splintered ice.

As I rounded the kitchen island, my hands smacked onto the tile of the kitchen floor. "Rebecca," I screamed again. Listened. And then, above the sound of my gasping breath, I heard it: a rush like water running in pipes.

I spit a mouthful of bile and looked up, my eyes so wet and glassy I couldn't focus. So I bent all the way down to the floor and wiped them with my sleeve, looked up, and everything was green. Bright green. And then I remembered the fancy French stove she'd bought a while back. A Lacanche, if I recalled. All green enamel and fancy trim. I started pushing myself toward it, the air getting viler by the foot, my lungs spitting it out as fast as I could force it in, until I made it to the far end of the kitchen and used one of the oven handles to lever myself to my knees.

It felt like somebody'd buried an ax in my forehead as I ran a hand over my face, trying to make out what it said on the stove knobs. I couldn't see, so I started turning knobs back the other way, and the rushing sound began to dissipate just as I lost my grip on the handle and flopped back to the floor.

I wanted to sleep, to close my eyes and just drift off into nothingness, but an inner voice was screaming at me to get up, to keep moving, to find Rebecca. I put my lips right down onto the tile, took in as much of a breath as my tortured lungs would allow, and forced myself upward again.

I lurched across the kitchen, threw an elbow at the window over the sink, and heard the glass explode. I felt a rush of fresh air wash across the back of my neck as I dry-heaved into the sink, so I straightened up and busted out the other half of the window, then pushed my face into the jagged opening, sucking air and coughing and sucking air and coughing until the jackhammer in my head began to quiet.

With a chest full of fresh air, I shuffled over to the guest bathroom and pushed open the door. She was lying on the floor naked, her eyes rolled back in her head and a syringe dangling from her left arm. I groaned and reached for her, terrified I was going to find her cold to the touch, but she wasn't. I put the palm of my hand on her chest. Her heart was fluttering like a breathless bird.

I grabbed her under the arms and lifted until I could feel her ragged breath on my neck. I wanted to reach down and scoop up her knees and carry her off, like in the movies, but I didn't have the strength. So I began to back out of the room, Rebecca mashed against me, weaving over the floor together like a pair of drunken tango dancers as I struggled back through the kitchen and living room and finally down over the rough concrete of the porch and out to the narrow strip of sodden grass that stood between the condos and Lake Washington, where I laid her gently on the ground.

I shouldered myself out of my coat and laid it over her. When I looked up, half a dozen of her neighbors were out on their porches, phones jammed to their ears as a chorus of sirens screeched above the drumming of the rain.

■ ■ ■

Might've been better if I'd passed out. I remember crabbing forward on my hands and knees, trying to shield her face with my body, and the sound of the rain pounding on my back as I swayed in the breeze, retching like I was trying to turn myself inside out. After that, everything seemed to happen at once.

The hands were on me, all over me, pulling me up . . . and the shouting and the voices talking to me, talking to one another. "Just relax, mister . . . Roll him over . . . Need a hand here . . . You got him, Frank? . . . One . . . two . . ." From over on my left: "We're losing her . . . No pulse, Tommy . . . No pulse . . ." And the rain, falling like mortar shells. "She's got a puncture wound . . . left arm . . . Anybody seen a syringe? . . . No pulse, Tommy . . . Take it easy, mister." And I can't sit up . . . the straps . . . there's a mask on my face. I puke into it. "Clean up his airway." Hands pulling the mask off my face, wiping my face as the rain beats down, cleaning out my nostrils. "Found this inside." I throw my eyes to the left. Little plastic syringe. Big yellow glove. Fireman. The EMT kneeling by her head. I watch him bring a finger to his mouth. "Heroin," he says. I want to tell them, No way. No way. Are you fucking crazy? But my throat won't spit out the words. "Narcan. Administering Narcan." And now there's four of them huddled over her. "We're gonna get him outta here. No pulse, Bobby." And suddenly we're rolling. Bouncing along with the rain slamming into my face. I can't sit up. "Take it easy, man. They're doing everything they can." Trying to roll myself free, thrashing with all I have left as they lift me into the back of an aid car. "Jesus, take it easy, mister." I can feel spittle running down my chin as I try to tell them, as I try to . . . and then the whoop whoop of the siren, and we're moving. The driver is talking into the radio, but I can't make out the words. The sweet air they're pumping into me cools my lungs. I'm getting light-headed. Don't want to pass out. I reach for the mask on my face. Somebody grabs my hand. Forces it down to my side. "Breathe. Breathe." And then somebody's pushing up my sleeve. "This will help you relax." And I collapse down inside myself, like one of those detonated buildings on TV: nothing but a rising cloud of dust and a sinking pile of rubble that used to be me.

■ ■ ■

I could see the purple streaks in her hair. She was standing right there, dressed all in blue, leaning over me saying something, but for the life of me I couldn't put the words together. She leaned closer. So close I could smell the mints on her breath. I watched as she reached over and picked up a blue plastic cup with a white straw. And then it clicked. It was one of those straws with wrinkles. Hospital straws. That's when it all came back to me in a rush.

I tried to speak. She brought the straw to my lips. Felt like I was washing a tennis ball down my throat.

"Easy," she said. "Easy."

"Rebecca," I rasped.

"Dr. Duvall?"

I nodded. It felt like my head was going to explode.

"Last I heard she was still in the ICU."

"Is she . . . ?" Something inside me just couldn't finish the question.

I watched as she refilled the glass and brought the straw to my lips again.

"I'm afraid that's all I know," she said. "We were busy with you."

I nodded my thanks. "Sit me up," I said. "Please."

She motorized me into an upright position.

"Where's my clothes?" I asked.

"Oh . . . I don't think . . . you've been . . ." Her eyes flicked over to the wardrobe by the bathroom door. "Are you sure?"

I nodded. She reluctantly let the safety rail down. I swung my feet over the edge and set them on the floor.

She looked dubious. "There's a couple gentlemen outside who'd like to have a word with you," she said.

I stood up. My legs felt like Jell-O. I wobbled a bit as I began to shuffle forward. She reached out and put a steadying hand on my arm. "I'm okay," I said. "Give me a few minutes to get dressed, and then send them in."

They were standing inside the door when I came out of the bathroom. Two of them. Matching gray suits, milling around like they owned the joint. Something about carrying a gun in one pocket and the power of the state in the other changes the way a person relates to the universe. For as long as I could remember, that particular sense of privilege had always pissed me off.

"Mr. Waterman?" the older cop asked. He was about forty. Short and stocky, beginnings of a wattle under his chin.

"Or what's left of him," I said as I tucked in my shirt.

The other guy looked to be fresh off the farm. Under thirty, blond, broad across the chest, and well put together. One of those guys who looked like he either had to be a cop or a football coach.

"This is Paul Nelson," the older guy said with a bob of the head toward his partner. "I'm Frank Krauss." He walked over and handed me their business cards. Investigators for the DA's office, both of them. I stuffed the cards in my pants pocket.

"We'd like to—" he started.

I cut him off. "You have any word on how my friend is doing?"

"Last I heard she hadn't come around yet," the younger guy said.

"We've got a few questions," Krauss began.

"That makes three of us then," I rasped as I zipped my pants. My throat felt as if somebody'd reamed it out with a wire brush. I shrugged myself into my damp coat.

"So you didn't have any idea that she was planning to . . ."

"To what?"

They passed a weary look. The air in the room suddenly thickened.

"To what?" I said again.

"To take her own life," Krauss said. "She hadn't said anything to—"

"Are you shitting me? Take her own life? You think she—"

"What with recent events . . . ," Nelson said.

"What events are those?" I growled.

"The charges . . . her suspension . . ."

I sidled over to the side of the bed and sat on the edge. "What the hell are you talking about? What charges? What suspension?"

They passed another one of those knowing cop looks.

"I've been out of town for a few days," I said.

"Story broke on Monday," Nelson said. "Dr. Duvall was suspended."

"For what?"

"Falsifying evidence."

"Pending a full investigation, of course," Krauss added.

I'm not often at a loss for words. Might be better if it had happened more often, but this . . . this reduced me to rubble.

"No" was all I could think to say.

"Front-page news," Krauss said.

They gave me a minute to process. Krauss broke the spell.

"So you didn't know anything about any of this?"

I shook my head. "I was down in Arizona on business. I spoke to her on Sunday. She didn't say anything . . . you know, about there being any sort of problem."

"I take it somebody down there can confirm your whereabouts."

I reached into my jacket pocket, pulled out my now-sodden boarding pass from the flight home, and held it out. Krauss walked over and took it from my hand.

"I wasn't supposed to get home from Arizona until tomorrow night," I said. "We finished up early, so I thought . . . you know . . . It was Valentine's Day. Thought I'd surprise her."

"The flowers and candy," Nelson said.

"Yeah."

Krauss was eyeballing the boarding pass. "First class," he said.

"Look to you like I'd fit in coach?" I asked.

I slid myself off the bed. My knees were very nearly knocking. "Listen . . . ," I began. "I get it. I can see how this could look like a suicide attempt. I don't believe it, but I can see how *you* might. But . . . you gotta listen to me. I've known Rebecca Duvall since I was ten years old. There is no straighter arrow on the planet. She's a by-the-book, by-the-numbers kind of person. There's no way she would ever even consider harming herself, and there's no way she would ever falsify anything. None. If—"

Krauss cut me off at the knees. "It's not just one instance," he said. "The investigation's been ongoing for the past several months. From what I hear, they've found multiple instances where forensic paperwork has simply disappeared."

"No fucking way," I said.

"Way," Nelson said quickly. "The DA's losing his mind. At this point, if he had a gun, he'd swallow it. The way this plays out, there's going to be a number of past cases called into question. Before this is over, every asshole her work ever helped convict is going to be wanting a new trial."

"And will probably get it," Krauss added. "I'm told they've got independent labs going back over her work and that it's not looking good for her."

I wanted to lose it. To scream at them. To make them understand what a crock of shit this all was. But, instead, I bit my tongue and got a grip on myself. "Unless I'm under arrest, I'm going downstairs to the ICU. Am I under arrest?"

Neither of them said a thing.

My resolve was steadier than my legs, but I managed to motor over to the door and pull it open. "I'm in the phone book," I said as I slipped out into the corridor.

■ ■ ■

Since my trust fund had finally found its way into my pocket a couple of years back, I'd pretty much given up my private investigator business—a life change that, not surprisingly, meant I spent a lot less time in emergency rooms than I used to. I'd forgotten how the air always felt like it was tinged with adrenaline, as if the split-second, life-and-death decisions they were forced to make every day somehow lingered for eternity just beneath the ceiling.

I was twenty feet down the hallway, trying to remember which way to go, when an orderly came jogging around the corner from my left. I stuck out an arm. He skittered to a stop.

"Duvall," I said. "Rebecca Duvall."

"Heroin overdose?"

"Yeah," I said.

"I think she's in number three."

That's all he said before sprinting off down the hall. I leaned back against the wall, forced several breaths into my lungs, and then continued on.

I made a couple of wrong turns before I found room three. All I could see through the window were heads. Four of them, working on whomever was hidden behind the privacy screens. I stood there with my nose pressed to the glass for what seemed like an eternity before one of the masked medics caught a glimpse of me.

A minute passed before he stepped back from the others and started my way. He pulled his surgical mask down with one hand and pulled open the door with the other. He was about my age. Maybe six feet tall. Bald as an egg, with big, strong-looking hands.

"You the significant other?" he asked.

"I am."

"You the one who found her?"

I said I was. "How's she doing?"

"She's breathing on her own," he said.

"So . . . she's gonna be all right."

He wagged a finger in my face. "I didn't say that," he corrected. "Her vital signs are improving, but she still hasn't regained consciousness." He reached out and put one of those big hands on my shoulder. "You have any idea how this happened?" he asked.

"No," I said. "The cops are treating it like a suicide attempt."

He pulled his hand back and shrugged. "The puncture in her left arm is the only needle mark anywhere on her body. Her lungs are clear and her sinus passages show no evidence of drug use, so it's a good bet she's not a heroin addict."

"Not a chance."

"So if it's not a suicide attempt, what is it? Either she did it to herself, or somebody did it to her."

"I don't know."

He looked dubious. "She was under a lot of pressure."

I didn't want to hear it, so I changed the subject. "So what's her prognosis?"

"We wait and see. She stopped breathing for quite a while. It's going to depend upon how long her brain went without oxygen. She'll either come out of it, or she'll remain in a persistent vegetative state, in which case we'll have to consult the next of kin as to what to do next."

I stifled a sigh. "I guess I'll hang around and . . ."

He was shaking his head. "We're moving her to critical care. There's no place to wait in the CC unit."

The stifled sigh suddenly escaped.

"Listen, Mr. . . ."

"Waterman. Leo Waterman."

He pointed over my shoulder. "Leave your contact info at the nurses' station. We'll let you know the minute anything changes."

I nodded wearily. "Thanks," I said. "For all you've done for her."

He shrugged. "You want to thank somebody, you thank that EMT who administered the Narcan. They tell me he used to have a drug problem himself, so he knew what heroin tasted like. He's the one who saved her life. Without him, we wouldn't be having this discussion."

The double doors bumped open. I watched as they wheeled her into the corridor. The collection of tubes coming out of her face forced me to look away. My gut was churning like a cement mixer full of auto parts. I must have wavered, because he reached out again and put his hand on my shoulder. "You okay?"

"I'll survive," I growled.

He turned and followed the gurney down the hall.

■ ■ ■

The sun was winking over the Cascades, backlighting the jagged spires of downtown Seattle, as I rolled slowly up Magnolia Boulevard with all the windows down. My head felt as if it had been stuffed with fiberglass insulation, and every muscle in my body ached. All I wanted out of life, at that point, was to lie down in my own bed and close my eyes.

Except . . . except that the front gate was wide open. I pulled to the curb and braked to a stop fifty feet short of the opening. Took a minute to wade through my mental swamp, but my memory was still in possession of a snapshot of the gate rolling closed behind me. Every hair on my body would have stood at attention, except the follicles were too damn tired.

I dropped the car into reverse, crimped the wheel, and backed into my next-door neighbor's driveway. The Morrisons were a kindly old couple who owned houses all over the world and thus were hardly ever home. Especially not in the winter.

I got out of the car, pocketed the keys, and walked down their driveway, moving left so I could slip between the north wall of their garage and my old man's stone wall, which separated their property from mine. When I was younger, this was how I used to sneak out after he'd closed the gate for the night. About a third of the way down, I stepped up onto the roof of an old derelict doghouse that had been there for as long as I could remember. The ancient, weather-beaten roof boards groaned under my weight. I levered myself onto the top of the wall, mustered my resolve, and slid into nothingness.

I landed like a sack of feed. I stifled a groan as I swept my eyes back and forth across the lawn. Nothing was moving, so I pushed myself to my feet and hurried across the matted grass to the garage, where I pulled out my keys, let myself in the side door, and closed it softly behind me.

I stood with my back against the door. Listening. Letting my eyes adjust to the darkness. Slowly, the familiar cabinets and workbenches that lined the garage walls began to come into view.

I tiptoed across the empty garage to the tall metal cabinet looming along the north wall. Took me some fumbling, but I eventually found the correct key on my ring, slipped it into the ancient cabinet, and eased the door open. I leaned in and felt around until my hand hit the old army blanket in the back corner.

I pulled the bundle from the cabinet, carried it over to the workbench on the rear wall, and rolled it open. Inside was my granddad's old Ithaca double-barreled 12 gauge. The one he supposedly used for goose hunting in British Columbia. At the bottom of the blanket bundle was a half-empty box of shells. Old-time lead shot. I thumbed the release, cracked the gun, slid in a couple of shells, and then jammed the rest of the ammo into my coat pockets.

I must have looked like Elmer Fudd out duck hunting as I crept up the flagstone walkway to the back door. Through the screen, I could see the kitchen door hanging open. I eased back the screen door, stuck my foot into the crack, and then stepped up onto the back porch with the shotgun waving out in front of me like a flag.

Took me the better part of twenty minutes, but I went through the rest of the house, room by room, upstairs and down, until I was satisfied that I didn't have any unwanted company. They'd opened every cupboard and drawer. Spread the contents all over the place like they were looking for something, but as far as I could tell, nothing was missing. By the time I made it back to the kitchen I was madder than a bipolar terrier.

I worked off some of the pent-up anger by retrieving my car from the Morrisons' driveway, closing the gate behind me, and locking the car in the garage. Once I'd hauled my gear inside, I was pretty much back to being exhausted, except for the part of me that was still seriously pissed off.

Whoever had rummaged through the place hadn't even bothered being covert about it. They'd gone through everything I owned and hadn't given a rat shit whether I knew it or not. That arrogance stuck in my throat like a fish bone.

I undressed in the laundry room. Before throwing my jeans into the washer, I went through the pockets. That's when I came across the pair of business cards the cops had given me at the hospital. A twenty-watt bulb went off somewhere in my head. Way I saw it, when it came to arrogance, the cops were a tough act to follow.

Stark naked, I padded down the hall to my bedroom, where I pulled my bathrobe from the closet and slipped it on. I sat on the edge of the bed and made a few calls. Nothing new from the hospital, so I dialed again and made arrangements to have Rebecca's kitchen window and front door fixed. Then I called her condo association office, who assured me they'd keep an eye on things until everything was shipshape. All the while I was talking, my eyes kept flicking over to those two cop business cards on the nightstand. I dialed the number on Frank Krauss's card. The operator patched me through.

"Krauss," he answered.

"Leo Waterman," I said.

I could hear him breathing into the phone.

"What can I do for you, Mr. Waterman?" he asked finally.

"Did you guys go through my house?"

Another breathy pause ensued.

"You mean, like, did we search it?"

"Yeah."

"If we searched your house, there'd be several copies of the search warrant somewhere where you could find them."

I started to say something, but he cut me short.

"This isn't the Wild West anymore, Mr. Waterman," he said. "If I wanted a search warrant for your house, I could have one in less than an hour." He gave it a minute to sink in and then said, "I hear they're going to indict Dr. Duvall on Thursday. Assuming she's still among us, of course."

"Thanks for sharing," I snapped.

I thought maybe I heard him chuckle. "Anything else I can do for you?"

"No . . . I guess not."

Click.

In disgust, I flipped the phone onto the bed. Krauss was right. I wasn't thinking clearly. The cops would have done it by the book.

The phone rang. And then again. I heaved a sigh big enough to fill a hot-air balloon, turned around, and picked it up. Oh joy. No caller ID.

"Yeah" was the best I could manage.

The voice sounded like a space-movie robot. Whoever was on the other end was using one of those gizmos that electronically alters your voice. "One o'clock. South 116th Street where it dead-ends at the river; and make damn sure you don't have any company."

That was it. Whoever it was broke the connection.

I sat on the edge of the bed for a full five minutes, running the possibilities around my fevered brain, but everywhere I looked just led to another question. This thing with Rebecca. Somebody searching my house. Phone calls to meet in out-of-the-way places. Hard as I tried, none of it made any sense to me.

What I was sure of was that I was going to have to show up for the mysterious rendezvous. Could be it was a wild-goose chase. Could be somebody wanted me dead. Could be a lot of things . . . But I was going.

■ ■ ■

I showed up twenty minutes early, left the car three blocks away in the parking lot of Winters Wholesale Plumbing, and then walked the rest of the way, weaving in and out and around buildings and storage yards, keeping an eye peeled for anything that looked out of place. I had a Walther PPS semiautomatic .40 caliber stuffed under my belt at the small of my back. The way I saw it, when you had this many unanswered questions, it was better to be safe than sorry.

Last night's rain had turned the potholes into ponds. Keeping my feet dry took a lot of cutting back and forth. By the time I made it down to the river, my lungs felt like I'd run a marathon on Mars.

I'm sure that somewhere in east King County, five thousand feet up Blowout Mountain, the Duwamish River begins as a shimmering silver trickle. Up there, in the lush, pine-scented forest, the water is probably as clean and fresh as a Perrier commercial.

Fifty miles later, it's not even a river anymore. The last five miles or so before it dumps into Elliott Bay are now known as the Lower Duwamish Waterway, lest you confuse it with an actual river and do something suicidal like drink it or dive in.

Here at the foot of South 116th Street, a couple of miles short of downtown Seattle, the water was the color of used motor oil and smelled a lot like something's ass. I picked my way through the rubble and litter over to a big pile of old truck tires somebody'd dumped onto the bank. I backed myself into the pile, pulled the Walther out of my belt, slipped it into my coat pocket, and settled down to wait.

He was ten minutes late. I heard him coming along the bank. The sound of the black mud sucking at his shoes. I pulled the semiautomatic from my coat pocket, leaned back into the tires, and waited. The footsteps stopped. I held my breath. The deep rumble of an engine wafted in on the breeze. Out on the waterway, a yellow-and-blue tugboat motored slowly into view, and then the gravel barge it was towing meandered by.

"Waterman. That you behind the tires?"

The voice startled me. I brought the weapon up by my right ear.

"Waterman," the voice said again. Second time was the charm. Suddenly I knew who it was. I pushed myself out of the steel-belted mountain and stepped into view.

He was a ferret-faced little runt with one of the worst comb-overs I'd ever laid eyes on. Timothy Eagen was also a very savvy lieutenant in the Seattle Police Department and my longtime rival for Rebecca's affections.

"Why all the cloak-and-dagger?" I asked.

"There's no cameras down this part of the river," he said. "Damn near the only place in the city these days where you're not on CCTV."

I slipped the Walther back into my belt and walked down the embankment.

"I take it you're not anxious to be caught on camera with me."

"You're a quick one, you are."

"So . . . wadda you want?"

He wiped the corners of his mouth and stared off into space. "I hear you saved her bacon last night."

I shrugged. "Right place, right time."

"Such modesty."

"Humble are us."

"Your name came up at a senior staff meeting yesterday."

"How's that?"

"The powers that be figure you're a good bet to stick your nose into this thing with Rebecca. They're planning on clapping your big ass in jail the minute you show your face anywhere near an ongoing investigation."

I started to say something, but he waved me off. "Lotta important people in this town are still pissed off about how much of the city's money you ended up with."

"Lotta important people are gonna have to get over it."

He moved up the bank so our eyes would be level. "I'm hearing they got Rebecca dead to rights on this thing."

"It's horseshit," I said.

He shook his head. I could tell; he wasn't sure. Cops live in a black-and-white world. Ambiguity makes them nervous. "I asked some questions," he said. "From what I've heard . . ." He cut the air with the side of his hand. "I'm hearing they could convict her right now of gross dereliction of duty. There's evidence files missing. We're talking capital cases here. We keep everything in capital cases until somebody either throws the switch on the perp or he runs completely out of appeals. There's important paperwork missing. They're telling me there's an obvious pattern of at least dereliction, if not outright falsification."

"That why you called me?" I asked. "To share this shit?"

"I called you because I'm up in the air over this damn thing." He shuffled around in a tight circle. "I'm not used to shit like this."

"More than a little out of character for Rebecca, don't you think?"

"Penitentiary's full of people did things out of character," he snapped.

"Somebody tried to kill her last night."

He shook his comb-over. "DA's calling last night a suicide attempt."

"My ass."

In this part of the world the DA was actually the PA, or prosecuting attorney, but old habits die hard. Everybody still uses DA. A toothsome clotheshorse named Paul Woodward had held down the job for the past seven years or so. All show, no go. Only thing Woodward knew for sure was where the camera was.

Eagen jammed his hands into his coat pockets. Looked me hard in the eye. "Woodward's playing this thing real close to the vest. SPD's not in the loop."

"I met a couple of his minions last night."

"From what I hear, the investigation's been active for a while now. What started it was that Kevin Delaney filed another appeal. Wanted his genetic material retested by an independent lab. The court said he had that right, so they went looking for his file and couldn't find it.

None of the precincts had it. According to records, the files were all at the medical examiner's office. So they start going through every felony case she's handled for the past five years and find a bunch of other files have somehow grown legs and walked off. Total of five whole case files have apparently disappeared. If this shit holds water, there'll be enough reasonable doubt floating around to raise the *Titanic*. There's multiple murder convictions at risk here, man."

"I need to know which files are missing."

He was making faces before the words were out of my mouth. "No way I can be seen working on this." He shooed the thought away like a fly. "All the ducks are lined up on this one. The mayor, the commissioner, the AG, the DA, all of 'em. Full cover-your-ass mode. Nary the cheek in sight. Anything I do, I'll have to do on the sly, which will take longer and just naturally be less reliable."

I held up a hand. "Let's assume that Rebecca is being set up."

He winced and rolled his eyes. "I'm not much on conspiracies, man." He waved a disgusted hand. "Coincidences neither. If it looks like a duck and quacks like a duck, it's generally a duck." He pinned me with an angry glare. "Somebody wanting to fuck with you—that I could see. Easy. But not her. She don't have that knack for making enemies like you do."

"It's genetic," I allowed.

He shook his head. "The brass is right about you. You're just the kind of asshole who's not gonna leave this to the authorities." His thin face took on a pained expression. "I'll help if I can, but it's gotta be big-time under the radar. I get caught sticking my nose in this, my ass is grass."

I kept my mouth shut. The cop part of him was telling him she was guilty as charged. Another part of him thought maybe the whole thing just didn't smell right. Way I figured it, ambivalent allies were better than no allies at all, so I just stood there and listened to the carcinogenic waves lapping the mud.

He checked his watch. "I've got a meeting," he said. "I'll see what I can find out, but don't hold your breath." He dug around in his pants pocket. Came out with a wrinkled piece of paper and handed it to me. Phone number. "It's a throwaway," he said. "Buy yourself a gross of them. You need me, call that number and give me the numbers of your whole batch. Then trash the one you used and keep trashing them every time."

I nodded.

He turned his collar up, poked his nose into the wind, and sloshed off down the riverbank.

▪ ▪ ▪

Looking for a shortcut to my car, I mamboed into a narrow alley that ran between a razor-wired storage yard and The Ludlow Lumber Company. I was busy checking my phone for messages, so I got a dozen paces into the alley before I looked up and saw the truck. UPS. Big Brown. "The World Is Our Parking Lot," jammed hard against the brick building on the right, making it so I was going to have to turn sideways and inch my way past on the driver's side.

I took another step and . . . bingo! It hit me like a pie in the face. One of those times when you wonder how you could have been so goddamn stupid, even though you long since knew the answer to that question. The truck. Those huge brown pachyderms that park wherever the hell they want—there was no truck! Last night at Rebecca's joint. Those two guys in UPS uniforms. There was no UPS truck! The only other car in the lot was that black van, and United Parcel Service doesn't deliver things in murdered-out Dodge vans.

I felt like smacking myself in the side of the head but resisted the impulse. Instead, I closed my eyes and tried to conjure their faces. White guys. Both over six feet tall. One was darker than the other, with hairy legs and a big Fu Manchu mustache. The other guy was a complete blank to me. Everything else was wind, water, and gas.

My shortcut turned out to be wishful thinking. Took me a full twenty minutes of bobbing and weaving around chain-link fences to make it back to my car. By the time I hauled myself up into the seat, I'd broken into a full sweat and was pretty much out of gas. My body felt like I'd been threshed and baled.

I drove to the Walgreens on Rainier Avenue South. I used the ATM, so I could pay in cash, and then bought myself half a dozen disposable phones. The kind where you don't have to sign up for a plan. Took me the better part of thirty minutes to get six different numbers set up and running, at which point I stepped out onto the sidewalk, found the piece of paper in my pocket, and used one of them to call the number Eagen had given me. It went right to voicemail. I recited the phone numbers of the other five disposables, hung up, walked over to the nearest storm drain, removed and pocketed the SIM card before I dropped the phone onto the pavement, stomped it to rubble, and then kicked the remains down the drain.

I climbed into the car, threw the bag of phones on the passenger seat, and fought the building traffic all the way over the hill and down into Madison Park.

The contractors had the front door back in place and were in the process of replacing the kitchen window. Boris, the foreman, handed me a new set of door keys and assured me that they'd stay at it until the place was buttoned up tight, which, as nearly as he could tell, was likely to be sometime tomorrow afternoon. I thanked him and headed for the master bedroom, where I gathered up an armload of Rebecca's clothes, shoes, and anything else I could think of. Realizing there was no way I could carry all of it to my car, I lumbered back into the kitchen, found a big plastic bag under the sink, and stuffed it all inside.

I had the bag thrown over my shoulder like a deranged Father Christmas and was easing out through the freshly painted doorway when I nearly ran headlong into a millennial in a tight blue suit coming the other way.

"Oh . . . excuse me," he mumbled.

He had one of those modern escaped-mental-patient hairdos. Everything gelled straight up, like he'd been left hanging by his feet overnight.

"What can I do for you?" I asked.

He pulled a folder out from under his arm. "I'm from the property management company." He made an expansive gesture. "We manage this property for the Lakefront Village Condo Association. And you would be?"

"I would be a friend of the owner."

He pulled some sort of form from the folder. "I'm here to deliver this," he said, pushing it toward me.

"What's that?" I asked without extending a hand.

"A notification," he said.

"Of what?"

"That we . . . the company, that is . . . considering"—he checked the form—"considering that the company considers Rebecca Duvall to be in violation of the bylaws of the association—"

I took a step forward and got right into his wheelhouse. "What bylaws are those?" I asked.

He began to stammer. "Her . . . the . . . she . . . there's a personal conduct clause."

"This property management company of yours."

"What about it?"

"How's the medical insurance?" I asked, taking another step forward, chest bumping him down off the porch.

He stumbled backward and began to scuttle up the sidewalk like a beached crab.

His mouth opened a couple of times, but nothing came out. I stood on the porch and watched until he was out of sight, then fumed my way back to the parking lot.

I'd no sooner buckled up and started the car again when my phone began chirping like a crazed canary. I fished it out of my pocket and pushed buttons until I figured out it was a text. All it said was: HARBORVIEW HOSPITAL. I groaned out loud, flipped the phone onto the passenger seat, and dropped the car into gear.

■ ■ ■

Sometimes you just know. It's not like the sight of police cars at Harborview is unusual or anything. Quite the contrary. Harborview is the primary trauma center for the area. You get shot seven times holding up a Circle K, they send you to Harborview. You extrude yourself through the windshield of a smart car, they send you to Harborview. There are cop cars parked all over the place, all the time.

But something about the haphazard cluster around the front entrance, doors flung open, light bars painting the front of the building blue and red. Something sent my stomach tumbling in the direction of my shoes. Whatever was going on, was going on inside the building, and it wasn't good.

I wedged my car into the fire lane, jumped out, and ran for the door. I made it down the elevator and as far as the ICU waiting room before a pair of SPD uniforms stepped into my path and brought me to a screeching halt. Through the small window in the door, I could see officers sweeping the area, zigzagging back and forth between the rooms, assault rifles thrust before them like spears.

"This area's closed," the one on the left said.

The other one held out a gloved hand. "Lemme see some ID."

That's when the first cop tried to move me over toward the corner and out of the doorway. I was reaching for my wallet when he slipped an arm around my waist and, as luck would have it, put his big hand squarely on the Walther semiautomatic tucked in my belt.

In a single motion, he jerked the gun from my waistband and slammed me face-first into the wall. I put my hands on top of my head and left them there. I was pretty sure the cold, hard thing pressing against the back of my head wasn't a fountain pen.

"Spread 'em! Spread 'em!" one of them screamed in my ear while the other used the side of his foot to kick my legs apart.

"I've got a license for that piece," I said.

"Shut up," the cop bellowed in my ear.

"It's in my wallet over there on the floor."

"I told you to shut up."

"In the folding money section," I added.

"Gimme your hands . . . one at a time."

When I left them laced on top of my head, he grabbed my right hand and wrenched it down behind my back like he was trying to break it off. Same with the left. The handcuffs were cold. The hookup was tight enough to stop the flow of blood. They forced me to my knees. "Don't move," one of them yelled.

"What's going on here, officers?" a third voice piped in.

"Need you to keep back, doctor. Tactical's still clearing the unit."

"But I know this man," the voice said.

"Excuse me?"

"I know this man."

I looked back over my shoulder. It was the ICU doctor from last night.

"He was carrying a gun."

"For which I have a permit in my wallet," I said.

"Weeeell?" the doctor said.

They took their sweet-ass time about it. They found my carry permit, read it thirty or forty times, and then called it in just to make sure it wasn't bogus. Then they checked to see if I perchance had any outstanding warrants. Their disappointment was palpable. Only then did they bother to unhook me from the handcuffs and give me back my gun.

I was about to get shitty with them, but the doctor read my mind. He put one of those big hands on my shoulder and steered me down the hallway to the nurses' station.

"What's going on in there?" I asked. "Is it—"

"No," he said quickly. "Not Ms. Duvall."

Felt like somebody'd lifted a Subaru off my chest.

"She woke up. We moved her up to the fourth floor."

"Well . . . what's all that SWAT team crap about?"

"Someone attacked an ICU patient. Killed her, I'm afraid. And severely injured one of our orderlies in the process."

The great weight returned to my chest. "'Her,' you said?"

"Yes . . . why?"

"What happened?"

"As nearly as the police can tell, two men entered her room and turned off her ventilator." He heaved a sigh, then shook his head. "Apparently one of our orderlies responded to the ventilator alarm and was stabbed several times. He's in surgery right now."

My body was vibrating like a tuning fork. I tried to keep the question nonchalant.

"What room was she in?"

"The murdered woman?"

I nodded. I had that picture of Rebecca being wheeled out of the ICU welded in my brain somewhere. I could envision the oxygen mask and all those tubes coming out of her face. Her own mother wouldn't have recognized her under all that medical paraphernalia. My guess was that the intruders had the same problem.

"Why . . . number three." He picked up on my vibe. "Oh . . . I see where you're going. Yes . . . quite a coincidence," he said with a grim smile. "Quite fortunate your friend woke up when she did."

"Fortunate," I repeated. "Yeah . . . very fortunate."

■ ■ ■

She was asleep, and I was thankful. I hadn't decided whether to tell her what I was thinking or wait until she was on her feet and out of here, which would have been tough, because she always knew when I was holding something back. It was like she had some kind of Leo bullshit radar. No matter how I sliced it, it looked to me as if somebody was determined to kill her. First time, they tried to make it look like a suicide. Second time, they didn't give a shit how it looked as long as she ended up dead.

Had to have something to do with the missing files that got her suspended. Somebody didn't want her around to dispute the accusations. If I hadn't shown up last night, her suicide would have sealed her guilt. Nobody would have bothered looking any further. She got caught. She couldn't face it. She opted out. End o' story. Bunch of jerks get a get-out-of-jail-free card and life in Amazonville goes on.

Now . . . Now it was another matter. If they'd tried to kill her twice, there was no reason to assume they wouldn't try again. On the contrary: I figured you could pretty much make book on the fact that these people weren't going away anytime soon. First thing I needed to deal with was how to keep her safe.

For about three seconds, I considered going to the cops. Then I had a spasm of lucidity. There was no way they were going to believe what I was thinking, and, even if they did, all they'd do was put somebody on her door for a couple of days, and then, before you knew it, Officer Friendly was gonna be needed someplace else, and we'd be back where we'd started.

No . . . I needed somebody I could trust, and, due to a misspent youth that had lasted well into middle age, I had a real good idea where to find just such a person.

I eased myself out the door and walked down to the fourth-floor waiting area. The place was deserted. Nothing but me and three dozen dog-eared magazines. I picked a chair where I could see the door to Rebecca's room. I sat there with my phone in my hand, trying to come up with a viable alternative to making the call I was thinking about making. Nothing came to mind.

It wasn't a number I kept stored on my phone. Despite the fact that I'd known him for most of my life, Joey Ortega wasn't someone whose personal cell phone number I wanted to have in my possession when the roll was called up yonder, so I kept it spread out over several old business cards in my wallet. Two numbers here, one there, three on the next. Lay the cards out in reverse alphabetical order and you had Joey's number.

I hadn't needed his services for a number of years, and we sure didn't run in the same social circles, but Joey and I were joined in a way that people with the same last names often aren't. Joey's father, Frankie Ortega, had been my father's chief leg breaker and bagman for thirty-five years.

Joey Ortega and I used to play in my father's backyard on summer days while Frankie and my old man hatched their schemes inside the house. We even double-dated a couple of times. The toothsome Lombardi sisters, Connie and Donna.

Unlike me, however, Joey had followed in his father's footsteps. While Frankie had handled his own wet work, Joey outsourced. All Joey did these days was manage a dozen strip clubs and casinos scattered around the Pacific Northwest. At least that's what he told the cops and the IRS. Truth be told, he had his finger in every illegal enterprise in the region. Women, illegal gambling, fake green cards, dope . . . you name it, and Joey was getting his cut.

I spread the business cards out on the chair seat next to me, shuffled them around a bit, and dialed the number. Somebody picked up but didn't say anything.

"I need to talk to Joey," I said.

Nothing.

"Tell him it's Leo."

I heard the sound of someone walking away from the phone. Then nothing for a minute or two, then, "Been a long time."

"Too long," I said.

We did this dance every time I called.

"To what do I owe the honor?" he asked.

"I've got a big problem," I said.

"Tell me about it."

I did. Everything I knew so far.

"Takes big stones to walk into a hospital in broad daylight and off somebody."

"That's why I need a babysitter," I said. "Whoever did this is either desperate, crazy, or both."

"I saw in the *Times* where your girlfriend got suspended."

"It's bullshit," I said.

He didn't believe it but said nothing.

"Howsabout it?" I pressed.

"I might know somebody."

"Right now she's in Harborview. After that, probably at my place. I'm gonna need him till this thing is over."

"They tell me you finally came into your old man's pile."

"Yup."

"Gabe's a thousand a day, plus expenses."

"Done."

"We'll settle up afterward."

"So Gabe will be here when?"

"What room?"

"Four oh eight."

"An hour tops."

"Thanks."

"You need anything else, give me a jingle."

I assured him I would.

■ ■ ■

Forty minutes, actually. Rebecca was still zonked out. I'd pulled the faux-leather chair over by the window and was gazing mindlessly out over the newly refurbished Yesler Terrace neighborhood when the door eased open.

Before I'd moved back into the family manse, I'd lived up on Capitol Hill for a decade or so. That's where I discovered something about myself that I hadn't known before. I'm a classifier. I look at something and just naturally begin to find a slot for it. Ugly car. Good-looking woman. Tough-looking dude. Runt. That sort of thing. Everything's got a slot.

What I discovered was, when it came to people, my unconscious classification system began with gender. I found this out when a business in my neighborhood hired a person whose gender was a complete mystery to me.

As a result, I found myself at a loss. I'd go to another, longer, checkout line just so my brain didn't have to deal with the accursed uncertainty. Not because I didn't approve, but because my psyche didn't have a plan in place to deal with somebody I couldn't classify.

So when the door opened and Gabe stepped into the room, I sunk into full mouth-breather mode. Gabe was maybe five ten. Stocky. Within spitting distance of two hundred pounds. Old-fashioned crew cut. Carrying a black leather Gladstone bag. Walked like a man but looked like maybe it was a woman. My brain began singing that old Kinks song about Lola . . . L-O-L-A, Lola.

"You Gabe?"

"That's me," Gabe said.

"Joey fill you in?"

"Says there might be a couple hitters trying to take her out."

"They damn near got it done . . . twice."

"Not gonna happen while I'm here."

Normally, I would have questioned his or her bona fides, but Gabe came from Joey Ortega, so I had no doubt he or she was up to the task.

I stood up, pulled one of my old business cards out of my wallet, wrote my cell number on the back, and handed it over.

"Call me when she wakes up."

Gabe pocketed the card, walked around me, and sat down in the chair. I watched as he or she shed the coat, pulled out what looked like a GLOCK 9, slipped it between the fabric folds, and leaned back in the seat.

"You need anything before I go?" I asked.

"I'm good" was the answer. "I get hungry, I'll order out."

I stood in the doorway for an extra beat or two. Gabe leaned back into the chair and read my mind.

"Somethin' you want to ask me?"

"No," I lied.

Gabe smiled. "Does it matter?"

I thought about it. "No," I said finally. "I guess not."

"If you're lookin' for a pronoun, I prefer *they*."

"They? Like plural?"

"It's like Walt Whitman said: *there are multitudes of me*."

I pulled open the door, stepped partway into the hall, and then looked back. "Sounds like you've got a tapeworm," I said with a grin.

■ ■ ■

Nothing like getting back to your car and finding a ticket on the windshield. A hundred and fifty-nine bucks for leaving it in the fire lane. Matter of life and death, you say? They could give a rip. Just make damn sure we get paid. And promptly too. And if you want to pay over the Internet—you know, make it so no human being has to actually do anything—that'll be an extra four bucks. Convenience charge, you know.

I was sitting there stewing over the infamy of it all when the phone began to ring. I pulled my cell out of my coat pocket, but it wasn't lit.

I pushed the button. Nada. I shook it. Nothing. Another ring. Still no light on the phone. And then it hit me.

I reached over, grabbed the bag of throwaways on the passenger seat, and dumped them out. Another two rings before I found one that was lit up. I got there just in time to hear the break in the connection.

I checked voicemail. It was Eagen with his Robby the Robot contraption.

"There's five files they can't find. Kevin Delaney, Terrence Poole, Willard Frost, Gilberto Duran, and Lamar Hudson. Gone with the fucking wind." Click.

I wrote down what he'd said, then checked the mirrors, removed the SIM card from the phone, dropped it in my pocket, and got out of the car. I placed the phone behind the rear wheel, climbed in, and backed over it on my way out of the parking lot.

I pointed the car downhill, feathering the brakes all the way to Western Avenue, where I turned right and headed north toward Ballard and points beyond. What I needed now was everything I could get on Willard Frost. As luck would have it, I knew just how to make that happen.

Overhead, fluffy, white clouds marched across the sky like a ghostly train as I blew through Belltown and out onto Elliott Avenue, rolling past the steel-and-glass techno temples that lined the shores of Puget Sound these days.

Fifteen minutes later, I stepped out of the car. The wind had grown colder. I hunched my shoulders and stepped up onto Carl's front porch.

A while back, a couple of goons had tried to hammer Carl's head flat, so these days the place was buckled up like Fort Knox. Burglar bars covered every downstairs window, and you'd need a bulldozer to get through the steel front door.

I rang the bell and listened to the whir of the camera. Ten seconds later, the door buzzed, and I stepped inside. The place smelled like nobody'd opened a window in four or five years, which probably wasn't too far from the truth.

Twenty years ago, Carl Cradduck had been a famous battlefield photographer. A real name. Coupla Pulitzer nominations, a regular in *Time*, *Newsweek*, *Life*. Five years in Vietnam without a scratch, and he kept rolling—right up until Bosnia, September 1993, when a hunk of shrapnel insisted he start doing his rolling in a chair. Which he did, with nary a bump, putting his photographic chops to use building a highly successful surveillance business. For going on twenty years, Carl and his guys handled all my peeper work.

The advent of no-fault divorce was even worse news for the surveillance industry than it was for the private eye trade, and Carl wanted no part of industrial espionage, so Cradduck Data Retrieval was born. Now he was a skip tracer par excellence—the scourge of fled felons, freeloaders, and deadbeat dads. If he couldn't find you, you weren't there.

He came rolling out of the kitchen in his mechanized wheelchair. Looked like he'd been wearing the same set of clothes since early in the Truman administration.

"Where the hell have you been?" he demanded.

"Arizona," I said. "I was late to the fair."

"What else is new?"

I told him the story as I knew it so far. Flowers and candy, UPS guys and gas, the break-in at my house, and somebody killing the wrong woman in intensive care. How the cops didn't want to hear about it. Calling Joey. Gabe showing up. All of it.

His face took on a pained expression. "You sure about this?" he asked.

"About what?"

"About your girlfriend."

I started to protest, but he cut me off. "I been following this thing with Rebecca in the papers. The DA's makin' a whole lotta noise about this thing. The kinda noise they only make when they've got a slam dunk. You know—regular case, they don't want to give the defense anything they can use, so they clam up. But when they've got a sure thing, that's when you see 'em on the news making hay for the next election. And that, my old buddy, is what I'm seeing now." He showed his palms to the ceiling. "What if . . . ?"

"What if what?"

"What if she's got something going on in her life that you don't know a damn thing about?" he asked. "What if she really did all this shit they say she did?"

Somewhere in my brain, I could still hear Eagen telling me that prisons were full of people convicted of doing seriously out-of-character things. As far as I was concerned, Rebecca had always been the straightest, do-it-by-the-numbers person on the planet. But who knew? One of the great lessons of having worked as a private eye for twenty-some years was the revelation that you never know what's going on behind closed doors. Only chumps imagine they do. And that you never know other human beings all the way down to the bottom of their souls, because we all hold something in reserve. Some atoll of secrecy to which we can retreat when the ocean of life goes rogue.

Rebecca and I had been apart for the better part of four years. That part of her life was a complete blank to me. She'd married some asshole yacht salesman drug runner who'd damned near gotten us both killed. Was there something hidden in those years? Something that hadn't gone away but had, instead, lingered in the shadows of her life? The possibility depressed me.

I took a deep breath, shrugged the idea to the floor, and pulled my notebook from my pocket. "This whole thing with Rebecca got started when a guy named Kevin Delaney filed his umpteenth appeal of a murder conviction. Wanted independent testing of his forensic material. The Ninth Circuit Court said he had a right to have the material tested by an independent lab. When they went to get the file, it was gone, so they started checking. They found five files were missing. Kevin

Delaney, Terrence Poole, Gilberto Duran, Willard Frost, and Lamar Hudson."

Carl sat there for a few seconds deciding whether to let it go, then said, "And you want everything you can get on them."

"For starts."

"What else?"

"The DA's office has been checking Rebecca's work for the past few months or so. We need to know why these five guys. Do they have something in common? Are they known associates of one another? Have they done time together? That sort of thing."

He waved a cautionary hand. "Whatever's on public record, we can have a look at, but, like I've told you before, there's no outright hacking these guys. They've got serious firewalls. So not only would it be a long process to get inside—weeks, at least, maybe months—but if anything goes wrong, we end up in Walla Walla with our pants around our ankles, which ain't how I plan to spend my golden years. Capiche?"

He rolled over to the bank of monitors on the south wall and started pushing buttons. The screens came alive. I stood there with my mouth hanging open for about five minutes, watching the flashing screens like a monkey with a mobile.

I was rescued from my stupor by the buzzing of the doorbell. I checked the monitor above the kitchen door. It was Charity, with an armload of white plastic bags.

Charity was a local Jamaican guy who looked after Carl. Made sure he ate, called the maids, and got the place hoed out once in a while—that sort of thing. Once a day, he showed up with takeout, and the two of them chowed down on whatever he brought.

Carl buzzed him in. I watched as Charity elbowed the door open, ducked his shoulder into the crack, and slid inside. Proof positive that stereotypes are true at least some of the time, Charity moved from place to place as if a Bob Marley tune were playing somewhere in his brain at all times.

"Leo . . . my man," he sang.

"What's up?" I said.

He raised the bag. "Curried goat be up," he said with a grin.

I tried to recall the last time I'd eaten. The only image I could readily bring to mind was of airline peanuts puked onto Rebecca's toney Berber carpet.

"Got some jerk chicken, got some Geera pork and Aloo pie too," Charity cooed as he slithered toward the kitchen. "You hungry, man?" he asked over his shoulder. "'Cause I got plenty. Sheere was gonna come, but she had to go help her mama wid something."

"I'll choke some down. Thanks."

Charity swivel-hipped it straight for the kitchen, with Carl rolling along hard on his heels. I stopped on the way and took a leak. By the time I got to the kitchen table, they'd already fanned out paper plates, found some mismatched cutlery, and were at the swallowing stage of things.

I was so hungry I was halfway through my second jerk chicken leg before my mouth got hip to just how hot this shit was. Felt like another couple of degrees and my eyebrows would burst into flame.

"Why do you guys from hot countries always like spicy food?" I groused.

"Meat tends to spoil in hot countries," Charity said between bites. "Spices got antimicrobial qualities." He grinned. "Cover up the smell too."

"Makes ya sweat," Carl piped in. "Helps the body cool off."

"If this shit cools you down, you should look for a fireman, 'cause your ass is on fire."

By the time we finished, I was sweating like a racehorse, and my stomach had turned to ash. Everything from the roof of my mouth to the pit of my stomach felt like it must be glowing by now. I was barely being manly about my discomfort, when, out in the front room, the computers began chirping like gerbils. Carl wiped his mouth with his sleeve, rolled himself back from the table, and motored out of the room.

I helped Charity with the cleanup, gargled another glass of milk, and then wandered out toward the front of the house.

"Willard Frost. Homegrown, standard-issue scumbag," Carl announced. He looked up at me. "You know in the movies, that moment when they find out the fresh-faced boy next door is really the serial killer and everybody shakes their bewildered heads and says"—he raised his voice two octaves—"'But he was such a nice boy'?"

"Yeah."

"Well . . . I'm bettin' nobody *ever* said that about Willard Frost. Willard came out of the chute as a full-blown pain in the ass." Carl lobbed a hand into the air. "This shit isn't even interesting." He pointed at the monitor on the right. "Breaking and entering. Burglary. Lewd and lascivious behavior. Receiving stolen goods. Theft of services. Grand theft auto. Assault two. Menacing. Stalking. Felonious assault . . . Pandering . . . Pandering . . . Pandering . . . It goes on and on. This son of a bitch has spent more time behind bars than he has on the street."

He pointed up at one of the other screens. The photo was of a scowling Asian man. Spiked hair. Fierce macho snarl.

"Don't look much like a Willard Frost," I commented.

Carl pushed a few more computer keys. Two new figures appeared on the overhead screen. Nondescript, all-American couple in their fifties. Standing by a red Chevy crew-cab pickup. Smiling, arms around each other. **Boeing** emblazoned on the building in the background. The blue-collar American dream.

"Willard Senior and his wife, Bonnie," Carl intoned. "Adopted Willard Junior when he was four. He's either Cambodian or Laotian. The United Nations relief agency that assisted with the adoption couldn't pin it down any closer than that." He pointed again. "A sealed juvie file when he was eleven and another when he was fourteen. I'm betting they're not for overzealous charity work."

"They seal 'em, it's usually got some sort of sexual element," I offered.

Carl grunted and pushed some more buttons.

"He could have been the *victim* of abuse," I hedged.

Carl sat back in his chair and folded his arms across his bony chest. "Yeah," he said after a minute. "That's a definite possibility."

The printer began to hum. I ambled in that direction.

I reached down and pulled a handful of paper out of the printer tray. About the time I straightened up, my phone began to buzz down in the bottom of my pocket, creating a sensory experience considerably more user-friendly than the present situation called for.

I made a quick stab for the phone just as the wad of papers slipped from my grasp, spreading themselves over the carpet like refugees.

"Yeah?" I said into the phone.

"She's awake," Gabe growled. "She needs you to bring her some clothes."

"Tell her I'm on the way," I said, as I broke the connection and began raking the story of Willard Frost's misspent life into a ragged pile.

Charity came bopping out of the kitchen. Carl waved goodbye with one hand and hammered the keyboard with the other.

"Bath tomorrow," Charity said as he pulled open the front door.

Carl looked horrified. "Like hell," he said. "I ain't takin' no bath."

"Bath tomorrow," Charity said again.

"You and whose fucking army?" Carl snarled.

"Gonna bring my cousin Tommy. Gonna scrub your moldy ass wid a stiff brush."

"I'll lock you the fuck out."

"Got me a key . . . remember?"

When Carl didn't respond, Charity turned my way. "Good to see ya, Leo."

"You too," I said as I tried to pat the porcupine of paperwork into some semblance of order. I turned to Carl. "I gotta go too," I said.

Carl pointed at the unruly paperwork wedged in my armpit and smirked. "Take that pile of shit with you. I'll keep at it on this end. I get anything worth a damn, I'll give you a jingle, but I'm tellin' you right from the get-go, before we start getting into this shit—I don't see how a low-life bottom-feeder like Frost comes into this thing. Who'd be going to any trouble to spring him? What's that little shit doing in the pile?"

As usual, Carl had a point. "Yeah," I said. "I'm thinkin' we better find out."

"See now? Things are improvin'. At least you're thinkin' for a change," Carl muttered as I stepped out onto the porch.

■ ■ ■

Gabe was sitting in the visitor area leafing through a dog-eared *Guns & Ammo* when I stepped off the elevator. "They want you to stop at the nurses' station and sign her out."

"You ready to roll?" I asked.

Gabe favored me with a wry smile. "Which *you* is that? Singular or plural?"

"Whatever works," I said.

"Ready when you are."

"We won't be long," I said, as I headed up the hall.

I stopped at the nurses' station and signed everything but the Magna Carta. Then took the corridor to the left, found the right room, and stepped inside.

Rebecca had the bed cranked all the way up. "Hey," she whispered as I walked in the door. She looked like she'd recently lost her lunch.

I had a black trash bag full of her clothes slung over my shoulder like a homeless troll. "How you doing?" I asked as I set the bundle on the floor.

"I'm fuzzy," she said. "I'm having trouble holding a thought for very long."

"I'm guessing that'll get better with time" was the best I could come up with.

She shrugged but didn't say anything. I'm not good with elephants in the room, so I just blurted it out. "Wadda you remember about yesterday?"

She didn't answer right away, which wasn't like her at all. She'd always been the smart-ass in the front row with her hand up, while I was low-ridering it in the back.

"There were two . . ." She stopped, took a deep breath. "Two guys in . . ." She brought a hand to her throat. Massaged it and swallowed hard.

"UPS uniforms," I finished.

She nodded. Before she made me go through how I knew about the UPS guys, I staged a quick segue. "The cops are convinced you tried to kill yourself," I said.

She blinked several times. "Me? Suicide?"

I held up a cautionary hand. "You gotta understand," I said, "they're working from the assumption that you're guilty of all that shit you're accused of doing. The way they see it, you couldn't take the pressure and decided to take the easy way out." I waited a beat, thinking maybe she'd jump in with a denial. Instead, she looked away again, so I kept talking. "And at this point it's not gonna do any good to be telling the cops about the UPS guys either. They're just gonna think you're trying to cover your ass." Her eyes told me she knew I was right and didn't like it even a little bit.

"Is that what Gabe is about?" she asked. "You're afraid I might . . ."

"Nope," I said. I reached over and put a hand on her shoulder. "Not to worry, honey," I said with a big grin. "It's *way* worse than that."

"Do tell," she said.

I did. At length. About how everybody in the known universe seemed to agree that the case against her was a foregone conclusion. And then about the unfortunate woman they'd moved into her vacated

ER room. About how somebody had stabbed the orderly and killed her dead as a herring.

Furrowed brow. "And you think it was me they were . . ."

"I'm not big on coincidences," I said.

She shook her head. "That's quite a stretch."

"So . . . let's go back over the past couple days," I suggested. "Two fake UPS guys force their way into your condo, do their best to make it look like you tried to OD, and then disappear into the night. And then, the very next day, a woman in the same room you'd occupied a half hour earlier has a couple of hitters come in, turn off her ventilator, and stab an orderly in the process." She started to say something, but I waved her off. "And to make matters worse, the cops not only don't believe a damn word of it, but, as far as they're concerned, you're the worst kind of traitor. Somebody who's about to be responsible for putting a bunch of felons back on the street. I know it doesn't seem possible, but right now, they might actually dislike you more than they dislike me, which is sayin' somethin'."

It got quiet again as she thought it over. "But why? Why would anyone want to do this to me? Why would anyone want me dead?"

"I don't know, but think about it. If you'd died the way they planned it, the whole damn thing would have been over in a heartbeat. She got caught. She couldn't take it. She offed herself. End o' story. Onward and upward."

Silence settled in. I watched as she leaned back against the bed and ran it through her circuits. I was watching the movement of her eyeballs behind the lids when the tick of raindrops on the window hijacked my attention. I watched as one of those Northwest maritime squalls raced over south Seattle, blowing hard and raining sideways as it rushed across the urbanscape. Sitting there in that rarified hospital air, my brain conjured the smell of wet pavement, equal parts hope and decay. Rebecca jerked me back to reality.

"When you look at it that way, it makes perfect sense, doesn't it?" she said after quite a while. She looked over at me, like now it was my turn to say something.

As usual, I didn't know my lines.

"Aren't you going to ask me if I did it?" she said.

"Nope."

"I'm scared, Leo," she said in a voice I'd never heard before. "Nothing like this has ever happened to me."

I didn't know what to say and didn't want to make promises I couldn't keep, so I kept my trap closed.

When it got quiet enough, for long enough, my ears began to tune in to the building's underlying hum—a matrix somewhere between a note and a hiss—that loitered in the hospital air like old cigar smoke.

"Let's get outta here," I finally suggested. "We can hole up at my house until we figure out what to do next."

Her eyes narrowed. Like I'd figured, she hated the idea on principle. After twenty-plus years of keeping each other's company, the one thing we'd always avoided was moving in together. It was as if maintaining separate spaces somehow allowed self-contained souls like us to experience the best of both worlds.

She already knew the answer, but she asked anyway. "Why your place?"

"It's got a wall and a gate."

Also like I'd figured, that was a tough one to argue with. Like many politicians, my old man had made legions of enemies. Between his personal button man Frankie Ortega, a succession of beefy bodyguards, and the house's architectural fortifications, he'd pretty much created the kind of privacy a man in his position required. A kind that came in handy at a time like this.

"And I take it Gabe is coming with us?"

"For the duration."

She nodded grudgingly and looked around the room. "I'm prepared to do a Lady Godiva if I have to," she announced.

I reached down and picked up the trash bag full of clothes. "Won't be necessary," I said. "Got a bunch of your stuff in here." I dropped the bag onto the foot of the bed.

She cast a jaundiced eye at the ugly plastic pile resting on her feet. "My clothes, I presume," she said. "My mother would be appalled."

"Your mother was born appalled."

She slid off the bed and turned her back to me. I took the hint and undid the pair of ties holding her hospital gown together. She shrugged it to the floor, leaving her standing next to the bed wearing nothing but a pair of those little green hospital socks.

"Nice booties," I said with a smirk.

She arched an eyebrow. "Was that singular or plural?" she intoned.

■ ■ ■

The squeak of overhead footsteps jerked me awake. I held my breath and listened intently. A full ten seconds passed before my addled brain clicked into gear and I remembered. Gabe. It was Gabe. How, several hours back, we'd gone upstairs together, pulled the dust covers off everything in the guest room, and gotten Gabe settled in.

The bedside clock read 2:47. Rebecca and I had talked our way through the situation six or seven times. I must have nodded off in one of the silences. Last I remembered, Rebecca was stretched out next to me, going over her suspension order line by line. I'd lost track of how many times she'd muttered "Bullshit."

I exhaled slowly, ran a hand over my face, and looked in her direction. She was leaning back against the headboard with her eyes closed. I figured she must be asleep, and, as usual, I was wrong. She opened her eyes and pinned me with an icy glare. Like she'd just been waiting for me to wake up.

She said, "I don't understand how anyone could pull this whole thing off. Or why. I mean . . . why those five files?"

"No idea," I admitted.

"So that means . . ." She stopped herself.

People faced with ugly situations very often can't bring themselves to admit it out loud, so, human nature being what it is, they try to get somebody else to say it for them.

Rebecca shook her head in disbelief. "I still can't believe one of my guys swiped those files. I mean . . . putting aside the fact that I just can't believe they would, or would have any possible reason to—how would they have done it? The files are either locked down in my office vault or they're at the precinct that made the arrest. My vault is secure, and precinct evidence rooms are locked down tight. You have to scan your ID to take anything out. Another officer watches as you do whatever you're going to do. Same thing when you return it. The guy in the cage checks it again and then scans his ID. How does anybody circumvent that?"

That was pretty much what I'd been asking myself all along. Ever since the drug-crazed eighties, when kilos and kilos of cocaine regularly turned up missing from precinct evidence rooms, the SPD's protocols and procedures regarding evidence room security had become absolutely draconian. No way anybody was walking away with anything. Union or no union, it was a no-appeal, firing offense.

"And there's more than one precinct involved," she added.

"How do you know that?"

"They told me when they escorted me out of the building."

"So there's no way whoever did this could possibly corrupt two different evidence locker cops. One maybe. More . . . no way."

Used to be that the cop inside the evidence room cage was always some ancient flatfoot waddling his way toward that gated retirement community in the sky. Guys more interested in the quality of their impending leisure time than they were in the integrity of the chain of evidence. These days it was a regular part of duty.

She nodded at the pile of paperwork under my chin. "Anything useful there?"

I shook my head. "A life misspent."

I could see the worry pressing in around her eyes when she asked, "So what's your plan for morning?"

I thought it over and then said, "Willard Frost's the only one of them who's still out on the street. According to his sheet, he got his ass arrested two or three times at the same address down in Pioneer Square. Figure I'll mosey down there in the A.M. . . . kick over some paving stones and see what scuttles out. What about you?"

"Well . . . I'm going to have to find an attorney."

"Call Jed. Ask him for a referral," I said. Jed James had been my best friend and attorney, until they'd hauled off and made him a judge. He's still my buddy, but his firm's associates now handle my legal work. Conflict of interest and all that. He'd know exactly who Rebecca should call. Probably make the call for her, if I knew him.

"But most of all, I need access to my files," she said suddenly. "Without the files, there's no way I can even look for a connection."

"So?"

She folded her arms across her chest and frowned. "They took my keys. Just walked into my office, first thing on Monday morning, handed me the suspension order, demanded I turn over my keys, and then walked me out to my car. I'm forbidden to have contact with any member of my department until this matter is resolved."

"So you're completely locked out?"

"I've got backups of everything on the off-site, but I'm willing to bet they locked me out of those even before they served the suspension order."

"And?" There was an *and*. I could tell.

"I've always made it my policy to keep a copy of my records outside the protocol." She shrugged and looked a bit guilty. "Just in case," she added. "You never know." She shrugged again. "Life's uncertain."

"A copy you obviously don't think they'll find."

She shrugged. "I suppose they'll eventually follow my footprint and get there, but not right away," she said. "It's in an encrypted human resources folder."

I threw a crooked look in her direction. "Doesn't the suspension order cover messing with digital stuff like that?" I asked.

She shook her head. "They haven't updated the suspension form in about twenty years. I read it top to bottom. There was no such thing as off-site data storage when they wrote that thing."

She was just the type to read the whole damn form too. A few months back, I'd trembled in awe as she read all the way through the Terms and Conditions for a new iPhone she was about to buy.

"Then do it," I said. "But make damn sure you get everything you need on the first try, 'cause as soon as they figure out you've been in there, that door's gonna close in a big hurry."

"The system's locked during nonbusiness hours, so if I don't want to set off every bell and whistle they own, I'll have to wait till morning and hope," she said.

I'd like to tell you how we lay there in bed and worked the whole thing out, kinda like Sherlock Holmes sitting in his rocker with his pipe, laying it all out for John Watson. I'd like to tell you that, but it wouldn't be true, because before we rolled any farther down Detective Drive, the house's intruder alarm went off, bleating its singsong screech from all directions at once. I snapped my eyes toward the hall just as the outdoor lights turned my end of the street into a film noir set.

I rolled off the bed, reached into the bottom drawer of the bedside table, and found my little Smith & Wesson Shield napping under a pair of dirty socks. A stick-it-right-in-his-face gun that felt like a toy but packed the punch of a 9 mm. I checked the thumb safety and then started across the room. When I looked over my shoulder, Rebecca had one foot out of the bed and was throwing back the covers.

"Stay here. Gabe and I can handle this," I said.

She hated it, but slowly pulled her foot back in. I turned and hurried out of the room. The hall was dark.

Gabe was waiting at the bottom of the stairs, fully dressed, big black automatic in hand. I hustled down the hall, Gabe following in my wake. Just inside the front door, I pulled open the closet, leaned in, and checked the security control panel.

What I'd expected to see was a blinking green light from one of the motion sensors in the yard. It happens whenever seagulls decide to land and do whatever dumb shit it is seagulls do. The lights drive my neighbors crazy, which is why I don't generally leave the system on all the time.

No blinking green light, though. Not this time. Red instead. Somebody had breached the gate. I reached in and turned off the alarm but left the yard lights on. I grabbed an old leather jacket from the closet and shouldered myself into it.

"Front gate," I whispered.

Gabe nodded.

I pulled open the front door and stepped out into a starless night. It wasn't raining, but there was enough of an onshore flow to dampen your cheeks as you moved. Beneath my bare feet, the flagstones felt old and cold.

Gabe and I fanned out on either side of the driveway. Gabe moved out into the orchard and began sliding from tree to tree, from shadow to shadow. I hotfooted it over to the stone wall that separates my property from the Morrisons' and began to weave my way forward through the dense shrubbery.

Up ahead, the cast-iron bars on the front gate threw prison shadows along the asphalt driveway. I swiveled my head as I weaved forward. Everything in sight was stark black and white, like I was walking in a life-size negative.

Over to my right, Gabe had made it all the way to the front wall. I quickened my pace, slaloming through the flower beds, until Gabe and

I were parallel with each other, backs against the front wall, guns at the ready. We made eye contact.

And then suddenly my ears picked up the rhythmic thump of an engine. I listened hard. Thought maybe I heard somebody answer, but couldn't be certain. A car door slammed.

I found Gabe's eyes again, then reached up and pushed the button. The chain clanked. The motor began to roll the gate aside. As I stepped through the crack, I could sense Gabe coming hard my way.

I held the Smith & Wesson in front of me with both hands as I swiveled on the balls of my feet and checked both ends of the street in the second before Gabe's back was suddenly pressed against mine.

My yard lights threw enough long shadows for me to make out the TV truck backed into the driveway of the vacant house across the street. "This way," Gabe said from behind me. I craned my neck. Another TV remote was staging a K-turn up the street, digital satellite dish folded along the roof like a limp dick.

The scrape of a shoe pulled my head back around. I stifled a moan and dropped the semiautomatic to my side. It was Harley "Snowdrift" Dawson, channel eight's newsman on the scene for the past thirty years or so. One of those guys who started out in the Jimmy Olsen cub reporter role and somehow never quite graduated to the newsroom, instead spending his career reporting natural disasters from the side of the road. Thirty-six-foot snowdrifts, gas explosions, floods, flaming forests, droughts, infestations . . . Harley was there, squinting into the camera, hair on fire, teeth at full grit. *"This is Harley Dawson reporting from . . ."*

"Sorry about that," he shouted with quite a bit more jocularity than the situation called for. "We tapped the gate when we were turning the truck around." He waved a dismissive hand. "And then the yard lights came on and all that."

I tilted my head and whispered in Gabe's ear. "Let's go." We staged a U-turn worthy of the Rockettes and hurried back toward the house.

"Excuse me . . . please . . . sir . . . excuse me . . . are you Mr. Waterman?" he shouted from across the street.

I heard the slap of running feet. Dawson was heel-and-toeing it in our direction as fast as a man his age was able. "Excuse me, sir," he panted. "Could you please . . ."

I kept walking. Halfway back to the house, the alarm began to sound again. I pitched a glance back over my shoulder. Dawson had shoved his microphone between a couple of gate slats and was holding on to another with his free hand. I stopped and turned back toward the gate.

There was no leaving him there. He'd keep setting the system off. So I walked slowly back in his direction. Dawson pushed the microphone as far out as he could.

"You're on private property," I boomed. "I'm officially asking you to leave. If you don't, I'm calling the cops, and then I'm calling your employer."

Awkward silence to follow. He knew the rules. He spit out some bullshit about the public's right to know as he eased the mic back through the gate and began to flow backward at the speed of lava, slip slidin' away until his feet were on the public roadway.

The second TV truck pulled to the curb just north of the gate. The truck's halogen headlights lit Dawson up like a bike reflector. Two guys in white coveralls got out of the second truck and started our way. One of them said something I couldn't make out.

I turned and walked away, Gabe hard on my hip.

Dawson wasn't ready to quit. "In light of tonight's events, would either you or Dr. Duvall like to comment on the grand's jury action?" he shouted to our backs.

Once inside the house, I bolted the front door, turned off the yard lights, and then spent ten minutes going over the operation of the security system with Gabe, who, like I figured, was a real quick learner.

I gave Gabe a restrained clap on the shoulder. "Thanks for the help tonight."

"We're always glad to be of service," Gabe said.

We parted company at the bottom of the stairs, Gabe tramping back up into the stratosphere while I barefooted it for the back of the house. Halfway down the hall, I noticed the kitchen light was on, so I veered in that direction and found Rebecca sitting at the kitchen table, wearing one of my old, scruffy bathrobes and sipping at a cup of coffee.

"There's a couple TV remote trucks camped out front," I said, as I headed across the room, found a cup, and poured myself some coffee. "Snowdrift Dawson among them."

"Does that mean we're officially a wreck on the highway now?"

"That remains to be seen."

"What do they want?"

"A statement from you."

She emitted a short humorless laugh but didn't say anything, so I kept talking. "Which begs the question: How in hell did they know you were here? An answer that pretty much has to be Harborview hospital."

"Hospitals aren't allowed to give out that sort of information."

"From my experience, they're pretty much fanatics about it," I agreed.

"Then what?"

"If it wasn't you, and it wasn't me, and it wasn't Gabe . . . then it's gotta be them." I shrugged. "Unless you can think of something else."

"Could somebody have followed us?"

"Gabe would've seen 'em."

"Sounds like you have a lot of confidence in Gabe."

"Gabe is as advertised," I assured her.

We lapsed into silent sipping. I was trying to decide whether to tell her what Dawson had said about some sort of a grand jury proceeding. I was thinking, you know, since there's nothing we can do about it until morning anyway, might as well get a few hours' sleep and then tackle it in the A.M. I have few peers when it comes to the *do-it-later* rationalization.

On the other hand, there was something about this whole shit storm that chafed me. Something that didn't make the narrow kind of sense my feeble brain required. First off, I couldn't fathom who could have enough clout to set this kind of conspiracy in motion. Maybe back in my old man's time, when everybody was in everybody else's pocket, but not now, not in this white man's paradise.

A pair of killers in UPS uniforms was one thing. There are lots of scumbags you can hire for a gig like that—cheaper than you'd imagine too—but a plan that hinged on fully compromising a public employee, and possibly more than one? That's a whole different zip code. Same with having almost instantaneous access to highly confidential hospital records. How's that done? And then it gets really scary, when the first murder attempt fails, and somebody's either stupid enough or desperate enough to waltz in to the busiest hospital in town, in broad daylight, and try it again. To say my mind was boggled didn't begin to cover it.

I watched her get up, walk over to the sink, and rinse out her cup. She dried her hands on a plaid dish towel that had belonged to my mother, then leaned back against the sink and said, "It's always been you before."

"Me what?"

She gave me a wan smile. "You've always been the one with some kind of disaster going on, not me. You've been arrested and needed me to call Jed more times than I can count, or you've gotten beaten up and needed a ride home from the ER . . ." She shook her head in mock disgust. "And now it's *me*, and you know what?"

"What?" I asked.

"You know, as we've gotten older and people we know tried to cope with the normal disasters of life—illness, family problems, money problems, all of it—I know this sounds weird to say, but I never really felt as if any of that applied to me. I realize now that a little part of me always thought that when something went terribly wrong for somebody I knew, that they must have made some sort of mistake. You know, some miscalculation or momentary inattention that got them into the fix they were in." She heaved a sigh. "I thought I was immune to things like that."

"I've known you for a long time, babe, and, more than anybody else I know, your life has turned out pretty much the way you planned it."

The muscles along her jaw rippled like snakes. "But I never realized how arrogant I'd become," she said. "Just standing here now, I can think of a dozen things I should have handled differently, if . . . if I hadn't been so damn self-righteous. If I'd just shown a bit more empathy." She went quiet.

I had a feeling we'd reached the point where I was supposed to say something soothing. I rifled my brain for a suitable homily but couldn't muster anything more therapeutic than something about how maybe it was just her turn in the barrel, which, I felt pretty sure, wasn't what she wanted to hear at this juncture.

I was spared the dilemma when a shout of "Hey" resounded from the hallway.

I got up, walked over to the door, and peered down the hall. Gabe was standing about three stairs up, leaning over the ornate wooden bannister. "You all probably ought to watch the news. There's shit going on."

"Thanks," I said.

"Oh Jesus," Rebecca said. "What now? Locusts?" She'd wandered over and wedged herself between my shoulder and the door frame. In the fluorescent light, her skin looked nearly transparent. There was something strangely tentative in her eyes. I pretended not to notice. She picked up on it anyway.

"I've worked all my life to . . ." She stopped. "How can anyone think I would . . ."

She stopped again and then pinned me with an angry glare. "Do you hear me? I sound like some, some frigging soap opera heroine." Out of the blue, she stomped her foot. "GODDAMN IT," she bellowed. "I CAN'T FUCKING BELIEVE THIS IS HAPPENING."

Scared the shit out of me. Don't think I'd ever heard her yell before. Certainly not in anger anyway. I stood there and waited for her echoes to exit the eaves, then stepped over and stood next to her.

"Sorry," she said. "I lost it there for a minute."

"This must be—"

She cut me off. "It's just that people seem so gleeful about it. Unless I'm getting paranoid, I can feel a certain . . . like . . . a certain delight down at the bottom of it. Like there's a whole bunch of people out there sniggering about what's happening to me."

I put a hand on her shoulder. "Something about human beings likes to see the mighty come undone," I said. "Almost like it's part of our DNA. That's what tragedies are about, isn't it? Some sort of a universal schadenfreude."

She leaned her head on my shoulder.

"Go turn on the TV," I said. "I'll be right in."

She slid her hand across my back as she squeezed by me and padded off toward the bedroom. I went the other way, rinsed out my cup, checked the lock on the back door.

Commercial on the tube. Sonic Drive-In. Two dickheads sitting in a convertible discussing their milkshakes. I sat on the edge of the bed, returned the Smith & Wesson to the nightstand, and then began picking an armada of embedded beauty bark shards from the soles of my feet.

A familiar fanfare lifted my gaze to the TV screen. *"Eyewitness News Eight. Your Northwest Eye in the Sky."* Shot of a helicopter veering over downtown Seattle. Taken by another helicopter veering over downtown Seattle. Trumpets blaring. Talking head appears. New Asian woman I'd never seen before. Stacy Chen. Pretty. Dead-ass serious. There I go categorizing again. Gotta work on that.

"In today's top story, Prosecuting Attorney Paul Woodward has announced that he has taken the unprecedented step of convening an emergency grand jury for the purpose of securing an indictment against suspended King County medical examiner Rebecca S. Duvall."

Cut to one of the conference rooms at city hall. Bunch of ceremonial flags, a dozen guys in gray suits lined up behind a rostrum with the county seal glinting gold. Right on cue, Paul Woodward strides to the podium, nods at the assembled multitude, clears his throat, and then looks solemnly around the room.

If you needed somebody to play a prosecuting attorney, Woodward was the guy you'd hire. Fiftysomething. Even features, except for maybe a bit too much chin. Personal-trainer trim. Walking around beneath enough hair to stuff a morris chair.

He had his funeral face on as he leaned into the unruly thicket of microphones. *"My office has determined that, in order to avoid any appearance of bias or favoritism, it is in the public's interest to impanel a special grand jury for the purpose of obtaining an indictment against currently suspended King County medical examiner Rebecca S. Duvall."* Lots of shuffling around and whispering from the crowd. *"The normal protocol for an internal matter such as this would be to allow civil procedures to run their course. But—"*

"Oh Christ, he's not going to quote Franklin, is he?" slipped from my lips.

"—as Benjamin Franklin said so long ago, 'the law holds, that it is better that ten guilty persons escape, than that one innocent suffer.'"

"Which means he's got five attorneys so far up his ass he can taste hair gel," I said.

"The maintenance of the public trust demands that matters of official misconduct be rectified with great dispatch. To that end, a special grand jury is being impaneled at this moment. It is our intention to seek a bill of indictment on Friday, February seventeenth, and to arraign Dr. Duvall the following Tuesday, February twenty-first."

Woodward folded his notes and nodded gravely. Shouted questions arrived from about five people at once. Woodward bobbed his leonine mane a couple of times and then strode out of sight, entourage in hot pursuit.

Back to Stacy Chen. *"Channel Eight, your Eye in the Sky, continues with exclusive interviews with the families and loved ones of some of those whose convictions have been called into question. Back in a minute."*

"Sounds a lot like you're already guilty," I said.

"I could go to prison," she said.

"Nah," I scoffed, with quite a bit more bravado than I actually felt.

She wasn't buying it. "I've been being an idiot about this," she insisted. "I've been treating this thing like it was a nuisance . . . like it was so ridiculous it was going to go away if I didn't feed it any negative energy. And it's not. This is . . . This is serious."

On the tube, a commercial for a local pest control business. Stop Buggin' Me. Some asshole dressed up like Superman, whuppin' on some giant termite.

"Some of those cases are from several years ago. I need to look at my notes again," Rebecca said, as Superman launched the six-foot vermin like a javelin.

"I'm working on it," I said. She had to know Eagen was helping out, but if he got caught coloring outside the lines on this one, he'd be out on the street, so I was keeping the details to a minimum. Gotta have deniability.

Besides, truth be told, I was harboring a few lingering doubts myself. Not about her honesty. That was above reproach. But I couldn't help wonder if perhaps, during the years we'd been apart, her life hadn't gotten out of hand in some way I didn't know anything about. Maybe she'd just gotten sloppy from the stress. I gave up expecting people to be perfect a long time ago. Makes life a whole lot more pleasant.

I pointed at the TV.

"Welcome back. Stacy Chen for Channel Eight Eye in the Sky News. Continuing our story of Prosecuting Attorney Paul Woodward's surprise announcement of his intention to convene a special grand jury in the matter of disgraced King County medical examiner Rebecca Duvall. On the condition of anonymity, a highly placed source has told Channel Eight that the prosecuting attorney's office has notified five families that convictions involving their loved ones have been called into question by the charges of dereliction and evidence tampering currently being leveled at suspended King County medical examiner Rebecca Duvall."

Cut to the face of an older Hispanic woman. Midfifties. Blunt featured and stout. The banner under her face read: **CARLOTTA DURAN.** Under that: **MOTHER OF GILBERTO DURAN, CONVICTED IN 2014 OF THE ROBBERY OF A CAPITOL HILL CONVENIENCE STORE.**

"You remember Gilberto Duran?" I asked.

"Nope."

"I always know my son not do what they say," Carlotta Duran said in a thick accent. *"They hadda be some mistake. He's no that kind of boy. Dey took his life away. Poot him in prison. They keel him for no-thing in dat prison. For nothing. Deese woman gotta pay for what she done. Deys gotta be some kinda—"*

This didn't seem to be going anywhere we wanted to go, so I pushed the "Mute" button. Like most of TV, it was better without the sound.

Another mug shot appeared. "What do you remember about *him*?" I asked.

Took her a second to drag her eyes from the TV screen.

"Not a damn thing," she said.

Stacy Chen was back. I pushed "Mute." *"Also among those notified by the prosecutor's office was Mrs. Patricia Harrington, whose daughter Tracy was murdered earlier this year, by convicted killer Lamar Hudson."*

"Oh yeah," Rebecca said. "The Harrington business."

A new image flashed onto the screen. Well-to-do woman in her late sixties. Margaret Thatcher cast-iron hair, string of pearls the size of pigeon eggs. The second I saw her face, I remembered who she was.

That was because the Harringtons were Seattle's version of the Kennedy family. Everybody knew who they were. A big old-money clan for whom the trappings of great wealth had often seemed to be little more than a gilded invitation to tragedy.

As I recalled the story, they had a junkie daughter who was found strangled in Volunteer Park. Just the sort of sordid tale the media felt compelled to trumpet to the far corners of the earth, and just the sort of story with which an old-money family like the Harringtons were least prepared to deal.

Mrs. Harrington's husband—I was drawing a blank on his name, but I was pretty sure it wasn't Harrington—had found Tracy dead in the park. By the time the feeding frenzy was over, it had been revealed that the family had an autistic son who did not live with them and that the kid was found unconscious at the murder scene but was later exonerated of any wrongdoing. Just the sort of story that intensely private people like the Harringtons wanted plastered all over the front page.

The next day, the cops arrested a semisentient citizen named Lamar Hudson, who up and confessed to the crime; which, of course, gave the media an opportunity to dredge up the whole family soap opera once again. Took a jury all of two hours to hand Lamar Hudson life without the possibility of parole.

Just when it seemed like the media onslaught was over, however, Lamar Hudson's plight found its way back onto the front page when the matter of his fitness to stand trial caused considerable debate in national legal circles.

Didn't take Sigmund Freud to see that Lamar wasn't playing with a full deck.

Any damn fool could see that he was barely able to form complete sentences, let alone assist in his own defense. Unfortunately for Lamar, both the social status of the victim and the heinous nature of the crime were sufficient that the system didn't really give a shit whether he was crazy or not. Lamar had unwittingly stumbled into the place in our society where Old Testament vengeance replaces new age law, and reason and metaphorical teeth and eyes start disappearing into the ozone. Last I'd heard, the Innocence Project had gotten involved with Lamar's plight and were pushing for a new trial.

Patricia Harrington blinked at the camera. *"I don't quite know what to say,"* she began. *"There is, of course, no closure for us."* She stopped and allowed herself a small sigh. *"Our family has done our best to cope with the matter of Tracy's death. It has been a long and painful process. And now"*—she set her jaw and stifled another sigh—*"it is our sincere hope that this matter will be resolved as quickly as possible."*

Back to Stacy Chen. *"Stay tuned. We'll be back in one minute, after this word from our sponsors."*

We sat in silence, watching the same Sonic Drive-In commercial as before. Same car. Same two dickheads. *This is how we Sonic.*

"So I'm going to be in court on Tuesday," she said.

"Presuming Woodward gets his indictment," I hedged.

She made a rude noise with her lips.

Couldn't argue with that. There was a corny old adage that a grand jury would indict a ham sandwich if a DA asked them to. Unfortunately, it was true.

"Woodward's got no choice," I said. "Next year's an election year; he's gotta come out of this smelling like a rose. If he needs to throw you under the bus, he will."

"He never liked me much anyway. Told me once I wasn't a team player."

"Really?"

"Right after he got elected for the first time, he came to my office on a couple occasions. He didn't come right out and say it, but he was trying to tell me what it would be *nice* if I would find. Like I was going to adjust my findings to suit his need to make a case. I set him straight on the subject. He's never been too fond of me since."

Before I could think of anything else to say, Stacy Chen was back. *"Continuing with our story."*

Voice from the great digital beyond: *"The following may be disturbing to some of our viewers. Parental discretion is advised."*

I was hoping the disclaimer was for something fun like nudity but got a pair of beefy specimens in plaid flannel shirts glaring into the camera instead. Looked like they had to be brothers. Big, bushy, black beards, eyebrows that met in the middle; they gave the impression that they might be haired over like gibbons.

They were standing out in front of the downtown courthouse, a bunch of reporters pushing microphones into their fuzzy chops. Three or four equally beefy city cops were circling behind them like caged lions. Apparently, the situation had already gotten somewhat tense. SPD was taking no chances with these two.

A banner appeared at the bottom of the screen. **CORY AND BRUCE DELANEY. BROTHERS OF KEVIN DELANEY, CONVICTED OF THE MURDER OF FRANCIS BOSSIER AND HER SIX-YEAR-OLD DAUGHTER, EMILY.**

The brother on the right stepped forward. He waved a disgusted hand at the cops behind him. *"I don't care how many *beeping* cops they send out here. That *beep* has got to pay for this. That *beeping beep* needs to spend some time behind bars. My little brother's spent years in a mother*beeping* jail cell, 'cause this *beeping* medical examiner lied her *beeping beep* off."*

The other brother reached out and put what I took to be a restraining hand on his shoulder. The first brother angrily shrugged it off. Instead of calming down, he jabbed a thick finger at the nearest TV camera and then stuck his hairy mug right up into the lens. His eyes were rolling in his head like a spooked horse. Flecks of spit had collected at the corners of his mouth. *"You out there, *beep*? That Duvall *beep*.*

You watchin' this?" He jabbed again. This time he hit the lens. The TV camera wobbled and pulled back. *"We're comin' for you, *beep*. One of these dark nights, you're gonna pay for what you done to our family. You're gonna pay for all those *beeping* years you took from my little brother. I'm gonna come to your house, I'm gonna grab hold of your—"*

Mercifully, that was as far as he got. The circling cops had heard enough and decided to put a stop to it. A pair of uniforms stepped into view, grabbed brother number one by the shoulders, and pulled him back from the bank of microphones, at which point, the other brother, who I'd been seeing as a peacemaker, stepped in and head-butted the nearest cop full in the face. The cop's nose exploded, instantly sending a river of blood and mucus rolling down over his chin.

The sound of the struggle and sight of blood sent the crowd scurrying in all directions at once. The sounds of shouts and slapping feet filled the air. Brother number one hauled off and punched an Asian policewoman, who went down in a heap. Brother number two had another officer in a headlock and was pounding him in the top of the head with his free hand.

That's about the time it started raining cops. Must have been a dozen of the boys in blue out there by the time they finally got the brothers handcuffed facedown on the sidewalk. From the look of it, both brothers were still screaming themselves purple despite the six hundred pounds of cop kneeling on the backs of their necks.

I decided I'd had enough of this gaiety and turned off the TV. We sat there for several minutes without saying anything. I could hear water rolling through the pipes in the ceiling.

Finally, Rebecca broke the silence. "Kevin Delaney I remember," she said. "His girlfriend finally had enough of his abuse and told him she was leaving. That miserable son of a bitch beat her to death with a claw hammer, right in front of her little daughter. Then he raped and strangled the child. It's not the kind of thing one forgets."

A chain saw couldn't have cut the air in that room. Seemed to me we'd reached the point where things couldn't get a hell of a lot worse, so I sucked it up and fessed up to something I'd been holding back all day.

"You know . . . evidence rooms being what they are today, if somebody really did steal the files . . . then I'm guessing the theft pretty much has gotta be at your team's end."

She was generally very defensive about her department and her employees, so I was expecting serious pushback, but, as usual, she surprised me.

"Yeah," she said in a low voice. "I know it does."

We hadn't spent any time talking about how her department operated because we both already knew. Rebecca and Patrick Dovel performed all the autopsies. They had a couple of other forensic pathologists on call in case they got buried, but day to day, it was just the two of them. When all the tests were done, she signed off on everything, locked up the remaining evidentiary material, and then submitted the results to the PA/DA. If the PA/DA decided there was enough evidence to go to court, she had one of her three assistants hand deliver the evidence material to the arresting officer's precinct. Files got shifted back and forth between the medical examiner's office and the various precincts all the time. All very on-camera, scan-your-badge-and-sign-here kind of stuff. In capital cases, the evidence files and the forensic material were stored until the last appeal had been exhausted.

"Ibrahim, Micah, and Forrest have worked for me forever," she said. "I just can't believe one of them would . . ." She stopped herself.

"Every chain has a weak link," I threw in.

"They're all suspended too, until the matter is resolved."

I ran that news through my circuits. "Which has gotta mean that all of them signed off on at least some of the missing stuff."

She looked blankly in my direction.

"If all five files had been picked up or delivered by one guy, he'd have been the only one suspended. Pretty much says to me that each of them signed off on at least one of the files in question. Which means there's not only multiple precincts, but multiple messengers involved."

"And that's just way too many people," she said. "Way too many moving parts. Has to be simpler than that. There's only one person with access to all of the files." She shrugged. "And that would be me."

"Yeah . . . pretty much looks that way."

"This can't be happening."

If being a PI for twenty years had taught me anything, it was that you never know what's going on behind someone else's closed doors. Any notion that you do is outright dangerous. Everybody has secrets, some of which are best left that way.

"Weird shit happens."

"You don't say," she deadpanned.

Chapter 2

Willard Frost had teeth like toenails. Big ones, little ones, some of them far enough apart to finger floss, and all of them the color of very old piano keys.

The building at 407 Walter Street was a six-story dump, with a rippled brick facade and a faded serape covering one of the windows on the third floor. A class joint, I could tell.

It had taken me forever to get out of the house this morning. Something in me wanted to mansplain everything to everybody, to feel like every detail was firmly under my control before I walked out. Eventually, about the time Rebecca's new attorney was about to arrive, she and Gabe lost patience and shouldered me out the door.

I'd arrived at 407 Walter Street about three minutes before ten in the morning and was standing across the street wondering why the city hadn't condemned this dump thirty years ago, when Willard Frost jerked open 407's steel front door and began jogging directly at me, leaving me very little choice but to move in his direction. We passed, shoulder to shoulder, no more than a foot apart. I gave him the standard macho nod. He grunted, flashed his rat teeth, and quickened his stride.

I may have been a bit late for private eyes, but, by scumbag standards, Willard was a crack o' dawn guy. I'd planned on easing into this, asking a few questions around the neighborhood and having a couple more cups of coffee before I got around to getting up close and personal with Willard. Now that he'd seen me, though, I was going to have to switch to plan B, so I kept walking, stepped up onto the opposite sidewalk, and, first chance I got, hooked a quick right onto First Avenue.

Soon as I was out of sight, I cut diagonally across the street, pulled a Mariners cap from my jacket pocket, and put it on; then I took my jacket off, tied it around my waist, and hurried back to the corner. Willard was jogging away from me.

He was a stocky little specimen, with a bowlegged gait. One of those guys who wasn't small; he was just short. The kind of runt who'd be tough on the shins.

Willard was a little man in a big hurry. To keep pace, I had to stretch my legs as he jogged down South Main Street toward the water. I hustled over to the sidewalk on the north side of the street and kept loping along, weaving among the construction debris like a matador. The closer we got to Puget Sound, the fresher the air got, which was good, because long-distance running wasn't exactly my strong suit.

Two blocks in front of me, Puget Sound folded green and white. The far side of Alaskan Way looked like a war zone. They were rebuilding the century-old seawall; everything was torn to shit. Construction equipment loomed in the shadows of the Alaskan Way Viaduct like steel predators.

Halfway down South Main, Willard skidded to a stop, pulled out a ring of keys, and let himself into the last door before the alley. I hurried across the street and grabbed the door handle. It was locked. I took a step backward and stared up at the brick face of the building. I was still working on what to do next when the commotion started.

Shouts seeped through the door like rainwater into a basement. And then louder shouts and banging. Sounded like somebody was rolling a cobblestone down a flight of wooden stairs, getting closer and louder with every impact.

I hustled across the mouth of the alley and stepped up into the next doorway. The glass door read: **Robert A. Christophel, CPA**. I leaned back against the door, and, of course, somebody immediately pulled the door open, sending me staggering backward into the foyer just as Willard Frost and another guy boiled out onto the sidewalk, arms and legs piston pumping, a tight, grunting knot of humanity, rolling around the sidewalk like fighting dogs.

I steadied myself and looked back over my shoulder. Tall, middle-aged bald guy. "Can I help you?" he asked.

I pointed at the melee on the sidewalk.

"Things were getting a little dicey outside," I explained.

He nodded his understanding, reached around me, and closed the door.

Willard and his adversary had, by this time, rolled over into the mouth of the alley, improving our view considerably. The other guy had the classic look of a biker. Long, greasy, braided hair, lots of tats, earrings, and a long, billy-goat beard with two green rubber bands holding it together.

If he'd had the slightest idea how to fight, the biker should have dispatched our boy Willard fairly quickly. Despite a noticeable advantage in height, weight, and reach, it looked like Bikerman was more accustomed to sucker punching people and having them curl up on the floor so he could kick 'em a few times. Willard, however, was not being nearly so accommodating.

When they regained their feet and the guy started a haymaker whistling toward Willard's head, Willard sneered, stepped left, let the punch rocket past his ear, and then kicked the guy square in the nuts. Almost lifted him off the pavement with the force of it.

"Oooooh" escaped from the throat of the accountant behind me.

Funny thing was, the nad mashing didn't seem to bother the biker guy a bit. He sucked in a big mouthful of air and then started another death punch in Willard's direction, and, not surprisingly, got pretty much the same result. Willard easily avoided the blow, stepped up belly to belly, and then used the power of his legs to drive his head up under the guy's chin. Hard.

Bikerman went all bobblehead. His eyes rolled back in his skull as he staggered backward across the sidewalk. The blood rolling down his chin announced that, somewhere along the line, his tongue had neglected to avoid his teeth. It got worse for him. He brought his hand to his mouth and then pulled it away. He was still staring stupidly at his bloody fingers when he stumbled one step too many across the sidewalk. I watched in horror as his back foot begged for traction but found only air. Took all I had not to close my eyes.

Pioneer Square was built before the turn of the *last* century. The curbs are solid pieces of stone, intended for horses and wagons, not for modern cars. Lots of places in the square the curbs are so tall that, if you park next to them, you can't open the passenger door, so it was a long way down for Bikerman when he executed an impromptu swan dive and went hurtling toward the street like a sack of rolled oats.

The thump was audible through the glass door as Bikerman bounced his forehead off the rear of a green Subaru Outback and then pinballed down into the canyon between the Subaru and the black Lexus snugged up behind it.

Willard didn't hesitate. He bodysurfed across the hood of the Lexus and then hopped down into the street, where he grabbed the guy by the hair with both hands and began to haul him out from under the parked cars.

The trouble with street fights is that there's a strict time limit. You have only about three minutes before the excess adrenaline in the air convinces some bystander he's just got to get involved, or, worse yet, some concerned citizen dials 911 and the heat show up. This one was getting up around the red line.

I assumed Willard had yarded Bikerman's ass out from under the car so's he could whomp on him some more, but Willard had other ideas. Once he'd dragged the guy out into the street, instead of beating on him, Willard bent over and started going through the guy's pockets, and kept at it until he found a thick roll of bills hiding in the guy's jeans.

That's the point where I noticed the door they'd rolled out of was standing wide open. I couldn't see what, if anything, was inside, because the door opened in my direction and completely shielded the entranceway from view.

And then Willard looked up at the doorway for long enough to tell me somebody was standing there. Then, whoever was in the doorway said something. Willard replied. I watched as he pocketed the wad of cash and scrambled to his feet.

He shouted something at the guy on the ground, kicked him twice in the ribs, and then shinnied up onto the sidewalk, where he checked the street in both directions before disappearing into the building and pulling the door closed behind him.

I turned and stuck out my hand. "Leo Waterman," I said.

He took my hand. "Bob Christophel."

"Thanks for the hospitality," I said.

"Don't mention it."

"You got any idea what goes on over there?" I asked as I eased open the door.

He shook his head. "Not a clue," he said. "It's always older guys, though. They come and go all day long. Asians, mostly. Never seen a woman go in the building."

"Really?" I said as I stepped out onto the sidewalk.

He stuck his head out the door. "You know, during tax season, I sleep in the office once in a while. Nights get really busy over there," he said, jerking his thumb toward the joint next door. "It's a revolving door. There's somebody in and out every five minutes." He raised a finger. "That little Asian guy . . ."

"Yeah?"

"At night he's the one that lets the guys in and then shows them out."

Sounded like a bouncer to me. And Willard had sure turned out to be a significantly bigger badass than I'd imagined. Question was . . . bouncing for what?

I thanked him and started up the sidewalk.

Bikerman was back on his feet and moving now. He'd found a blue bandanna and had it pressed to his mouth as he zigzagged up the sidewalk toward First Avenue, leaving thick drops of blood behind him on the concrete like bread crumbs. I stood and watched his grim visage part the remaining crowd like Moses at the Red Sea.

I considered hanging around for a while—see if maybe Willard wouldn't put in another guest appearance—but I was feeling way too itchy for anything that even resembled a stakeout. I had too many loose ends dangling to stand around waiting for a skell like Willard Frost.

▪ ▪ ▪

In Seattle, old-fashioned gin mills are getting to be relics. Everything is becoming gentrified. Shit-hole taverns have become gastropubs, complete with twenty-dollar hamburgers and duck-fat French fries. Neighborhood bars have morphed into Château Le Douche. Sustainable and locally sourced, you know.

The Eastlake Zoo was a remnant of a bygone era. No plastic. Cash only. If you wanted to nosh, you better have a hankering for packaged peanuts or beef jerky, otherwise you should feel free to visit the pizza joint next door. And by the way, shut that fucking cell phone off before you come in here. The Management Thanks You.

I stood in the doorway, letting my eyes adjust to the deep-space dark. Serious speed metal blasted from the speakers. Young music. Angry music. I vaguely remembered being an angry young man, but, for the life of me, couldn't recall what I was so pissed off about. I covered my ears and started for the back of the room.

George Paris, Ralph Batista, and Harold Green were the last living members of my father's political machine. George had been one of Big Bill's bankers. Money launderer, the authorities said. At the time of my old man's demise, George had owned a big house over in Madrona Park, had a high-society wife, and was thinking about buying a second condo on Maui for his daughter. When the shit hit the fan, George was fired by the bank, divorced by his fancy wife, and summarily convicted of misappropriation of public funds. George served eighteen months in the county cooler before being jettisoned back onto the streets like a wadded-up gum wrapper. He'd been sharing an apartment with a telephone pole ever since.

Ralph Batista had been my old man's Port of Seattle connection. According to the cops, he'd been the one who'd looked the other way while hundreds, possibly thousands, of illegal Chinese were smuggled into Seattle. When my old man popped a heart valve out in front of the Fairmont Olympic Hotel and his whole house of cards came tumbling down, Ralph was picked up as a material witness. They grilled him for nearly a week before letting him go, which wouldn't have been so bad, except that fourteen Chinese nationals ended up locked in a shipping container on Pier 23 in ninety-five-degree temperatures for almost a week. Six of them died.

The cops never managed to work up a court-worthy case against Ralph, but it didn't matter. Ralph was his own judge and jury. As far as he was concerned, those six lives would always be on him. To my knowledge, he'd never been sober for a single day since. While George had retained his incisive eye and caustic wit through all of it, the years had not been nearly so kind to Ralph. A quarter century of debauchery had reduced him to a state of perpetual bewilderment. If George hadn't been looking out for him, he'd surely have been dead by now.

Harold Green's only sin was being a childhood friend of my father and trusting him implicitly. Unfortunately for Harold, he'd signed his name on various dotted lines, unwittingly making himself de facto CEO of several dummy corporations my father had set up to hide his ill-gotten gains, a misstep that cost Harold the better part of three years in the lockup and any remnant of self-respect he may have still possessed at the time.

I'd often wondered how different the trajectories of their lives might have been if they hadn't fallen in with Big Bill Waterman. They sure as hell wouldn't involve being shit-faced before ten every morning, I was pretty sure of that. Which probably explained why, all these years later, I still made it a point to keep track of them. To make sure they had at least a little of what they needed. Sins of the fathers and all that.

The Zoo's day bartender generally let the boys in about an hour before the actual opening time at eleven A.M. Like most steady drinkers, none of them slept worth a damn, so, by the time seven A.M. rolled around at whatever dump they were crashing in, most of them had already started their drinking day.

They required a couple of beers in bed before attempting anything serious, like walking. Once up and stumbling about, a man could surely be excused an eye-opener or two, followed, of course, by the obligatory phlegm cutter as a medicinal prelude to serious intellectual discourse. After that, they'd venture into the great outdoors for their daily pilgrimage to the Eastlake Zoo, where a little snooker and an ocean of beer would wash them gently into the prelunch cocktail hour, from whence a bracer of two would of course be required in order to approach the dinner hour in a civilized manner. Then, depending upon the state of their finances and world affairs, the revelry generally continued till about nine P.M. or so, at which point they'd stagger back to their flop and settle in for another night in dreamland.

The whole crowd was there. George, Ralph, and Harold, Nearly Normal Norman, Heavy Duty Judy, Red Lopez, Large Marge, Frenchie, Billy Bob Fung, and a few others I'd seen before but couldn't put a name to. Usually at least one of them was in the slammer. When you're down and out, running afoul of the law is pretty much a given. They'd get cited for pissing in an alley or something and then fail to appear in court, which, of course, was a far worse breach of legal etiquette than relieving oneself, and then the next time they surfaced there'd be a warrant out for them, which would inevitably lead to yet another joyous month behind bars.

I threw some money on the bar and nodded at the kid for a round of whatever they were drinking. How to know you're getting a tad long in the tooth: when you start making decisions about where you eat and drink based on whether you can abide the music they play. So whenever I came in, the kid and I had a longstanding deal. He could keep the change as long as he got rid of that fucking "I hate everybody" music he blasted all the time. He walked over and kept his end of the bargain. My ears thanked him. I heaved a sigh of relief and headed for the rear of the bar.

Norman saw me first. "Leo," he bellowed, and the place erupted. They came at me like mad lemmings. I was backslapped and hugged nearly into submission.

I grabbed an empty chair from one of the tables and pulled it up next to George.

"How's it going?" I asked.

He shrugged. "Passable, I suppose," he allowed.

These days, George had a face like an old satchel. His wardrobe looked like it belonged to somebody else, which it once had.

"Wanna make some money?" I asked.

He red-eyed me. "Doin' what?"

"Like old times," I said.

When I was still making a living as a private eye, I made work for these guys whenever I could. They were great for stakeouts, as long as it was somewhere downtown. They could hang around all day and nobody paid them any mind because society has trained itself not to see the poor and the destitute. That way, we don't have to think about how the richest society on earth allows so many of its citizens to live in the streets like stray dogs.

He took a sip of his beer, leaned back in the chair, and stifled a belch.

On the other side of the room, raised voices captured my attention.

"You're fulla shit," Red Lopez shouted. "You never done no such thing."

"Swear to God." It was a big, red-faced, Nordic-looking guy I'd never seen before.

"Ten dollars," Red yelled. "I'll betcha ten dollars you won't, you lyin' motherfucker."

"Let's see the money," the guy yelled back.

Red jumped to his feet, dug around in his pants pockets for way longer than was considered polite, and finally came out with a wadded-up bill, which he unwadded and slapped onto the snooker table with a clap. "There," he shouted. "*There's* my goddamn money. Where's yours?"

The guy pulled out a modest wad of cash, sorted through it, and clapped a ten on top of Red's money. He pocketed his roll and looked around the room.

"Anybody else?" he wanted to know.

Frenchie and Judy jumped at the chance. Once they'd anted up, the red-faced man strode across the room, pulled open the men's room door, and disappeared inside.

When I turned my attention back to the room, Ralph was tacking across the floor in our direction. "What's goin' on?" I asked him as he plopped down in the chair next to George.

He poured himself a beer and then downed it. "They got a bet," he slurred.

"About what?"

"The Swede says he'll eat one of those smelly things for ten bucks."

"What smelly things?"

"You know, man. From the pisser."

I didn't have to press for a clarification before the men's room door burst open and the guy he'd called the Swede came sauntering back into the room. I strained to see what it was he was bouncing in his hand. Looked like half a vanilla cupcake.

Across the room, the assembled multitude began to rumble and rise to its feet. "Do it, man," somebody yelled.

"Yeah, do it!" Judy screeched.

The place came unglued.

And then they began to chant like a soccer crowd. "Do it. Do it. Do it . . ."

Wasn't until he began to lift the cupcake to his mouth that I figured out what it actually was. When, with a great flourish, the Swede held it in two fingers and the rest of his hand got out of the way, I could finally see a little white cake . . . Awww . . . Jesus, nooo. It was one of those old-fashioned deodorant cakes that they used in the urinals.

"Do it . . . do it . . . do it . . ." rang through the room.

Instinctively, I started to rise. George put a restraining hand on my arm.

"Stay out of it," he growled around a mouthful of beer.

It was like a wreck on the highway. You know you should turn away, show some respect for the dead, but you just can't bring yourself to do it, as if some primal instinct insists that, for the sake of your own survival, you are required to pay attention.

I watched in horror as he chomped down and took a bite. Pieces dropped onto the wooden floor. Apparently, it was a bit flakier than my palate had imagined.

He chewed away. Swallowed. Took another bite. Swallowed.

"Do it . . . do it . . . do it . . ."

Took him about thirty seconds to get it all the way down. It was a toss-up. I couldn't decide whether to puke or applaud.

When he raised his fingertips to his lips and then pulled them away in a classic "bon appétit" move, wild cheering rattled the rafters.

The Swede smiled knowingly, snatched the money from the top of the snooker table, and strode regally toward the front door.

When things had settled to the usual mumble, I turned to George.

"I need a few guys to keep an eye on a couple places down in the square," I said. "You guys interested?"

"How much?"

"Fifty a day for each guy," I said. "It'll take at least four of you."

What I wanted could have been easily handled by one guy at each address, assuming, of course, that they weren't hammered—an assumption I'd long since parted with when it came to these guys. So I automatically double the manpower required, in case somebody needed an in situ nap.

"Where in the square?" he asked.

I pulled out my notebook and wrote down both addresses.

"When?" he asked.

I told him tonight.

"And we're just supposed to watch 'em?" he gargled around a mouthful of beer.

"See if you can get inside the Walter Street place," I said, sliding the page across the table to him. "I think he lives there."

"He who?"

I pulled the picture of Willard Frost from my inside jacket pocket and used my palms to straighten the creases. George leaned over and put his nose about an inch from the photo.

"His name's Willard Frost," I said.

"Sure as hell don't look like a Willard Frost," George said.

Great minds think alike. Scary thought, that.

"See if you can get inside the building and ask around about him. See what anybody knows about him."

"What about the other joint?"

"Find out what in hell they're doing in there. Seems like he's the muscle for some kind of operation they're running out of the building."

He gave me a mock two-fingered salute. "Gotcha, boss," he said. I slid him a fistful of money and got to my feet. Just as I was wondering if what I'd witnessed from the Swede could possibly have been real, I noticed that somebody'd stepped in the remnants of the deodorant cake and smeared it all over the floor. I was still swallowing hard and shaking my head in wonder as I headed for the street.

As I walked past the bar, I could hear George behind me calling out, "Harold, Billy Bob . . . get your moldy butts over here."

The kid came out from behind the bar and locked the door behind me. I'd parked my car up on Franklin, so I waited for the light, crossed Eastlake, and started hoofing it up the hill. Gravity seemed to be stronger than I remembered, but, what the hell, it wasn't raining. *Gotta look on the bright side,* I told myself.

One block up, a movement in my peripheral vision pulled my head to the right, and there he was. The Swede, sitting on a low stone wall that formed one side of an overgrown flower garden. He looked over at me and smiled.

He waved me over. I took a couple of steps in his direction and then stopped. I sure as hell didn't want to get close enough for that mofo to breathe on me, so I kept my distance. He pulled a handful of something from his jacket pocket and set it on the wall beside him. I watched as he peeled back the ends of a brown paper towel to reveal what appeared to be two more of those disgusting deodorant cakes. I swallowed hard. Wasn't till he peeled the cakes apart and set them beside each other on the wall that I noticed the slight difference in color between the two. I gravitated closer. He touched the whiter one with his grimy finger. It jiggled. I leaned in closer.

"Tofu," he said.

Took me a couple of seconds to blurt out, "What?"

"I carve the ones I eat outta tofu," he said with a gap-toothed grin. He nodded at the other cake. "But you gotta take the real one outta the john in case they check."

A colorful Odwalla truck ground slowly up the street and turned uphill on Louisa. The tops of the trees swung gently in the breeze.

I collected my lower jaw, fished around in my pocket, came out with a twenty-dollar bill, and handed it to him. He looked like he was going to ask a question.

"Just take it," I said, and walked away.

■ ■ ■

I'd known Rebecca's assistant Ibrahim for the better part of fifteen years. It was the kind of relationship that reminded me how little most human beings really knew about one another. How it's come to the point where we call people we met online "friends" and yet, at the same time, have almost no idea what the lives of those most familiar to us look like.

He was Sudanese and had seen terrible things. He and his wife had somehow escaped the carnage and made it to London. Once they got to the United States, they had kids. Gender and age unknown. That was about it. Oh yeah. . . and he didn't think I was a bit funny. Over the years I'd made several hundred jokes with him and had never so much as seen his lip quiver. All those years of seeing him on a fairly regular basis, and that was all I could bring to mind. Dude. An existentialist dream.

His wife answered the door. Two little girls in pigtails swirled around in her brightly flowered skirt, peeking out from the material to see the strange giant at their door and then slipping from sight.

His wife knew who I was. We met every year at the office Christmas party. She gave me a smile. As I recalled, her English wasn't so good.

The larger of the two girls poked her head from the folds of the dress. The little sister scurried back into the house, giggling all the way.

"What's your name?" I asked the older girl. Six or seven, I thought. I'm not good with kids' ages.

She looked up at her mom and got a nearly imperceptible nod.

"Nikka," she said, before disappearing back into the dress.

"Hi, Nikka," I said. "I'm Leo."

"Is Ibrahim here?" I asked the wife.

"My husband . . ." I didn't understand the next part. "A walk," the wife said, pointing at the little pocket park across the street. "A walk."

I thanked her and began to back down off the porch. Nikka poked her head out again as her mom withdrew from sight. "Bye, Leo the Lion," she said with a huge grin.

I gave her a wave and turned away, but she followed along. "Leo the Lion, Leo the Lion," she sang as I stepped down onto the sidewalk. She pointed in the direction of the park. "Papa's over there," she said. She grinned and spread her arms wide. "Way up on top."

I started to walk off, but she grabbed my hand and began to skip along beside me.

I stopped, squatted low, so our eyes were on the same level. She let go of my hand and threw an arm around my shoulder. I picked her up and carried her back to the porch.

"You watch out for your mama," I said as I set her in front of the door.

"Leo the Lion, Leo the Lion," she sang as she stepped inside the townhouse.

I waved bye-bye again and started up the sidewalk. I checked over my shoulder to make sure Nikka was gonna stay put and then picked up my pace.

The air was still and thick like soup. The newly planted trees in the median dripped with moisture. I stuffed my hands in my coat pockets, hunched my shoulders, and picked up the pace.

I crossed the street and followed the pristine white sidewalk up into the park. They'd built the park as a little hill, I suppose so the rainwater would easily drain back into the sewer system. No signage of any kind. Must have been so new it didn't have a name yet. Eventually, they'd name it after some neighborhood luminary. They always did. Couldn't have a park with no name. Google wouldn't stand for it.

The sound of voices pulled my head up. A phalanx of strollers was rolling my way. The plastic wheels of death. I stepped off into the grass and gave a nonthreatening nod. One of the mothers said something to me in a language I didn't understand. They all laughed. They kept looking back over their shoulders at me and laughing as I stood there on the newly rolled-out sod and watched them disappear into the gloom.

Up at the apex of the knoll, I could make out the shape of Ibrahim sitting on a bright-blue bench all by himself. Looked a bit like a pocket Rodin. He sensed me coming. I saw his body tense. He turned his head away and pushed himself to his feet. I sidled up to the bench. The fog had an acrid taste to it.

He was a skinny little man without an ounce of body fat. It was as if he had already used up every bit of his reserves. Bald in the front but not in back, he had enough coffee-colored forehead to post handbills.

"I don't think I should be talking to you," he said in a low voice.

His English was precise and perfect. All the *s*'s and *t*'s just right. Listening to him reminded me how sloppy most of us are when it comes to pronunciation.

"I read the suspension order, coupla times," I said with a shrug. "As far as I could see, my name wasn't mentioned anywhere. They said Dr. Duvall couldn't have any contact with you, but they didn't say anything about me."

I was splitting hairs, and he knew it. Ibrahim was a careful man. He looked at me hard, weighing his options. "She's a good woman," he said finally. "A good doctor. This shouldn't be happening to her. It's not right."

"You got any idea how this could have happened?" I asked.

He shook his head and sat down. "They didn't tell me anything." He shrugged. "Sometimes things happen," he said. "Must be . . . She would never . . ."

I shook my head. "They think they've got a sure thing."

I sat down next to him on the bench. I could hear the shrill sound of the strolling mothers in the distance. I spent the next ten minutes asking him everything I could think of and came up with a fat nothing.

As nearly as I could tell, Ibrahim was as confused as the rest of us. When I ran out of questions, we sat there and watched the fog fold around us like a blanket of wet felt.

Eventually, he got to his feet and began ambling slowly in the direction of his house. I kept pace. The sodden air felt like we were wading. I'm generally comfortable with silence. Most of what I hear in the course of a day is the same ol', same ol' anyway. I've always been of the opinion that if people could just bring themselves to say "I don't know" when they don't know, we'd all live longer and have to listen to a whole lot less bullshit. But that's not how people are. People hate to say "I don't know." They'll speculate, gesticulate, and just plain make up shit to avoid saying the words out loud.

We were nearly back to his front door before he said anything.

"They sent a man with a paper this morning. He came to my house."

"What paper?"

"I must appear in court on Friday."

"A subpoena?"

He nodded.

"Just tell the truth and you'll be fine," I assured him.

The look in his eyes said he knew better. "Dr. . . . she's like family to me," he said. "I don't want to . . . The last thing I would ever want . . ."

I put a hand on his shoulder. "Whatever they ask you, you just tell 'em the truth as you know it. That's all you can do."

He straightened his spine and tried to stare a hole through my skull.

"Family is all that matters," he said. "There's nothing else."

Hard to argue with that, so I didn't try.

■ ■ ■

Forrest Blaine lived way the hell up north in Pinehurst. Figured I'd get him out of the way before rush hour screwed things up. I decided not to mess with the freeway, so I bounced over the University Bridge and just kept on going, rolling through the neighborhoods until the sidewalks petered out and you could actually park for free in front of your own house. What a concept!

I parked on the dirt shoulder across Eighteenth Avenue from Forrest's sixties trilevel. The fog hadn't crept this far north, just the damp. I could see the bottom half of Forrest sticking out of a bush at the far end of the house. I walked that way. Cue the Aerosmith music.

He was whacking away at a blackberry bush with a machete. His body language made it plain that the blackberry bush was ahead on points. I've always figured that in the event of a holocaust, the only two things that were sure to survive were PVC pipe and blackberry bushes.

Forrest was a stocky local kid from Ballard who'd tried this and that after high school—construction, mortgage broker, property management, and such crap—until he came up with the medical examiner assistant gig and discovered the joys of unionization and the public dole. I'd always figured he was gonna be a city government lifer.

Interestingly enough, from the moment I'd met him at a Fourth of July picnic, he'd treated me like I was a long-lost buddy. Like somewhere in the past we'd shared something so profound that it automatically joined us at the hip for eternity. I was flexible on the subject. Way I saw it, buddy-buddy worked for me, so I'd always made it a point to keep up my end of the homeboy business.

He was running his sleeve over his brow when he noticed me coming across the lawn. "Hey, man," he said, waving the machete in my direction.

"Tough going, eh?"

He pointed the machete at the blackberry bush. A seeping red scratch adorned the back of his machete hand. "Shit bites back," he said.

"They're friggin' indestructible," I allowed.

"You got any idea what's going on down at the office?" he asked.

"That's what I came to ask you."

He hacked out a bitter laugh. "You come to the wrong place, bro. All I know is they suspended me *with* pay until this thing shakes out." He threw me a big grin. "Several months of this shit would be fine with me," he joked. "I might even get a few things done around here before the place sinks into the ground."

"We really can't do much until we know who signed off on the deliveries."

He looked a bit sheepish and turned away, like somebody who had something to say but wasn't sure it was a good idea. He checked the area like he was in a bad B-movie street scene.

"What?" I pushed.

Took him a second. "Findin' that out ain't gonna be a hell of a lot of help neither," he said.

"Why's that?"

"This is off the record, right? You're working for the Doc."

"Nothing we say here is ever going to be attributed to you."

He gave it some thought. "Because . . . you know, man, I'm real fond of the Doc. I feel like I ought to be straight with you here. Because you need to know . . ." He hesitated, then let it out. "Whoever signed off for the stuff isn't necessarily the same person who delivered it."

Gotta admit, I went full mouth breather for a second or three. We'd bet the farm on being able to find out who delivered the samples to whom and when. Neither of us had said it out loud, but both Rebecca and I were hoping that once we had the specifics, the mix-up would become obvious, and the current shit storm would magically disappear. My stomach felt as if I'd swallowed a basket of ball bearings.

"How's that?" I choked out.

"You know, bro. I don't have to tell you, man . . . city traffic's terrible. Getting to the precincts during the day is a first-class pain in the ass. You get unlucky, and you can waste half a friggin' day at it and then come back and have to finish your work on your own time. So . . . you know, like, we hear somebody else say, 'I'm going to the North Precinct.

Anybody got anything that needs to ride along?'" He showed his palms to the leaden sky, machete and all. "We sign the paperwork, slap one of the Doc's labels on it, and give it to whoever's going over there. It just makes sense. No extra trips. No extra budget items we gotta justify. End o' friggin' story."

"And nobody at the precinct end objects?"

He made a face. "Everybody knows everybody forever." He shrugged. "It's just business as usual, bro."

■ ■ ■

Micah Lowery, on the other hand, hated my guts. Somehow, despite seeing each other on a regular basis, we'd never managed to make the human connection necessary for a relationship. Which was odd, because, generally, if I see somebody often enough, I start to notice how we're similar rather than how we're different, and we manage to find some common ground. But with Micah . . . We'd always seemed to repel each other in the manner of opposing magnetic poles.

Micah was a morbidly obese little guy, somewhere between fifty and sixty. Bald as an egg, he'd always smelled a bit moldy to me, the way people who live on sailboats often do. Anybody who believes that gay men "decide" to be gay ought to spend a day or two with Micah. I'm betting they'd come away from the experience transformed . . . so to speak, anyway.

Problem was, unlike the other LGBT people I knew, the vast majority of whom just wanted to be treated like everybody else, Micah always seemed to feel that his sexual orientation entitled him to a little something extra. Some kind of universal forbearance because it was harder to be gay than it was to be straight. Like in figure skating, where you get extra style points for a triple toe loop.

As for me . . . I simply didn't agree. I figured out a long time ago that just because I was one of those blokes for whom sex was simple—you know, nothing more complicated than phalange A seemed to fit nicely into grommet B—that didn't mean that things were that simple for everybody. I treated Micah like I treated everybody else, a fact he sorely resented.

His roommate, Clint, told me I could find him over where Madison branches into Union. Take the second left. Half a block of flat black facade. Shimmering silver, **Leathers**, and a bevy of CC cameras spaced along the wall. According to the marquee, tonight's band was Throbbing Gristle. Be still my foolish heart.

Micah was sitting at the far end of the bar, swirling a flat beer round and round in a glass. Sinatra was crooning it *his way* over the sound system. Other than Micah and the big chin whiskers polishing glasses behind the bar, the place was deserted.

When I slipped onto the stool beside him, Micah turned his bleary little eyes my way. Took him a few seconds to focus. "Wadda *you* want?" he slurred.

"You got any ideas about what's going on with this missing evidence thing?"

He rocked on the stool. Wiped his lips with his sleeve. "My union rep says I shouldn't talk about it"—he waved an angry hand at me—"so get the fuck out of here."

He chugged the rest of his beer and banged the glass on the bar. Chin Whiskers had disappeared into the walk-in cooler. "Bobby . . . lemme have another," Micah yelled.

"So you got any idea what's going on?" I pressed.

"Bobby," he bellowed.

"Somebody was fucking with my livelihood, I'd want to know what in hell was going on," I said.

"Why don't you take your big homophobic ass out of here."

"I'm not homophobic," I said amiably. "I'm rectophobic. It's assholes, not gay dudes, I've got a problem with." I smiled wide and shrugged. "Probably explains why we never got along."

"Fuck you."

"Never on the first date."

Movement on my left pulled my attention back behind the bar.

It was Chin Whiskers, carrying a foamy draft beer. He set the beer on the bar in front of Micah. "This guy bothering you?" he asked, throwing me his most baleful stare. I stifled tears.

"Just another day-tripper," Micah said.

"'. . . a Sunday driver, yeah,'" I sang.

They both looked at me like I'd cursed somebody's mother.

"I think you better go," the bartender said.

"When I'm done talking to Micah here." I turned back to Micah. "You keep track of which samples you take to the precinct personally and which ones somebody else delivers for you?"

He had to chew on that one for a few seconds before his color returned and he straightened himself on the stool and said, "I don't know what the hell you're talking about." He gave me the finger and then twirled the stool so his back was to me.

"I'm not telling you again," the bartender said.

I thought about hopping over the bar and busting him in the chops a couple of times for practice but managed to stifle the urge. Good thing too.

The kitchen door burst open. A guy wearing a stained white apron appeared. He was holding a German shepherd on a purple leash.

I made a surrender sign with my hands and slid off the stool.

"Isn't it illegal for an animal to be in a place they serve food?" I asked, as I shambled across the room.

"He's a service dog," Chin Whiskers said.

"Exactly what service does he perform?" I inquired as I reached for the door handle.

Behind the porcupine beard, he smiled. "You wanna find out?" he asked.

I smiled back. "Nah. Think I'll take a rain check on that."

▪ ▪ ▪

The closer I got to salt water, the thicker the fog became. I'd tried calling Rebecca, but her phone went directly to voicemail—which, the way I saw it, was as good a reason as any to make a pit stop back home. You know, use the john, swap information, figure out what to do next, that sort of thing. At least, that's what I told myself.

By the time I got all the way down to Elliott and started rolling north toward Magnolia, the afternoon traffic was beginning to swell, and the glass tech palaces that line Puget Sound were winking in and out of the fog like half-erased pencil drawings.

Must have been a slow news day. The same two news teams as last night had returned. I pushed the button for the gate, swung the car all the way across the oncoming lane, and squealed through the opening before Snowdrift Dawson could even get out of the truck. I watched him in the rearview mirror, waving the microphone like a flag, shouting something at my back, as the gate slid closed in his face.

I pulled the car all the way around the back of the house and popped the door handle. I was halfway out of the seat when I noticed the bag of throwaway phones over on the passenger side. I grabbed it, got out, and let myself in the kitchen door. Two steps inside, the door swung closed behind me. I looked over my shoulder. Gabe was behind the door. I watched as the chrome Smith & Wesson disappeared under the wide black belt.

"How goeth the battle?" Gabe asked.

"He returneth," I announced. "Battered, bruised, and damn near dog bit, but undaunted." I threw the bag of phones on the kitchen table. "How long have those assholes been camped outside the gate?"

"Since about half an hour after you left. They've set the system off twice by touching the gate. I followed your suggestion and called the cops." Gabe grinned. "Of course, they sent the SWAT team right out."

These days in Seattle, anything short of a mass decapitation, and you could get an anchovy pizza delivered before the cops would show up.

Rebecca poked her head out of the hall. "Hey," I said.

I could see the strain gathering around her eyes.

"You retrieve your copies of those files?" I asked.

She brightened three watts. "Yep."

I leaned out the door and hung my jacket outside on the porch wall.

"You found a lawyer?" I asked as I closed the door again.

"Come and gone," she said with a wan smile.

I walked over to her, threw an arm around her shoulders, and pulled her up the hall with me. She leaned her head on my shoulder. Gabe followed along.

"Nancy Pometta. Soon to be the newest partner at Kellogg and Haynes."

"And she said?"

I steered her into what had once been my father's office. The inner sanctum from which I'd been perpetually banned, and from which all Big Bill's nefarious schemes had once been hatched. Gabe lounged in the doorway.

A while back I'd completely renovated the first floor of the house and turned the office into what has become popularly known as a man cave. Nothing crazy. No neon beer signs or any schlock like that, just a flat-screen TV the size of Vermont and enough soft furniture to accommodate a football team. And . . . oh yeah . . . the big ol' stainless steel refrigerator back against the far wall. No sense traipsing back to the kitchen every time I . . . you know what I mean.

Rebecca sat down heavily in the red leather chair. "Nancy said . . ." She heaved a massive sigh. "You know how lawyers are. She wasn't making any promises." Rebecca leaned back and folded her hands in her lap. "She didn't say so, but I don't think she liked the lay of the land at all. She's down at the courthouse right now pushing back against the timeline the DA wants to establish. Claiming she hasn't been given sufficient time to review my case."

"Good."

She shook her head. "But she doesn't think it's going to do much good."

"Why's that?"

"Because, like you and I figured, Woodward and his minions want this thing to make as much noise as possible. She thinks they're going to call in every judicial marker they own to milk every PR drop out of it they can."

"Can't she do anything about it?"

"Not until we get to the trial phase of things, by which time the media will have long since moved on to something else, and the other side is in a better position to manage the news, which, according to Nancy, is the object of the exercise. At the trial phase, we'll have a right to know what the prosecution has in the way of evidence and a right to sufficient time to prepare a defense. Before that, though, we're more or less at their mercy."

"Ibrahim said he's been subpoenaed to appear on Friday."

She looked surprised. As if she'd been so busy handling her end of things that she hadn't had time to wonder what I was up to. "You saw Ibrahim?"

"I visited all three kings."

Her face wanted to know whether I'd come up with anything.

"Just about what you'd expect. Anybody trying to get anything out of Ibrahim had better heat the pliers red hot, because that old boy is tellin' nobody nothin'. Forrest is enjoying the time off, and Micah wouldn't piss on me if I was on fire."

"You're way too alpha for him."

"Personally, I'd like to beta the crap out of him."

I brought the Olympic eye-rolling finals to halt when I said, "I did come up with one not-so-minor problem."

"Yeah?"

Discretion being the better part of valor, I took an extra second to choose my words. "I'm guessing you weren't aware of how your guys handled the evidence delivery on a day-to-day basis."

"What do you mean?" Something in her eyes told me she wished I'd shut up.

I told her what Forrest had told me. Not the *Reader's Digest* version either. The whole damn thing, about all of them covering for one another on evidence deliveries. She went from red to white and back to red. An uncomfortable silence slipped over the room. And stayed there for what seemed like a year and a half.

"It's my fault," she said finally. "The buck stops with me." She threw a hand in the air. "I sign whole sheets of ME seals at the beginning of the week." She caught the surprised look on my face. "It's not like they can come running to me every time they need to ship something over to a precinct. Most of the time, I'm up to my elbows in someone's remains." She shook her head in disgust. "Besides which . . . shit rolls downhill, and I'm the one who's forever carping at them over the damn budget." She appeared to be having an argument with herself and losing. "And, much as it pains me to admit, delivery was one of those things I made it a point not to be too aware of . . . if you know what I mean."

Did I ever. Me and denial were friends with benefits. I couldn't think of anything sufficiently self-serving to say, so I didn't bother to try.

"Forrest's right," she said after another tense interlude. "It *is* silly to make more than one trip to a precinct on any given day." She made a rueful face. "I've always known what we were doing was at odds with the protocol, but that's the way it's always been done. The way Harry Doyle did it before me and, for all I know, how the guy before Harry did it.

"I suppose this is the place where I'm supposed to beat myself up about all the things I coulda-shoulda done, but . . . you know what?

When I think about it—the staffing and the workload and the budget constraints—I really don't see any other way it could be accomplished."

"The evidence room's surely gotta be under CC surveillance," I threw in.

"Like they're going to share that with us," she scoffed.

"Which raises the question of what to do next."

That's when I remembered that I hadn't checked to see if there were any messages from Eagen. I looked over at Gabe, who was still holding up the door. "You know that bag I dropped on the kitchen table?"

Gabe nodded. I didn't have to ask. Gabe levered off the door frame and disappeared down the hall.

"What about that Frost guy?" Rebecca asked. "Did you find him?"

I told her about my little morning adventure down in the square. I finished up with, "I've got the boys working on it."

"Oh . . . I feel so much better now."

Gabe strolled back into the room and handed me the bag. I dumped it out onto the bed and began to pick through the phones. That's when the security system alarm began to bleat.

Gabe heaved a sigh. "Those TV assholes again. Goddamn it." Gabe headed for the front door.

"I'm scared," Rebecca said out of the blue. "Every direction we turn in seems to be a dead end."

I was working up my famous "the darkest hour is just before the dawn" speech when Gabe returned, looking vaguely amused. "It's the cops."

"They got a warrant?"

"Nope. Say they wanna talk to you."

I thought it over. "Let 'em in," I said.

Gabe disappeared. Rebecca cocked an eyebrow at me.

I shook my head. "Maybe they found out I saw Ibrahim and the guys today and want to warn me off. They're big on that intimidation thing."

Took about three minutes to find out how wrong I was. Gabe followed Krauss and Nelson into the TV room. The DA's bruise brothers each gave Rebecca a polite nod, and then Krauss got right to the point. "Did you see Ibrahim Durka earlier today?" he asked.

Here it was. The old keep-your-nose-out-of-this-case speech.

"Why?"

"Mr. Durka was involved in an accident."

"What kind of accident?" Rebecca asked.

"Hit-and-run," Nelson said.

"Is he okay?"

"No," Krauss said quickly. "Mr. Durka was DOA at Harborview."

I felt as if somebody were standing on my chest. Rebecca brought a sob-stifling fist to her mouth. It didn't work. I watched as her shoulders began to shake.

"You want to tell us where you were at noon today?" Nelson said.

I thought about telling them to get the hell out of my house, but managed to quell the urge. "In a leather bar up on the hill."

Krauss couldn't hide the sneer.

"Yeah, that's right," I said. "It's the rough trade for me. Nothin' quite like somebody rubbing their stubbly chin over my nuts."

Gabe hid a smile behind a hand.

"We'd like you to come along with us," Nelson said.

"Where to?" Gabe threw in.

Both cops staged a slow turn toward the voice. "And you'd be . . . ?" Krauss said.

"I'd *be* standing right here," Gabe replied.

The tension in the room started to tingle my cheeks.

"Am I under arrest?" I asked.

They grudgingly turned back my way.

"No. Not at this time," Krauss growled.

The answer annoyed me. It reminded me of a woman friend of my father's who once had introduced me to "her present husband, Robert."

At the time, I'd wanted to bust one of them in the lip but couldn't decide which one. Now Krauss was giving me that same urge.

"Where is it you want to take me?" I asked.

"To the accident scene."

"Why would you need me to go there?"

"Just covering our bases," Krauss said.

Cops are like that. They want to know every goddamn thing about you but are never willing to part with any information. Nelson could tell I didn't like it.

"Other than his wife and kids, you were, as far as we can tell, the last person to see Mr. Durka alive," he added.

I looked around. Rebecca was teary but under control. Gabe looked like I felt: like rearranging Krauss's face held a great deal of appeal.

"I'm coming along," Rebecca announced. "I can't just sit here."

"Any place the Doc is going, I'm going," Gabe said.

I looked over at the cops. "Give me the address; we'll meet you there."

▪ ▪ ▪

No surprises. Same address as this morning. I pulled the car to the curb directly across the street from Ibrahim Durka's townhouse. The home's front door hung open. The townhouse was full of neighbors. Rebecca wanted to offer her condolences to the wife, but since the suspension order forbade any contact between Rebecca and *any and all representatives of Mr. Durka*, we decided it would be better if she and Gabe stayed in the car. She wasn't happy about it but went along with the program.

I got out and followed Krauss and Nelson into the cotton-ball fog. Unless I was mistaken, we were taking the same route I'd taken this morning. Without visual clues, it was hard to tell. A minute later I could make out a pair of SPD cruisers parked nose to nose, blocking the entrance to the park, and then, as I got closer, the three miles of yellow cop tape strung from sapling to sapling all the way around the perimeter.

We crossed the street to the park. The sidewalk rolled down the slope at us like a concrete tongue. It wasn't as clean and white as it had been earlier this morning. A pair of muddy tire tracks came down over the hill and disappeared into the street right where the SPD cruisers were parked.

Ahead, up at the top of the knoll, light bars were feverishly painting the underside of the ground fog alternately blue and red and yellow.

"He got run over in the park?" I said as much to myself as to the cops.

"They're thinking maybe somebody got confused in the fog," Nelson said.

"It's a fucking park," I groused. "This thing we're walking on is a sidewalk, not a street. That doesn't make any sense."

"Parks and Rec hasn't gotten around to installing the pole barriers or the park signs yet. They're thinking somebody turned in by mistake, didn't see him in the fog . . . Or I'm thinking maybe it was another one of those assholes who likes to tear up fresh grass with his tires, and Mr. Durka just got in the way."

"Could be whoever did it never even knew they hit somebody," Krauss added as he started waddling up the incline.

The forensics guys had a yellow tent set up in the middle of the sidewalk about three-quarters of the way up the hill. Half a dozen men and women in white plastic jumpsuits were milling around the area, a couple of them snapping away with cameras.

Nelson led us around to the left of the tent, looping way out onto the sod so we wouldn't interfere with the accident scene. From the top of the rise, I could see the spot where whoever it was had jumped the curb and come blasting up into the park. Where they'd looped out wide to the south, tearing the crap out of the new grass as they'd fishtailed all over, fighting for traction. What really got my attention, however, was the bright blue bench where I'd found Ibrahim sitting earlier in the day.

They'd set up temporary posts and run cop tape all around the perimeter. The bench stood on a single pedestal anchored in a concrete slab. Didn't take Sherlock Holmes to see that the hit-and run vehicle had plowed into the bench hard enough to bend solid steel. The damn thing was bent all the way over backward. What used to be the seat back was now parallel to the ground. I walked as close as the barriers would allow. The ground around the bench was littered with automobile debris. Major portions of the plastic bumper. What looked to be parts of the grille. Broken glass, both clear and yellow. But all the debris—all of it, except for the glass—was black. Flat black. Murdered-out black. I shivered.

I leaned against the tape, getting as close to the bench as I could. And there it was. Blood. Almost black in the flat light. All over the bench and the concrete slab beneath. Impact splotches of crimson bigger at one end than the other, telling anyone who cared to look which direction the vehicle had come from.

The torn-up grass showed how the vehicle had roared up the hill, plowed into Ibrahim and the bench, then backed up, and cut across the grass to the sidewalk. No skid marks at all. Looked to me like the driver was still on the throttle when he'd made contact with Ibrahim Durka. I shuddered at the thought.

I had one of those "is it just me or . . ." moments. And suddenly the fog was colder. I looked back at the yellow forensic tent, which I'd figured for the spot where the body had been found. Then back to the bench. Forty feet maybe. Certainly no more than that. But Jesus . . . how did anybody who'd lost that much blood get even that far?

When I glanced over at the tent again, Krauss was hard by my shoulder.

"So," he said, "you got anybody who can vouch for where you were at noon?"

I told him about that Leathers bartender named Bobby and that little shit Micah and the CC cameras out in front of the place. Telling him about the dog seemed like overkill, so I let it go. He wrote it all down.

I glanced over at the tent again. Krauss read my mind. "They think maybe Mr. Durka got caught up in the undercarriage of whatever hit him."

"You can't be thinking this is an accident."

Krauss stone-faced it. "Not our call," he said. "Only reason we're here is because SPD's computer flagged Mr. Durka's name as part of the case we're working on."

"And you think I had something to do with this?"

"Like I said before, far as anybody knows, you were the last person outside his family to see Mr. Durka alive." He shrugged. "And you know, Waterman, I've met the wife and kids. The missus don't even have a driver's license, and, I've gotta tell you, those two little girls don't look real dangerous to me. So if you're right and somebody did do this to Mr. Durka on purpose, then standard operating procedure says we look at you next." He spread his hands in mock resignation.

"Why would I want to do something like that?"

"Could be you found out earlier today that Mr. Durka was going to roll on Dr. Duvall in court on Friday and decided the best way to get your girlfriend outta the mess she's in was by getting rid of the unfortunate Mr. Durka."

Nelson strolled up from the tent area and joined us. I looked from Krauss to Nelson and back. "You guys really think I'm good for this?" I asked.

The glance they exchanged told me they didn't. Nelson's phone began to buzz. He stepped away from Krauss and me, listened for a minute, and then stuffed the phone back in his pocket. He pulled Krauss to his side and bent to whisper in his ear.

I sidled closer.

"Patrol thinks they found the vehicle," he hissed in Krauss's ear. "Parking lot of Jefferson Park Golf Course."

"They say what kind of vehicle?" I asked.

Nelson fixed me with an over-the-shoulder scowl. "Probably best you keep out of this," he said, as he pulled his partner farther up the sidewalk.

"Yeah," I said. "I'll be sure to do that."

■ ■ ■

They had the car running and the heat on when I got back.

"So?" Rebecca said.

"So . . . either Ibrahim was the unluckiest guy on the planet, or somebody ran his ass over on purpose, and I'm betting on door number two."

"Why's that?"

"Because whoever ran him over was still on the throttle when he hit the bench. There's no sign of any attempt to brake anywhere on the hill."

I fastened my seat belt while that was sinking in.

"Could it be . . . I mean, is it possible that we're getting a little paranoid here?" she asked. "Maybe we're reading more into this than there is."

"It could be, but I don't think so."

"Why would anyone . . ."

"Cops think they found the car that hit him over on Beacon Hill," I said as I eased the Chevy back into the street. "I want to have a look at it before they haul it off."

Took twenty minutes to cover the three miles or so to Beacon Hill. If anything, the fog was thicker on top of the hill. They'd already hoisted the van up on the back of a City of Seattle tow truck by the time we arrived. They'd turned off the sirens and light bars, but there was something about the three police cars and the city tow truck that got my attention as I cruised the golf course parking lot. It wasn't exactly tough to cruise, considering the fact that if you wanted to play golf at Jefferson Park, you had to leave your ride somewhere among the parking spaces they'd carved out of the Beacon Avenue median. So it was more or less made for a quick drive-by eyeballing.

I drove past the scene on the opposite side of Beacon, took the next turnaround, and started back south. The boys in blue had that segment of the lot blocked, so I played stupid and pulled in anyway, like I had no idea what was going on, and drove right up to the rear of the tow truck. There it was. Sitting up on the back of the truck. There was no doubt in my mind. This was the same van I'd seen the other night. Front end all busted up now, but that was the one, for sure.

"That's the same van the fake UPS guys were driving the other night," I said.

A uniformed cop was disgustedly waving at me to back up. I gave him a toothy idiot grin and began to ease back out the drive.

"You're certain?" Rebecca pressed.

"Positive," I said. "Same van."

"The cops know about this?" Gabe asked.

"They've got their own theory. They don't want to hear about ours."

"What now?" Gabe wondered out loud.

"Let's go get my car," Rebecca suggested. "I hate being stranded at your house."

I checked my watch and stifled a groan. 3:27. I dropped the car into drive and eased out into the street.

■ ■ ■

Took almost an hour to get down to Madison Park and then back over to the west side of the city, where I lived. Seattle's a white-collar town these days. The rush hour starts whenever they want it to, and the blanket of fog just made it exponentially worse. Average speed somewhere around 5 mph. Brewing myself a new pot of road rage about every five minutes.

Rebecca and Gabe were somewhere behind me in her Beamer as I eased up Magnolia Boulevard in the fog; or, at least, I assumed they were. Visibility was down to six or seven feet. I felt like I was driving through a bucket of whipped cream.

From the corner of my eye, I caught the outline of the Morrisons' windmill mailbox and slowed even more. I tried the high beams, but that just made it worse.

I could make out two TV remote units parked side by side in the driveway of the empty house across the street. A sudden breeze off the sound plowed a valley in the fog, and I could make out outlines of half a dozen people milling around in the street, directly in front of my gate. Even with near zero visibility, there was something off about their body language. Something was going on either inside or just outside the gate.

I braked to a stop, flipped the switch for the emergency flashers, and got out. Adrenaline hung on the fog like Spanish moss. Raised voices floated my way. Rebecca braked the BMW to a halt behind my car.

I walked back in her direction. Told her I didn't know what was going on but to stay in the car. Gabe didn't need to be invited to the party.

Gabe and I walked shoulder to shoulder as we closed the distance. Several people were shouting at once. Wasn't till we were ten feet from the nearest guy that I began to put it all together. A big red Dodge crew-cab pickup was parked diagonally across Magnolia Boulevard, with both front doors flung open. Somebody yelled, "Get that goddamn thing outta my face."

That's the point where I could make out Snowdrift Dawson waving his microphone in the face of a big guy with a beard.

"I tole you, motherfucker," the guy shouted.

What happened next will remain etched in my brain circuits until they slide me into the ground. It all happened in the space of about three seconds.

Snowdrift's cameraman was hopping around like an organ grinder's monkey, trying to keep the action in frame. Snowdrift brought the microphone up to his cherubic lips to record something for posterity, at which point Bluto with the beard took two steps forward and made a serious attempt to drive the microphone all the way through the back of Snowdrift's head. Swear to God, you could hear Dawson's front teeth snap off when that big, hairy fist made contact.

Snowdrift went from standing in his tasseled loafers to landing on the back of his neck, with no intermediate steps. Even through the fog, it was immediately apparent that the seeping maw formerly known as Snowdrift's mouth was going to require major cosmetic renovations. When the other bruiser then stepped forward, tore the camera from the TV tech's shoulder, and hurled it to the pavement, I finally snapped to the fact that these were the same assholes we'd seen on TV. The Delaney brothers—the idiots who had been fighting with cops out in front of the courthouse yesterday. Bailed out and bound to go.

The other camera crew had apparently decided that dealing with the Delaney brothers was not part of their job description. They came stiff-legging it back past Gabe and me, wobbling and wide-eyed. "Call 911," I said as they tottered past.

When I turned back toward the gate, I could see the remnants of the TV camera spread willy-nilly over the asphalt like roadkill. The camera operator was kneeling next to Dawson in the mouth of my driveway. I could hear the awful gurgling noises Snowdrift was making. The bottom half of the wireless microphone lay next to his head, but the bulbous top half was missing. I winced and hoped like hell he hadn't swallowed it.

Things got ugly from there. Rebecca told me later that she'd been leaning forward over the dashboard, trying to see through the fog, when she'd accidently blown the horn with her chest.

"That's that doctor bitch right there," one of the Delaney brothers shouted. He was pointing out over our heads, at Rebecca and the BMW. The brothers weren't big on meaningful discussion. Without another word, they forgot about poor Snowdrift Dawson, spittin' teeth there onto the asphalt, and started our way at a trot.

"I'll take the elephant," I whispered to Gabe. "Just keep little brother occupied while I—"

"See now, there you go being a sexist again," Gabe said. "I'll take Jumbo."

Before I could protest, Gabe cut in front of me and headed for big brother like a Scud missile. I thought later that it would have made a good public service message.

"What the fuck is this?" big brother growled through his chin whiskers. "Some kinda dyke bitch perv—?"

That was as far as the dazzling repartee got, because that's when Gabe hauled off and hit him full in the throat. Bluto brought both hands to his windpipe, took an unsteady step backward, and started making noises like an air compressor.

I was two steps behind the action when little brother emerged from the fog bank. "Hey, asshole," I said.

He lumbered my way. I closed the distance quicker than he anticipated and led with a stiff left jab that caught him coming in and spread his nose all over his face. It got his attention, but that was all. This ol' boy had been hit before.

He dropped his shoulder and bull-rushed me like a linebacker. My high school offensive lineman muscle memory kicked in. I got my feet moving and fended him off with my hands. He stumbled to one knee.

On my right, Gabe executed what I believe MMA fans refer to as a spinning back fist. Sounded like somebody'd dropped a Sunday roast from the roof as it connected with the side of big brother's head; the impact sent the older Delaney's Skoal ball cap flying into the air and hideously contorted the outline of his skull. When he dropped to one knee, Gabe drop-kicked him in the face. He went all the way down and stayed there.

The sight of his big brother napping in the street brought my guy up short, torn between trying to finish what he'd started with me and going to the aid of his brother. I was about to help him decide when the first siren began to wail in the distance.

And then another and perhaps a third—it was hard to tell them apart once the whoops wound together.

"You two have already gone a couple rounds with the boys in blue," I said to the guy in front of me. "Maybe you ought to collect your brother and get the hell out of here before you two end up spending another night in Casa Vomit."

He had a muley look to him. I half expected him to be stubborn about it and give me another try, but I was wrong. Something about how easily Gabe had handled his big brother had given him pause. Me too, for that matter.

He pushed himself to his feet, sidestepped me, and helped his brother up. He threw a shoulder under Bluto and began to half carry, half drag him toward the truck. He fixed me with an angry glare on the way by.

"This ain't over," he said. "That bitch gonna pay for my brother."

The bitch in question was out of her car now, around back with the rear hatch open. I kept a wary eye on the Delaney brothers until they were both inside and their truck had melted into the fog.

With Gabe following along in her wake, Rebecca jogged past me carrying the red blanket she always kept in the back of her car for emergencies.

There was enough adrenaline in my system to float a paddleboard. I closed my eyes and sucked in a couple dozen lungfuls of fog. Kept at it until I couldn't hear my pulse in my ears anymore. By the time I refocused, Rebecca had slipped the folded blanket under Dawson's head and was dabbing the area around his mouth with a handkerchief.

That's when the first wave of cavalry skidded to a halt behind the BMW. First to arrive were a pair of SPD uniforms, combat-stancing their way through the gloom, pointing drawn guns in all directions at once, like you see on TV.

Dawson's cameraman took one look at the approaching cops and began screaming at the top of his lungs, "Not them. Not them." He pointed furiously in the direction the Delaney brothers had gone. "That way. That way."

Took a while to sort things out. By that time, another police cruiser and an emergency-aid car had joined the vehicle conga line in the middle of the street, at which point somebody had a spasm of lucidity and suggested we get the cars the hell out of the street so the aid car could get up here.

My car was offender number one, but Dawson was still semiconscious in the mouth of the driveway, so Gabe and I and the first pair of cops had to pick him up and ease him over to the grassy edge of the street so I could pull both cars into the driveway and clear the way for assistance.

I pulled into the yard, took my car all the way to the back and locked it in the garage, then jogged back to the street and got the BMW. I stopped in the gateway and got out. Gabe and Rebecca were standing against one of the stone gate pillars watching as the emergency personnel trussed Snowdrift Dawson and carefully rolled him onto a gurney. The noises he made when they moved him would stay with me for a while.

Somewhere along the line, a couple of plainclothes cops had arrived and taken statements from Snowdrift's cameraman and the other TV crew, who by this time had decided it was safe to go back to work as professional carrion eaters and were now tiptoeing across the street with a microphone and camera at the ready.

The medical crew had Snowdrift up in the back of the aid car. The backup lights came on. The light bar snapped on. Red and white. The aid car started to move. Rebecca and I made eye contact.

I nodded at the open door of the Beamer. "You guys better go inside," I said. "I'll finish up out here."

She was about to get ornery when she spotted the camera crew approaching and made a dash for the car. Gabe was hard on her heels when a new voice intervened.

"Gabriella," the voice said.

I turned toward the sound. One of the plainclothes cops had wandered over. Cheap suit. Maybe forty. Only five-ten or so, but thick in the torso like a Turkish wrestler. Not somebody you wanted to end up rolling around on the ground with.

"Detective Greenway." Gabe flashed a crocodile smile. "'Fraid I've gotta go."

I watched as Gabe got into the passenger seat and Rebecca threw it in gear.

"You'd be Mr. Waterman," the cop said, as they disappeared into the gloaming.

"I'd be."

"Nice company you're keeping there."

I tried to sound shocked. "Whatever do you mean?"

"Gabriella Funicello."

"Like Annette?"

"What?"

"Great tits."

"Gabriella?"

"Annette."

"She's a hitter for Joey Ortega."

"And here I thought she was a Mouseketeer," I said.

I started walking toward the gate. "If you'll excuse me," I said without turning around. I walked to the far side, found the "Close" button, and pushed it. Took the gate about ten seconds to roll all the way shut. Ahead in the gloom, the house lights were dim and fuzzy and inviting.

I heard a loud snap, crackle, and pop when the aid car backed over the remains of the TV camera. I couldn't help but smile.

Took less than an hour for them to get Snowdrift Dawson's dental realignment on the air. Nice to see they were every bit as willing to compromise the dignity of their own people as they were that of the general public. Equal opportunity jackals somehow seemed more palatable to me. Somebody's camera had been rolling when the bigger Delaney brother dropped the unfortunate Mr. Dawson like a bad habit.

They put up the old **This may be offensive to some viewers** sign and then pixilated the moment where Delaney's fist blasted Snowdrift's front teeth and half a wireless microphone down his throat, but the rest of the disaster was pretty much cinema verité. The public's right to know and all that.

Somewhere along the way, we remembered that none of us had eaten a thing all day and called Bite Squad to remedy the situation. Forty minutes later enough mediocre Chinese food to feed a Polish artillery division arrived at the front gate. We ate like a pack of wild dogs, after which Rebecca repaired to my office with her computer files, Gabe headed upstairs for a shower, and I went in and turned on the tube again.

When I woke up about two thirty, she was still pecking away at the keyboard and wasn't in any mood to chat, so I tottered into the bedroom, crawled up under the comforter, and slipped into the arms of Morpheus.

She was still at it, and still crabby as hell, when I woke up a little after eight in the morning, so I took a shower, got dressed, and headed for my car. Along the way I stopped in the kitchen, grabbed a semistale pancake from the counter, filled it with leftover mu shu pork and plum sauce, and stepped out into the morning, in a full chomp.

■ ■ ■

"Whorehouse," George said. He downed a draft beer and ran a hand over his shaggy head. "Hundred bucks a pop. Little Korean girls. Some of 'em don't look no older than twelve. Don't none of 'em speak a worda English neither, so they probably ain't legal."

Above us, the line of old-fashioned windows that ran along the Zoo's mezzanine began to tick, tick, as raindrops from the west began to throw themselves on the ancient panes.

The clock over the restrooms read 10:09.

"You're sure?" I pressed.

"I have it on good authority."

"Such as?"

"Red," he yelled. He made a come-over-here gesture with his arm. Red came weaving over from the snooker table, dragging the big end of the pool cue along the floor as he made his way.

Red was a native of somewhere up in the Northwest Territories. The poster boy for genetic intolerance for alcohol. Just a few drinks and he was either puking outside in the alley or drooling among the peanut shells on the floor. As if that weren't enough of a social impediment, Red also had a lifelong penchant for exposing himself in public, an unfortunate fetish pretty much guaranteed to put a stop to upward social mobility. His habit of whipping it out and asking "Ain't that a beauty?" proved to be a social faux pas of truly epic proportions, earning him both repeated stretches behind bars and a level-one sex offender designation. He and I had long ago reached an area of accommodation. I wouldn't show him mine if he wouldn't show me his.

"Tell Leo what you seen inside that joint on South Main," George said.

Red lurched closer, leaned the pool cue against the nearest pillar, and then took a seat. "Ain't right, Leo. Ain't right," he said.

"Tell me."

"I like dipping my wick as much as the next guy, but these wasn't even growed-up women. These was just kids."

"So you didn't . . ."

He looked horrified. "That ain't nice, man. I may be a drunken bum, but I ain't stealin' nobody's childhood from 'em. I got kids a my own, Leo." He shrugged. "Someplace. They doan let me see 'em no more. Not since they was little."

"So what happened?"

"I done like George said. I slipped 'em a yard at the door, and a thick little Asian guy took me upstairs, where the whatcha-call-her was."

"What whatcha-call-her?"

"You know, like the head honey."

"The madam."

"Yeah, madam. Real painted-up Chinese broad. Meaner than a snake."

"Yeah . . . and so?"

"They sent me down the hall to this room. Little tiny Korean girl." He looked up at me. "Poor thing wasn't even haired over."

When I didn't say anything, he went on.

"So you know . . . I was tryin' to do what Georgie tole me—you know, pick up as much info as I can—so I told 'em I wanted some other girl. Somethin' a little older, maybe. Somethin' with a thatch. So we went to another room. I kept doin' that till I could tell the musclehead bouncer was thinkin' about throwin' my ass out, so I stayed with the last one he took me to. I figured I could at least talk to her and maybe find out somethin' about what was goin' on."

The pool cue slipped from where Red had leaned it and clattered to the floor. Nobody in the joint batted an eye. Gotta love it.

"Well . . . turns out she don't speak nothin' I speak, and the poor little thing's so fuckin' scared of these people she's whoring for, she keeps tryin' to get my meat outta my pants, and I'm tryin' to keep it in, and she's tryin' to get it airborne, and I ain't lettin' her, and she starts wailin' at the top of her lungs, and then that leg-breaker motherfucker shows up to see what in hell's goin' on, smacks her one upside the head, and throws my ass back out in the street." He shrugged. "That was it."

"Nice work, man," I said.

"And the building," he said. "I forgot about the building."

"What about it?"

"Up on the third floor—you know, up where the girls are doin' their thing with the customers . . ."

"Yeah?"

"Well, up there, that building is connected to the buildings on the next block south. You can walk all the way through and go out a door on Jackson Street."

"No shit."

George leaned close. "When Red told me about it, I checked it out myself. Went through the alley, out on to Jackson. Only thing open that time of night was an all-night falafel stand. Guy workin' the counter told me they bring the girls out about two every morning. Load 'em in a big old van and drive 'em off someplace. He don't know where."

"How many girls?"

"Somethin' like ten or twelve."

"Your shot, Red," somebody shouted from over by the snooker table. George and I watched in silence as Red started across the room, remembered his pool cue, came back over, fetched it from the floor, and stumbled back over to the snooker table.

"I took the C-note I gave Red from me and Ralphie," George said.

I took the hint and forked out another hundred. "What about the other joint?" I asked as he pocketed the cash.

"Now that's where things get interesting," he said with a twinkle. "That Walter Street joint is just a low-rent crib. Got about twenty-five rooms to rent. Grifters. Pimps. Outta work Arthur Murray dance instructors. That sorta trade. That's where me and Ralphie started out last night. Red and Harold were handling the whorehouse for ya. Anyway . . . right . . . so we're just hanging around. Ralphie's panhandling anybody looks like he might have two nickels, when out of four oh seven comes this guy I know named Henry the Hittite. So he takes one look at me and goes, 'Hey, Georgie Boy, what's up?' and we get to yakking. Henry says this Frost guy is a nasty little son of a bitch. Likes to smack people around. Lives up on the top floor, but just sometimes. Henry lives up there too and says Frost don't sleep there but a couple times a month. Rest of the time he sleeps at wherever it is he works."

"Why rent a room if you're not gonna sleep in it?"

George held up a grimy finger. "'Cause we hear he don't pay no rent. Henry says he lives there gratis—on the owner." He paused for dramatic effect. "So I ask about this owner, and you know what I get?"

"What?"

"I get the exact same description I got from Red when he told me about the whorehouse madam. Middle-aged Asian broad, too much makeup and mean enough to frighten feral swine."

"Be interesting to find out who owns the buildings," I said.

"If your aunt Jean were still running City Records, I coulda found out in five minutes."

"Oh, we can still find out. They're public records. It'll just cost a hundred fifty bucks and take three weeks."

"Progress," George muttered.

▪ ▪ ▪

Sometimes I think the world can be divided into people who have a desire to tell other adults what to do and those who don't. I'm one of the latter, a live-and-let-live guy all the way. You do your thing; I'll do mine. The twain don't have to meet.

Don't get me wrong: if you're about to step in front of a bus, I'll stick out my am, but that's about it. Otherwise, you're pretty much flyin' solo, as far as I'm concerned. As long as whatever you've got in mind involves other consenting adults, I say go for it.

When it comes to kids, however, I get downright medieval. I fall right into line with penitentiary convicts, who consider it to be full-time open season on child molesters. I once asked a counselor who worked up at Twin Rivers prison in Monroe if she had any idea why they hated pedophiles so much, and she told me that she thought an ungodly percentage of them, whether they'd admit it or not, had been victims of some sort of abuse. She said she thought that they, at least on some level, knew better than most what the experience of abuse did to a person's soul, and that was why they were willing to accommodate decapitators, disembowelers, and every other kind of despicable dirtbag, but they don't tolerate baby rapers.

So I was a man in an emotional quandary. Part of me knew how desperate Rebecca was for some good news and how much I wanted to be the one to come up with it. Another part of me couldn't bear thinking about somebody's kids giving blow jobs for a living. Just flat-out gave me the willies, it did.

I was still kicking my feelings around when my car pulled itself to the curb across the street from Ibrahim Durka's townhouse. It wasn't the first time I'd driven somewhere on automatic pilot, but the older I got, the scarier those moments seemed to become. Like wherever it was I went to got farther away as the years passed. I looked around and heaved a sigh of relief.

I got out of the car and ran both hands over my face. The fog had blown away, leaving everything adrip. Ibrahim's front door was closed today. Somebody had left a pot of red geraniums on the porch. Nikka was sitting on the top step, playing a video game on a blue tablet.

A block up, in the entrance to the park, city workers were installing bright yellow concrete poles designed to prevent motor vehicles from driving into the park. At the insistence of the legal department, I was betting. Talk about a day late and a dollar short.

I wasn't even quite sure why I was there. Thought maybe I'd like to have another look at the park, or maybe see if there wasn't something I could do for his wife and family. But standing there in the street, both reasons suddenly seemed puerile at best, so I grabbed the door handle and started to climb back into my car. A shrill voice stopped me. "Mr. Leo the Lion man."

It was Nikka, off the porch and out on the sidewalk now.

"Hi, Nikka," I said.

She held out her hand. Mama had trained her well. She wasn't setting foot in the street, so I hip-checked the car door closed and crossed to her side. She grabbed me by the hand. "Come," she said. "Come see Mama and the social lady."

She began to tug me toward the door. "Come on, Mr. Leo man," she chanted as she pulled me toward the three concrete stairs.

"What's a social lady?" I asked as Nikka hauled me toward her front door.

Next thing I knew, she had the door open and was shoving me over the sill.

Bedlam. Ibrahim's wife and another woman held down the middle of the living room. Little sister was running in circles screaming her head off. Mrs. Durka was seated in a worn wing chair under the window, looking like she hadn't slept in a month.

The other woman was dressed in what I identified as traditional African garb of some nonspecific variety or another. If you counted the twelve yards of material she had turbaned on top of her head, she was damn near as tall as I was. Bright green and red and yellow flowers everywhere. Sure to brighten up any room.

"Mr. Leo the Lion man, Mama," Nikka shouted as she pulled me along.

Mama managed a wan smile and a feeble wave. The other woman looked me over like a lunch menu. "And you'd be?" she asked.

"Leo the Lion man," Nikka shouted again.

I told the woman who I was and how I knew the Durkas. "I thought maybe Mrs. Durka could use a little help," I said. Sounded lame as hell, but it was the best I could come up with.

"Of course she needs help," the woman blurted. "She's been made a widow. She doesn't speak the language. She has two little children to care for and absolutely no experience dealing with anything except the home." She stomped across the room and grabbed a thick pile of envelopes from the desktop. "Favor has never paid a bill in her life," she said. She dropped the pile back onto the desk. "Husbands do such tings in her culture. She has never written a check. Never written anything."

As if on cue, little sister came toddling back into the room in full scream. Mrs. Durka rose wearily from the chair, scooped her youngest child onto her hip, and carried her from the room with Nikka following along behind. I heard a door close. The noise level went down considerably.

I walked over to the African woman and held out my hand.

"Leo Waterman," I said.

Took her a while to decide whether or not to take it. Maybe it was a cultural thing, I don't know, but finally, she reached out and gave me a brief, limp shake.

"Talia Madibo."

"You friends with Mrs. Durka?"

"No. I'm from the South Sudanese Social Organization." Her face took on a rueful expression. "Which is part of the problem," she said. "Most of the Sudanese in Seattle are from South Sudan, which is where Mr. Durka was from, but Favor is from North Sudan. Her dialect is very different. I can understand some of what she says but not all of it. I'm trying to find an interpreter."

Even with the door closed, the child's crying was permeating the house now. Talia Madibo heaved a considerable sigh, excused herself, and strode off into the fray, leaving me standing alone in the Durkas' living room.

I wandered over to the desk and picked up a neatly stacked pile of bills: mortgage, car, Seattle City Light, cable, storage unit, the usual crap. Several raised voices flew into the room when somebody opened the bedroom door. I dropped the bills back onto the top of the desk, where they spread out like playing cards.

When I looked down, Nikka was standing at my side. She pointed down at the pile. "Papa's lockup," she said. She held a finger to her lips. "Shhhhh," she shushed. "Mama don't know about the lockup." Her big brown eyes rolled upward. "Papa say be quiet when the other men came."

"What other men?"

Her eyes grew big. "Scary men. They made Papa cry."

I patted her on the head and was about to say my goodbyes and sneak out the door, when it came to me. When they'd escaped the Sudan, they'd gone to London first, and a lockup was what the Brits called a storage unit. I walked back to the desk and found the storage unit bill. Sodo Moving and Storage. Ninety bucks. Address on South King Street. I looked over at Nikka.

"Papa got a key for his secret lockup?" I asked her in a whisper.

She squatted down, pulled open a small bottom drawer in the desk. Her little hand fished around inside the drawer and came out with a silver key on a white plastic Sodo Moving and Storage fob. She stood up and handed it to me. I used my ankle to slide the drawer closed. I bent down and put my face in Nikka's. I held a finger to my lips. "This will be our secret," I said.

"Shhhhh . . . ," she said with a grin.

I pocketed the key, figuring that, should this turn out to be a dumb idea, I could probably at some point find a way to return it. The noise from the other room had settled down. I figured this was as good a time as any to make my escape, so I said my goodbyes to Nikka and stepped out onto the porch.

■ ■ ■

Storage must be a hell of a business. Some of the most desirable real estate in Seattle—real estate that you'd think would long ago have been made into pricey-view condos—was covered with brand-new storage units. Must have something to do with the minuscule size of city apartments and the amount of crap we inevitably collect as we go along. That and the fact that you can run a ten-thousand-square-foot storage operation with a single mouth-breathing desk clerk.

Sodo Moving and Storage wasn't in Sodo, which is short for south of downtown. Interestingly enough, Sodo Moving and Storage was in the International District, which back before World War II was known as Japtown—back in the days before we shipped its namesakes all off to relocation camps and made political correctness the national religion.

The kid behind the desk looked up from his video game long enough to see the key and the fob, then pushed the button and buzzed me in. The key had *234* stamped in it, so I was pretty sure it was gonna be upstairs. Not much gets by old Leo.

The place was cleaner and warmer than several of my early apartments. Whatever they had in mind for a numbering system was lost on me, so I just kept walking up and down the aisles. Eventually, I found 234 by attrition.

Standard *shoot it with a bullet* padlock. I took it off and slipped the key and the lock into my pants pocket, where it hung dull and heavy like a cannonball.

The first thing that crossed my mind when I pulled the door open was why a guy on the city payroll, with a wife and two kids, would blow ninety bucks a month on a storage unit with very nearly nothing in it.

Sitting on the floor six feet in front of the rear wall was a red plastic tote, about two feet by three feet. The kind where the lid snaps on. That was it. Nothing else.

I've got to admit to feeling a bit squeamish. I'd visited the guy yesterday, and an hour later he was dead. Today I'd manipulated his beautiful daughter, stolen something from his desk, and was now about to pry into something he'd kept secret even from his wife. I gave up guilt for Lent, so I got over it in a hurry.

When I pried the lid from the tote, it took my brain a second to process what I was looking at. It was half-full of labeled manila envelopes. All of them in Rebecca's handwriting. I fingered through them. They were all there. Kevin Delaney, Gilberto Duran, Terrence Poole, Lamar Hudson, Willard Frost.

My brain was doing somersaults. Why would Ibrahim do such a thing? He was Rebecca's oldest and most trusted employee. I leaned against the side wall of the unit, trying to get a hold of myself. Must have stood there with my eyes closed for a full five minutes or so.

When I couldn't come up with an answer, I moved on to something my feeble brain could handle, like what to do next. I went back to the tote, pulled off the top, and rearranged things. Then I snapped the lid back into place and carried the tote out into the corridor, where I locked the unit back up and pocketed the purloined key.

On one hand, I was glad that I was going to return the conquering hero. Saving the land from pestilence was, after all, the specialty of the house. On another, I hated what this was going to do to Ibrahim's family. To extricate Rebecca was to indict Ibrahim. There wasn't going to be any middle ground in this thing. Whatever his reason for squirreling away these files, Ibrahim Durka was going to come out of this looking like a low-life scumbag. No way around it.

I grabbed the tote and headed for the elevator. The kid's thumbs were a blur as I backed out through the security doors.

■ ■ ■

The new silver Lexus sitting in my driveway belonged to Nancy Pometta, Rebecca's new lawyer. They were sitting together at the kitchen table when I came in the back door. I set the tote on the table between them.

The lawyer was a woman of about forty. Trim and fashionable, wearing enough gold jewelry to open a store. She didn't seem pleased to be interrupted.

Rebecca threw me an exasperated look. "Leo . . . we're working here," she groused. I was trying not to look like the cat who ate the canary but apparently wasn't pulling it off. Problem was, in all the years I'd worked as a PI, I'd never had a case just pop wide open like this one had. Yeah, I'd kicked over rocks here and there, found out this and that, contributed to the successful resolution of cases on many occasions, but I'd never gone from zero to a hundred in about ten seconds before. Not once.

"What's that look?" Rebecca wanted to know.

"It was Ibrahim," I said.

"Ibrahim what?"

"Ibrahim who stole the files."

Pin-drop moment. The two women exchanged puzzled looks.

I pulled the top from the tote, grabbed the envelopes, and put them on the table. "They're all there. All five of the cases in question."

I backed over to the kitchen counter and watched as Rebecca pawed through the files. I watched as she considered opening one of the files, thought better of it, and set it back down. She looked up at me in wonder. "How . . . how did you . . ."

"Dumb luck," I said and told her the story. How the whole thing sprung from the mouth of a babe and how I just happened to be standing in the right place at the right time.

She stood up, threw a bear hug on me, and waltzed me all over the kitchen. The whooping and hollering rattled the rafters. It lasted for quite a while.

"I don't understand," she said, once we'd disentangled and calmed down. "Why would Ibrahim do something . . . something like . . ."

"That's the Double Jeopardy question," I said. "Whatever was in it for him had to be real important for him to do something like that."

"But what?"

Rebecca may have been somewhat at a loss, but her lawyer wasn't.

"We'll demand a complete exoneration," she said. "In the press. In public. And then we'll talk about punitive damages."

Rebecca waved dismissively. "I don't know about punitive damages," she said. "Anything like that would just drag Ibrahim through the mud more than this is already going to. Might even give the county reason to think about not paying out his insurance and pension to his family." She looked up at the other woman. "I won't be party to that."

The lawyer got to her feet and shrugged herself into her coat. "Before we do anything, I want to run this by the senior members of my firm. I'll get back to you this afternoon. In the meantime . . . needless to say, mum's the word." She stopped. "And whatever you do, don't say anything to anyone about how you're not going to sue," she said. "The fear of God makes them ever so much easier to deal with."

Gabe was in the kitchen making grilled cheese sandwiches when Rebecca and I returned from letting Nancy out.

"Hail the conquering hero," Gabe joked.

Rebecca took a sip of tea and leaned back in the chair. She was torn, I could tell. Part of her was overjoyed to be out from under a cloud of suspicion. Another part of her was worried about Ibrahim and his family. She was like that. Nothing was ever simple.

"Why do you suppose Ibrahim hung on to those files?" she asked. "If the idea was for the files to disappear, why not just destroy them?"

I'd thought about it. Ascribing motivations to other people is always dicey. I don't even know why I do the things I do, so I've always been unable to imagine how anybody else could have a clue.

"If I had to guess," I said, "maybe he felt guilty about what he'd done. Maybe some part of him wanted to be able to fix it, if things got too ugly for you."

"So why do it to begin with?" Gabe asked. "You don't do the crime if you can't do the time."

"That's the question, isn't it?" Rebecca said to nobody in particular.

I gave it some thought. "Seems to me the idea had to be either to exact some sort of revenge against you personally—which, with the culprit turning out to be Ibrahim, seems ridiculous—or the whole mess was started in motion to get one of those people out of jail." I looked around. "Unless one of you can think of something else."

The silence suggested not, so I kept talking.

"You know . . . for a guy who started out dodging bullets in North Africa, Ibrahim's pretty much got the American dream going on. Steady union job. Beautiful wife, two beautiful daughters, car, nice new townhouse. I just don't get what could have motivated him to do this."

"He's up at the top of the salary schedule," Rebecca added. "Makes seventy-something a year. Full bennies . . . The whole ball of wax. It just doesn't make any sense."

"So I guess you crazy kids won't be needing me anymore," Gabe said.

I held up a restraining hand. "Let's wait till this whole thing shakes out before we make any changes," I said. "This thing's still got way too many loose ends for my taste."

Gabe chomped a grilled cheese sandwich in half. "My time is your time."

At four in the afternoon, the battle plan was fully in place. Rebecca and her lawyer were holding a downtown press conference at ten thirty tomorrow morning. By the time Rebecca got off the phone with Nancy and ran it by me, her lawyer had talked her into suing for punitive damages and using the money to start a trust fund for Ibrahim's kids, which pretty much made sense all around. It provided for the kids' futures and made it so Nancy's law firm came out of it with a goodly piece of change. A match made in lawyer heaven; assuming, of course, that lawyers and heaven were not, as many contended, mutually exclusive.

"What say we celebrate?" I suggested.

"Like what?" Rebecca asked.

"Let's go out to dinner. Maybe have a libation or two."

The idea was greeted with wild acclaim, so I called Lark and begged and pleaded and managed to get us in at six fifteen. A mite early for continental dining, but it was the only table they had open until next Wednesday, so I went for it.

And so it was with a slightly fuzzy head and a very full stomach that I found myself strolling contentedly down East Seneca Street a little after nine that night. Gabe had commandeered a toothpick and was working several pieces of pork belly out from between their teeth as we ambled back toward the car. Rebecca was hanging on my arm like it was a life preserver. All things considered, it had been a hell of a good day.

Maybe it was the liquor. Or just having the shit storm lifted from our shoulders. I don't know, but about a block and a half before we got to the car, Rebecca asked, "How's Nikka doing?"

"Beautiful kid. Sweet," I said.

"I mean physically? Is she still up and around?"

I stopped walking and looked over at her. "Why wouldn't she be up and around?"

"She's got Sanfilippo."

"Sounds like a vacation destination."

"It's a fatal metabolic disorder, dolt."

"You're sure?" I asked.

"Ibrahim's been fighting the insurance company for years now. I've written letters of support for him. It's genetically transmitted, so the insurance company claims it's the ultimate preexisting condition. I showed up at two insurance advisory board meetings in his defense. Things got quite heated."

"And they won't pay?"

She made a face. "Actually, until lately there hasn't been much to pay for. Up until recently, Sanfilippo was considered incurable. There's a couple new therapies being developed right now. Gene therapies. Some of them, I understand, are very promising, but they're superexpensive and still experimental, so, of course, the insurance carrier doesn't want to fork out for them."

"So why did you think Nikka wouldn't be up and around anymore?"

She went into textbook mode. "Sanfilippo affects mostly the central nervous system. Over time, brain cells fill up with waste that the body can't process. Children experience hyperactivity, sleeplessness, loss of speech, mental retardation, cardiac issues, seizures, loss of mobility, dementia, and finally death, usually long before adulthood. That's why they list it as a childhood disease."

"'Cause nobody survives childhood," Gabe tossed in.

"Seemed like a regular, healthy, happy kid to me," I said.

"I have everybody's medical files," Rebecca said out of the blue.

"I thought those were always superconfidential."

She shrugged. "They drive city vehicles. They're subject to drug testing. They sign away their confidentiality rights when they sign up for the job."

"But not the families."

"But the way the computer system works, if you have access to the employee account, you have access to all the accounts connected to it. They're all the same budget item as far as the county is concerned."

"Might be very interesting to have a look."

"What say we repair back to the family manse and do just that," she suggested.

The motion was seconded and thirded.

■ ■ ■

"One hundred forty-six thousand dollars and eighty-three cents," she said, pointing at the computer screen. "Out of pocket in the past year and a half. He took her up to Providence in Everett. Gene therapy. That's why it took a while to find."

"Ibrahim didn't have pockets that deep," I pointed out.

"No . . . he didn't."

"And the only one of the five cases they were pressing against you where somebody *does* have that sort of loose change is the Harrington case, but they don't have anybody they're trying to spring from jail. Quite the contrary. They've already got their daughter's murderer convicted and doing life without, over in Walla Walla."

"Then what?"

"Clueless."

"You know," Rebecca said in a low voice. "I feel a little better about the whole thing now. I sorta don't blame Ibrahim for what he did. We let people like him give their lives to public service, and then we nickel-and-dime them over the most precious things in their lives. It's just not right."

"He tried to tell me," I said after a quiet moment.

"Who?"

"Ibrahim. The last thing he said to me was to the effect that family was everything. I think he was . . . you know . . . trying to apologize. Trying to tell me that he'd only done what he needed to do."

"So who came up with the cash then? That's a lot of loose change," Gabe said. "Somebody had to set this thing in motion. And why?"

I just shook my head.

Rebecca pushed herself to her feet. "I'm on TV in the morning. I better see if I can put together something to wear."

Gabe was chewing. I leaned back against the sink.

"You made handling the brother look pretty easy last night."

"It *was* easy."

I waited for Gabe to swallow. "How'd you know that cop?" I asked.

"He tried to nail an assault rap to me once."

"Was he successful?"

"We're standing here talking, aren't we?"

I wasn't sure whether the "we" referred strictly to Gabe or to both of us, so I segued. "Gabriella Funicello, huh?"

"You make any Annette Funicello jokes, and I swear to God, I'll shoot you."

I kept my mouth shut. I could hear Rebecca thrashing about in the bedroom.

"You take a lot of crap about your name as a kid?" I asked.

"For a while," Gabe said. "Took a lot of crap about a lot of things. High school's tough that way. I wanted to play on the football team, but they wouldn't let me. You'd have thought I wanted to burn babies on the town square."

"Where was this?"

"Topeka, Kansas."

"What brought you out here?"

"Topeka was a tough place to be genetically ambiguous."

"I'll bet."

"My family wasn't much. Just livin' hand to mouth. Havin' a kid like me was hard on them. They weren't exactly deep thinkers. There was nothin' holding me there."

"Is it better here?"

"Around here you could marry the family pet and nobody'd give a shit, except maybe the ASPCA. In Topeka you'd look out the window and there'd be a mob outside with shovels and rakes and torches . . . with a squad of reverends leading the way, riding your ass out of town on a rail, for the glory of God and the brotherhood of man."

"So . . . you know . . . if you don't mind me sounding like a Topeka preacher, what exactly is 'genetically ambiguous'?"

Gabe grinned. "You know why I'm going to answer that instead of getting all up in your face, Leo?"

"Why?"

"'Cause you don't really give a shit. Not like it bothers you or anything. It don't threaten you. I can tell. You've just got a case of curiosity that killed the cat. You just can't *stand* not knowin'."

"Bad habit," I allowed. "Damned near got me killed on numerous occasions."

"I have no doubt," Gabe said, without a trace of humor. "So anyway. Just so your little brain can be at rest: If you ask gene doctors about me, they'll start to mumble something about my extraordinary combination of chromosomal genotype and sexual phenotype. If you recall from biology class, men are XY, and females are XX. I'm an other. I'm the exception to the rule. I'm both and I'm neither." Gabe wagged a finger in my face. "But remember, asshole: my multitudes . . . we're all Italian."

"And . . . you know, like . . . You prefer . . . ?"

"I prefer not to."

Didn't seem the place for a snappy rejoinder, so I kept my trap shut.

"I was kidding before," Gabe said after an awkward silence.

"About what?"

"When I said you guys didn't need me anymore."

"You think we do?"

"I work from the theory that if things seem nice and simple and cut and dried, I've probably missed something. You know what I mean? Every damn thing we needed fell into our laps like manna from heaven. And, oh yeah . . . the guy who *really* did it just happens to end up stone dead, so he's telling nobody nothing, and everything's rolled up nice and neat like a kid's birthday present. The Doc's exonerated. Her lawyer sues the crap out of the DA's office and everybody but them goes away feeling fuzzy and fulfilled. Except that I still feel like I'm missing something here," Gabe said. "Like when somebody tells you a joke and you just don't get it, and you're standing there wondering what in hell everybody else is laughing at."

"Yeah," I said. "That's how I'm feeling too. We've got everything we need except the answers to anything."

"Like what happened to the pair of hitters who tried to make it look like she killed herself and then tried to take her out again at Harborview? The UPS guys. They leave the country or what?"

"Same van ran Ibrahim down," I said. "I'm sure of it."

"Then those guys are still around, and this ain't over."

"Unless this whole mess has somehow or other accomplished whatever it was set in motion to accomplish."

"Like what?"

"Not a hint."

"Then we're running blind, and blind makes me nervous."

I thought about it for a while and finally had to agree. "Yeah . . . I guess we just take things one at a time. Let's see what happens with the news conference tomorrow and then go from there."

"Sounds like a plan."

I left Gabe standing in the kitchen and started up the hall toward the bedroom. Rebecca had dumped out the whole plastic bag of clothes I'd brought from her house. She was down on her knees rummaging through the mound.

"Do you have an iron?" she asked.

"Top shelf in the hall closet."

"I'm going to look like the wrath of God," she groused.

I walked over to the bed, grabbed one of the disposa-phones from the paper bag, and stuck it in my pocket.

"Yeah," I said. "But your strength will be the strength of ten because your heart is pure."

"Get out of here," she growled.

I did. When I strolled back through the kitchen, Gabe had gone upstairs. I took the phone out into the backyard and dialed the number Eagen had given me. Right to voicemail of course. I told him what was going on and that it was time to pull his head back into his shell, 'cause, for the time being anyway, we had things firmly under control.

The second it was out of my mouth, I knew it was the kind of thing you never wanted to say out loud. That's probably why I was still talking when the machine hung up on me.

■ ■ ■

Gabe shouldered the nearest photographer out of the way. The newshound would have ended up flat on his ass, except there wasn't enough unoccupied space in the hallway to fall down. I had one hand locked on Rebecca's elbow and was using my hip as a battering ram as we fought our way toward the elevator. The air was heavy with shouted questions and shuffling feet. I kept us moving down the corridor, hip-checking people out of the way as we moved along.

A junior member of Nancy's firm was waiting with my car in the building's garage. All we had to do was get there. We had a little over an hour to get back to my place. Prior to the news conference, Nancy had negotiated the terms under which we would surrender the newly discovered evidence. My place. One o'clock. We would hand the stuff over to duly appointed officers of the court, and we'd already worked up the formal deposition I was required to give concerning how the material had come to be in my possession. After that, the DA's office would review the situation and, after due diligence, respond accordingly.

We made it with ten minutes to spare. I left Gabe to person the gate, let Rebecca in the back door, and headed out to the garage, where I pulled the red tote down from the shelf and carried it back into the house. Gabe buzzed me from the gate to tell me our guests were there.

They arrived en masse. Nelson and Krauss in one car, a pair of nerds from forensics in a county van. And, just to add sufficient gravity to the situation, Prosecuting Attorney Paul Woodward decided to grace us with his most august presence. Woodward and a pair of toadies arrived like Caesar conquering Gaul. The toadies waited out in the driveway. Woodward immediately got busy giving orders. *Make sure of this; don't forget that. Has this been accounted for?* Let the record show, I kept my mouth shut. For a while anyway.

The nerds had their very own Igloo cooler. They put all the files inside, and one of them looked over at me. "Do these require refrigeration?" he asked me through the mask.

I tried, but couldn't help myself. "Nah," I said. "Those are already the cold hard facts."

The nerds chuckled behind their masks. Woodward couldn't stand it.

"We'll let you know what our findings are," he said.

I reached in my pocket and pulled out a blue thumb drive and a chrome key.

"Be sure to let us know what you think of these."

From the look on his face, you'd have thought I was trying to hand him a dog turd.

Wish I could tell you that what followed was a spur-of-the-moment thing, but truth was that Nancy and I had choreographed the scene in advance. Because both she and Rebecca were officers of the court, she decided it would be best if I did the talking.

The nerds headed for the front door with Gabe in tow. I dropped the thumb drive and the key into the palm of Woodward's hand.

"The key is to the storage unit. The thumb drive contains pictures I took with my phone on the day I found the storage locker. There's times and dates on them. Your techies are gonna tell you straightaway that the pictures haven't been doctored, and you're going to find out that the files are genuine too, and when that happens the first thing you're going to do is to throw Mr. Durka under the bus. That's what guys like you do. They get out from under at somebody else's expense."

His smooth face twisted in anger. "You'd know about guys like me, wouldn't you, Mr. Waterman?" He swept a hand around the area. "Living here in baronial splendor on money stolen from the Seattle taxpayer."

"My father was never convicted of stealing anything," I said. "He just did what everybody else was doing at the time. He just did it better than they did."

He opened his mouth, but I raised my voice a notch and kept talking. "But before you throw Mr. Durka to the wolves, I want to run something by you. Yeah . . . Mr. Durka took money from somebody to steal files. There's no doubt about that. Why somebody would pay for such a thing is a complete mystery. What isn't a mystery is why Mr. Durka agreed. He did it because his daughter has a rare childhood disease called Sanfilippo, and because children are everybody's weakest link. People will do things for their kids they wouldn't otherwise dream of doing."

"So you say" was the best he could come up with.

I threw a thumb at Krauss and Nelson. "You can have one of your boys here look it up for you. And guess what? The county insurance carrier won't pay for the treatment the girl needs to stay alive, so Mr. Durka did what he had to do, as a father. And you know what, Mr. Woodward, I don't think you want to be the villain of that little bedtime story. I'm thinking the sooner this thing fades into the woodwork, and the less public heat Mr. Durka takes, the better it will be for you come next November's election."

Nelson and Krauss were shuffling around in the corner of the kitchen, looking like they'd rather be strolling the surface of the sun.

"Are you finished?" Woodward sneered.

"Not quite," I said. "I've got one more thing you can do for me."

"What would that be?"

"You can take these two bozos," I said, nodding at Nelson and Krauss again, "and get the hell out of my house."

He went into a long bullshit speech about how the material would be subjected to the most rigorous scientific inquiry ever known to man and how if and when they reached their conclusions we either would or wouldn't be notified, after which he flounced from the room, with

Krauss and Nelson trailing along like flotsam. Gabe followed them out. Nancy stayed for another fifteen minutes or so and then made her exit. I closed the gate behind her.

■ ■ ■

The most rigorous scientific inquiry known to man took a little less than three hours. By the time the six o'clock news hit the air, Woodward had changed both his suit and his point of view. The lead story was about how Woodward's crack investigative team had unraveled a Machiavellian plot designed to thwart the ends of justice. Cue the music.

How they now believed an unnamed county employee had stolen police files for his own ends and had thus very nearly brought about the ruin of much-decorated county medical examiner Dr. Rebecca Duvall, who, but for the sterling work of Woodward's team, might have been spuriously convicted of the crime.

He went on for a while. The good news was that Ibrahim Durka's name never came up. Woodward got himself out from under by announcing that the matter was an *ongoing investigation* and therefore not something he could go into any detail about. He finished up by saying that the final disposition of Dr. Duvall's employment status was a matter for the King County Council and the mayor, but that his investigation had found no culpability whatsoever on Dr. Duvall's part, other than perhaps in the departmental protocols for the delivery of evidentiary material, which he was recommending be rigorously reviewed.

"He just had to find something," I said as he walked away from the microphones.

"He's right. We need to figure out something else."

"New budget item," I joked.

"Fat chance," she said. She leaned over and rested her head in my lap. "You know what I saw on TV?"

"What?"

"They said that on the night you pulled me out of my house, you'd showed up on the porch with flowers and candy."

"It was Valentine's Day."

"Seems like forever ago."

"Big bouquet from The Flower Lady and a two-pound box of Fran's."

"Sorry I missed it."

"Happy Valentine's Day," I said with a big grin.

She laughed and then stood up and took me by the hand.

"I think you should be rewarded for your thoughtfulness."

"I think so too," I said.

■ ■ ■

I'd like to tell myself it could have ended right there. That *there but for fortune* the whole matter could have been declared null and void, and everyone could have just gotten on with their lives.

A few days after Rebecca and Gabe had moved back to her place, I met with Eagen again down by the river. As usual he was late, so I spent twenty minutes standing on a carcinogenic riverbank, hopping up and down, trying to keep warm in a thirty-mile-an-hour gale, before he finally put in a guest appearance.

"I don't know what kind of fire you guys lit under Woodward's ass, but you've got him hopping around like a scalded rat."

"Glad to hear it," I said.

Eagen turned around, put his back to the wind, and turned up his collar. "I saw the results of the tests Woodward had done. Those are the genuine files you found. Haven't been tampered with."

"That's what I figured."

"Duran's dead. His mom cleans apartments for a living, so paying a hundred and forty grand to bribe a city employee is pretty much out of the question for her. Delaney—the stuff you found is the actual material from his file, all of which makes him out to be guilty as hell, so he's goin' nowhere, not to mention the fact that both his brothers look like they're going down for felonious assault on Snowdrift Dawson. Terrence Poole's doing life without for killing a grocer in Springfield, Oregon. We know where to find Frost."

"Which leaves us with the Harringtons."

"Who've got absolutely no reason to want anybody out of jail."

"The coroner's leaving the Durka hit-and-run open-ended."

"Which means what?"

"It means he met his death by misadventure, which leaves them a lot of leeway if they ever catch the guy and have to charge him."

"Any word on the van?"

"Not yet."

"You see the scene?" I asked.

"I dropped by."

"Son of a bitch was still on the throttle when he hit that bench."

We stood without saying anything for a while. The wind whistled around us, pushing my hair around, lifting pieces of litter from the ground, swirling debris and unanswered questions like pinwheels.

"I'm gonna let it go," I said.

"I didn't think you had that much sense."

"Anything I do is just gonna make it worse on Ibrahim's family."

He nodded but didn't say anything for a good bit. "And you've got no idea what all this shit was actually about?"

"Less than zero."

"Worst friggin' conspiracy I ever saw."

"Yeah," I said. "Makes no damn sense at all."

"Probably best to just move on," he said.

He was baiting me. I decided it wasn't fishing season.

"It's cold out here," I said. "Thanks for the help on this thing."

"No problem."

We sloshed off in opposite directions.

■ ■ ■

I thought she was a reporter. I stifled a groan, braked hard, and rolled down the window. "Howsabout you get out of my driveway," I said, as I reached up over the visor and pushed the "Open" button. The clank of the gate seemed to startle her. She collected herself and walked over to my side. Standard-issue young professional woman. Tiny little thing. Tortoiseshell headband. Medium-length brown hair parted down the middle, wire-rim glasses, and a Midwestern seriousness of expression to give Grant Wood hives.

I'll say this for her, she kept it short and sweet. "I'm Angela St. Jean," she said. "I'm with the Innocence Project, and I'd like to talk to you about Lamar Hudson."

I checked the street, thinkin' maybe this was some sort of media ruse. That some TV crew in clown makeup was about to jump out of the Morrisons' hedge and start filming like maniacs. But no. The only thing in sight was her little red Toyota Celica, fifty feet up the west wall, half in, half out of the street.

I checked the clock on the dash. 3:16 P.M. I was due at Rebecca's for dinner. We were gonna celebrate her reinstatement and the public apology on the front page of today's *Seattle Times*. Whoop it up a little, but mostly we needed to talk about what to do next. About how it looked like, despite all the unanswered questions, we were pretty much gonna have to get on with our lives and assume that whoever had put this together had accomplished whatever it was they were trying to do. I didn't like the idea one bit, but Gabe was still driving Rebecca to and from work and bunking in her guest room at night, a situation we couldn't keep up forever. Something had to give here. We just needed to work out the whats and whens.

"Better pull your car into the drive," I said. "I'll let you in the front door."

I put my car into the garage and walked back through the house. She and her briefcase were waiting on the front steps when I pulled open the door. I directed her into the front parlor. Over by the two-story fireplace and the *Architectural Digest* furniture—you know, all upscale home–like and cozy.

"So what can I do for you?" I asked as I took a seat across a hideous French provincial coffee table from her.

"As you may know, the Innocence Project has been looking into the matter of whether or not Lamar Hudson was capable of assisting in his own defense. We feel—"

"No sense preaching to the choir, Ms. St. Jean," I said. "As far as I'm concerned, Lamar Hudson wasn't capable of mowing lawns, let alone assisting in his own defense."

"We believe Mr. Hudson deserved a new trial."

"Deserved?"

"Yes. Past tense. We have evidence that links Mr. Hudson to the crime for which he is presently incarcerated."

Took me a minute to put it together. "And nobody connected to Mr. Hudson's defense, either then or now, has ever seen whatever it is before?"

"The prosecution is saying it's been there all along, but since Mr. Hudson repeatedly confessed and then pled guilty to the crime in open court, there was no reason to introduce other evidence, so they had no legal obligation to do so."

"I've heard crazier things," I said.

She opened her briefcase and pulled out a legal document. "This is an order from the Ninth Circuit Court granting Mr. Hudson a new trial. They granted it yesterday and then rescinded it this morning, when the results of the forensic analysis were made public."

"The large print giveth and the small print taketh away."

"Have you ever met Mr. Hudson?" she asked.

"Just seen him on the tube," I said.

"I have. Half a dozen times over in Walla Walla. He's the mentally challenged, totally unsophisticated black sheep of a fifth-generation oyster-farming family from the Willapa Valley. He has an IQ of eighty." She leaned forward. "Lamar Hudson was going home, Mr. Waterman. Other than his confession, there was absolutely no evidence of any kind that linked him to Tracy Harrington's murder. There's no appeal court in this land that would still support that Jim Crow conviction of his. Especially not here in la-la-liberal land. A month from now he would have been back on the street."

I didn't like where this was going. "They say timing is everything," I tried.

She made a wry face. "Except that now, after the evidence just happened to go missing for no reason anyone has been able to figure out and then almost magically reappeared, suddenly there's *new* evidence. I only know what everybody else knows, sir. What I've been reading in the papers. But, you know, regarding the suspension and reinstatement of Dr. Duvall, it almost looks to us as if that whole charade was designed to keep Mr. Hudson in jail."

Chapter 3

The booth was small and white; the guard was big and black. The Highlands was Seattle's oldest gated community. Political movers and shakers like my old man needed to be at the center of the action, so we'd always lived in the city. The Highlands was the opposite. These folks had money for so long some of them couldn't tell you where it came from. So, back in 1907, a bunch of local swells got together and bought a mountain overlooking Puget Sound. They built their own roads and private utilities, built perfect parks and bucolic walking trails, and then put up a fortified guard gate to keep out the riffraff. The American way at its finest.

I'd called ahead and made an appointment. It was either that or jump the fence somewhere out on their private golf course and take the Lewis and Clark approach; took me under two seconds to conclude that trekking over hill and dale held scant appeal.

I leaned out the window and watched his thick fingers pound the keyboard. He seemed surprised to find me on the guest list. He pulled a little handheld GPS from a shelf and fingered in the Harringtons' code, and a map appeared. He handed it to me.

"You can leave it at the Harrington house, or you can bring it back here on your way out."

I thanked him, dropped it into drive, and started down the road. Good thing I had the GPS map. No street signs. No house numbers. No mailboxes. No nothing. Just follow the yellow arrow. Interesting, and I suspected not coincidental, how you could come to visit a Highlands resident and leave without ever knowing their address.

The Harringtons' house had a turret. Having a turret is like being monomial. Like Cher or Elvis. Looked like somebody'd dismantled an Irish castle, flown it across the pond, and put it back together, throwing in a five-car garage and what these kind of folks probably called a carriage house for good measure.

The brass door knocker was some kind of spaniel. I gave it three good ones. The booms echoed through the cavernous interior.

Somehow I was expecting a prissy maid to answer the door, but, to my surprise, I found myself staring eye to eye with a guy dressed in an old-fashioned chauffeur's livery, shiny knee-high boots and all. He'd apparently put on a little weight, so it was hard not to notice the bulge under his left arm. I told him who I was and that I had an appointment. He told me to wait, took the GPS from my hand, then walked off down the hall and disappeared from view.

I'd never been comfortable dealing with domestic help. My old man's worst nightmare was prying ears around the house, so we never had any. If something terribly domestic needed to be done, either his sisters came over and took care of it, or he hired day labor. Drivers? Sure. Bodyguards? Lots of them. But butlers and maids? No way. I'd had to deal with them only when I was at other people's houses, and somehow I never felt as if I'd mastered just the right tone and attitude. Always felt a bit awkward to me.

Wasn't long before the driver was back. He led me down a short hallway and directed me into a large sitting room on the south side of the house. The exterior wall of the room was half a mile of French doors, looking out onto a professionally manicured garden. Half a dozen crows were squawking it up and frolicking in a cherub-encrusted birdbath out at the middle of the lawn.

Patricia Harrington was wearing a gold evening dress at ten thirty in the morning. She was sitting in an overstuffed chair, facing in my direction as I walked across the three acres of carpet. I felt like I was about to have an audience with the queen . . . or, at the very least, Helen Mirren.

"I wondered if you'd be big like your father," she said as I approached.

I smiled. "Not quite that big," I said.

She looked over to her left. "Sidney," she called. "Bring Mr. Waterman a chair, will you please?"

That's when I noticed the man puttering around over in the corner by the art deco bar. Midfifties, spare and elegant in a Fred Astaire sort of way. If the silver mustache had been a bit longer, he'd have been a dead ringer for the Monopoly man. Even from a distance, I could tell he was one of those people who'd never been fat. Picked on as kids for being skinny, they get their revenge in middle age when everybody else is growing beer guts and big asses, and they're the same weight they were in high school. When he walked over and grabbed a red wing chair, I saw that he was wearing a tuxedo. His smooth, unhurried movements gave the impression he had most likely slept in it.

I watched as he dragged the chair over the carpet to my side.

"My husband, Sidney Crossfield," Mrs. Harrington said.

He gave me a limp-fish hand. I pumped it up and down a couple of times and let it swim back into his pocket. We both said something highly intelligent like "Pleased to meet you" and let it go at that.

He gave the impression of a man disappointed by life. That somehow, whatever he had planned for himself hadn't quite worked out, so he'd hunkered down with Mrs. Harrington and her trillions, awaiting the final curtain call . . . in the style to which he was accustomed, of course.

I sat down in the chair. Sidney headed back over to the bar.

"My secretary said you had a matter to discuss with me."

I'd run this moment through my rehearsal circuit several times on the way over. If ever I needed to be careful with my words, this was it. Didn't matter who my father had been or how much cash he'd left me; offending Patricia Harrington was completely out of the question. Be like giving the Pope a wet willie. One call from her, and I'd be getting parking tickets in my own driveway.

"I'm sorry I wasn't more specific with your secretary," I said. "But what I'm here about is a painful and difficult matter, so I thought discretion might be in order."

Her face turned to stone. "Tracy."

"More specifically, Lamar Hudson."

She stiffened in the chair, folded her bejeweled hands in her lap, and looked at me with a pair of the chilliest blue eyes I'd ever seen.

"What about Mr. Hudson?"

Sidney had mixed himself a cocktail and was slaloming through the furniture, working his way back in our direction. He moved like he was on an escalator.

"Were you aware of the fact that the Innocence Project had recently managed to get Mr. Hudson a new trial?" I asked.

"They notified us when they first started to look into the matter," she said.

"They told us victim notification was part of their protocol," Sidney added.

"Then you were also aware that, in legal circles, there's always been quite a bit of heated debate as to whether Mr. Hudson got all the due process he was entitled to."

"The boy confessed," Sidney Crossfield whined.

"Strange as it seems, lots of people confess to things they didn't do," I said.

"Makes absolutely no sense to me at all," Crossfield huffed. "Why in God's name would anyone—"

I jumped in. "Skilled interrogators can make a person's life so miserable for so long, some people will say anything to get them to leave them alone. It happens a lot more often than you'd imagine."

"The jury certainly seemed to have no doubt," Mrs. Harrington said.

She had a point. The jury had taken only two hours to put Lamar Hudson away forever.

"And as you said . . . he confessed."

"That's what I hear."

"Then I'm afraid I'm a bit at sea as to why you've come here, Mr. Waterman."

"As it turns out . . . his confession was the only evidence of his guilt." I paused for effect. "If it turns out that Mr. Hudson is, as most legal scholars think . . . if he wasn't competent to assist in his own defense, then his confession isn't valid, and I'm told that without anything forensic to connect him to the crime, Mr. Hudson was about to be released from the penitentiary."

Sidney sounded like he was offended. "They assured us we'd be notified prior to Mr. Hudson's status being altered."

"You haven't heard anything because the appeals court rescinded Mr. Hudson's order for a new trial the very next day."

"Why would they do that?" he wanted to know.

I told them about what I'd found in the storage locker, leaving Ibrahim's name out of it. Just referring to him as a city employee. Halfway through the story, Sidney got up and fixed himself another drink. By the time he got back, I was finishing up.

"And now, suddenly, new evidence has come to light. Evidence that connects Mr. Hudson to Tracy's death."

"What sort of evidence?" Crossfield wanted to know.

"I don't know," I said.

"Why didn't it come out in court?" Patricia asked.

"Prosecutor says they didn't need it to get a conviction, so they didn't bother."

"That animal got off easy," Crossfield spat. "They should have taken him out and put him down like a lame horse."

I decided not to go into my spiel about a kinder, gentler America and instead asked, "During the trial . . ." They both stiffened. I could still recall the pictures in the newspaper. Patricia Harrington and Sidney Crossfield sitting alone in the front row of the courtroom, ramrod straight, dressed to the nines, security guards keeping the media at bay.

The press lapped it up. Front-page news for days before the trial. Mercifully, the court proceedings were over in a couple of days, and the family was able to slip back to The Highlands and away from the public eye.

"Not even his attorney seemed to have much interest in his defense," Patricia Harrington said.

"His mother spoke on his behalf," Crossfield said. "Dreadful woman."

"According to the social workers whom they called as defense witnesses, Mr. Hudson didn't have a friend in the world," Patricia Harrington added.

"He'd already spent major portions of his youth behind bars," Crossfield added. "They should have left him there."

I kept at it. Asked them everything I could think of that might shed some light on the situation, but I came up dry. All they seemed to know was that somebody had killed and mutilated their daughter and that the miscreant had gotten what he deserved. I was about to give up the ghost when a female voice from the hall tugged at my attention.

"Mama," it called.

"In here," Mrs. Harrington said.

A woman in her forties entered the room. Dressed nicely, but conservatively, in a blue-and-white patterned dress and a pair of red high heels. Her resemblance to Patricia Harrington was unmistakable. Same even features and wide-set eyes.

"Oh," she said when she caught sight of me. "I'm sorry . . ."

I stood up, like my mother taught me to. Old habits die hard.

"Mr. Waterman. My daughter Jessica."

She walked across the room and shook my hand. Good firm handshake.

"Jessica is chair of the Political Science Department at Seattle University."

Didn't take Dr. Ruth to hear the maternal pride in Patricia Harrington's voice.

"Mr. Waterman came to talk about Lamar Hudson," Crossfield said.

She didn't say anything, but the muscles along the side of her jaw suddenly rippled like snakes. I could feel the tension level in the room move up a notch or three. While it wasn't unusual for a tragedy such as theirs to drive wedges into an otherwise close-knit family, it felt like the animosity floating in the room was something far more tangible than simply collective grief.

"I've got a department meeting and then a graduate seminar at one," she said after an awkward moment. "Nice to have met you, Mr. Waterman." She looked over at her mother. "I'm going to take the Rover."

"Will you be home for dinner?"

She shook her carefully coiffed head. "I'm having dinner with Cindy Holmes and her new husband. I'll be home about nine." She nodded goodbye to me and then turned and strode from the room. The tension lingered in the air like artillery smoke.

I didn't want to quit, so I asked, "Does your son Charles live here also?"

"Charles has special needs," Patricia Harrington said. "He requires full-time care." The stone face and icy tone of voice made it clear she wasn't particularly comfortable with the subject of Charles Harrington, so I didn't bother to ask what Charles's problem was and precisely where he was being cared for. Seemed like that might be pushing it. To my surprise, Patricia Harrington spoke directly to her husband. Like I'd walked in on the middle of a long-standing disagreement.

"He's stagnating out there, Sidney."

"Charlie's doing the best he can," Crossfield said.

"He needs some therapy. Some direction. Everyone needs some direction."

"He's in the best place he can be," Sidney said.

"Out there in the woods. Doing nothing. Stagnating. We should have listened to Dr. Thorpe. He thought Charles was on the verge of a breakthrough when . . . when you . . ." She stopped herself. "There must be something more we can do."

I suddenly felt like I was eavesdropping on a private conversation, so I got to my feet. "Thank you for seeing me," I said. "I wish it could have been under more pleasant circumstances."

"Thompson will see you out," Patricia Harrington said.

When I looked up, Thompson and his bulge had magically reappeared in the doorway.

I followed him down the hall. "I take it they don't agree on Charlie's care."

"Big-time bone of contention," he said as we walked along.

"How long you been with the Harringtons?"

"Forty-seven years," he said.

"Long time to do anything."

"It's a living."

I nodded at the bump under his arm. "They really need armed security?" I asked.

"Money changes everything."

Couldn't argue with that either.

■ ■ ■

"Charles Malcolm Harrington the Second," Carl announced. "Legal name change about three years ago."

"Changed from what?" I said.

"Don't say. Malcolm was Patricia Harrington's grandfather's name," Carl said. "He's the one who loaned Bill Boeing the money to build that first seaplane. That family's been shittin' in tall cotton ever since."

"They told me Charles doesn't live at home. That he requires round-the-clock care, but . . . you know . . . the missus didn't seem comfortable with the arrangements."

"Shouldn't be too hard to find. They must have medical insurance. You don't stay that rich by spending any more than you have to. Cheapest fucks I ever met all had more money than they knew what to do with. That's how you stay rich.

"Got something else for ya." He started pushing buttons. The overhead screens started to blink and roll. Half a minute later, five nearly identical text documents appeared all in a row on the biggest screen. Carl pointed upward. "Ya see it?" he asked.

I scanned the screens for a couple of minutes. Arrest jackets for each of the five missing files.

"Look at the dates," Carl suggested.

I stood up and walked closer to the screens. "Four of them . . . Poole, Duran, Frost, and Delaney got themselves arrested on the night of September eleventh, twenty twelve. Everybody except Lamar Hudson, who wasn't arrested for Tracy Harrington's murder until the next day." Carl pointed at one of the screens. Article from the *Seattle Times* on Tracy Harrington's death. Carl read it out loud.

"On the night Tracy Harrington was killed, they found her brother Charles passed out on the grass next to her. I remember it. They musta taken him to juvie." He spread his hands. "No record of it whatsoever. Like it didn't happen."

"How do we get a look at those sealed juvie records?" I asked.

"We get somebody else to do it for us. Somebody who moves around a lot."

"You know such a somebody?"

"Charity's got a cousin."

"Charity's always got a cousin."

"He ain't cheap. But it won't come back at you."

"How much?"

He told me. "Jesus," I said. "That's more than my first car cost."

"Hey, man . . . this is serious shit. He's gonna have to get online someplace public but with no CCTV, which is damned near impossible these days. Whatever computer he uses is going to have to disappear from the universe. And then he's gonna have to get his own ass lost for a while, 'cause they're gonna know somebody's been in the cookie jar just as soon as it happens. About two minutes after he gets ahold of those sealed records, there's going to be an army of cops headed his way."

I sighed. "Okay. Okay. Howsabout you give him a jingle."

"I'll make the call. Won't be any data till tomorrow at the earliest, though."

"Okay. What about the medical insurance angle? Can we find out where Charles lives and what's wrong with him? That sort of thing."

"Half an hour or so," he said, and then went back to pushing buttons.

I hate standing around waiting for computers to do their thing, and I was hungry enough to eat the Harringtons' brass door knocker, so I said, "I'm gonna run down and get a Cuban sandwich at Un Bien. You want anything?"

"Bring me a number two with extra jalapeños," he said, without taking his eyes off the bank of overhead monitors.

Un Bien was only about a half a mile down the hill, but, as usual, every construction worker in town had his hard hat in line, so it was the better part of forty-five minutes before Carl buzzed me back in the front door.

I followed Carl into the kitchen, where we sat at the chipped Formica table and ate like rabid wolves. The Cuban pork and onions was the best damn sandwich in town. No doubt about it. I had to put the thing down once in a while just to make it last.

Carl wiped his mouth with his sleeve, balled up the sandwich bag, and lobbed it at the garbage can. He missed the can but didn't give a shit.

"Tiger Mountain," he said around a toothpick. "Tiger Mountain Lodge."

"What about it?"

"That's where your boy Charles Malcolm Harrington lives. It's a real fancy rehab center slash loony bin. He employs a pair of full-time caregivers with Croatian names. I couldn't find anything on any of them. I also couldn't find out how much Harrington pays the joint 'cause he apparently doesn't, so I ran the Tiger Mountain Lodge itself. His mama owns it. Turns out the Harringtons are invested in rehab centers in a big way. Forty or so different facilities in five states."

"Addiction's big business."

"'Get-tin' better ev-ry day,'" Carl sang.

"Any idea what's wrong with him?"

He pointed up at the screen on the far left. "No medical records that I can find, but here's a list of the medications he makes co-payments for."

"Print that," I said. "I'll ask Rebecca what they are."

We kept at it for another half hour or so, at which point Carl looked up from the keyboard. "I thought he was supposed to have special needs."

"That's what his mother told me."

"Says here he graduated from Lakeside School."

Lakeside School was Seattle's most elite private school. Grades five through twelve, if I recalled. Bill Gates graduated from Lakeside School, immediately prior to becoming the richest man in the world. Like Bill, most Lakeside graduates toddled off to Ivy League universities and then came back and ordered the rest of us around.

"Attended?"

"Nope . . . graduated. June two thousand twelve. Three point four five GPA. Number thirty-seven in a class of one hundred sixty-three."

"Lakeside wouldn't have me," I said. "My old man inquired."

"So that means that whatever happened to him must have happened the night his sister got killed. There was a rumor that the junkie sister injected him with something."

"How long has Charles been living in Issaquah?"

He hammered a few keys. "Five months. Ever since his sister was killed."

"Maybe the rumors were true," I tried. "And that was just the kind of thing the Harringtons didn't want to be reading about."

"Or . . ."

My phone began to buzz in my pocket. I fished it out. It was Eagen on his own phone. I'd left him a message this morning saying I wanted to meet.

"Meet me at Vito's in an hour," Eagen's voice said, and he hung up.

▪ ▪ ▪

Vito's was the kind of retro fifties joint where you half expected Sammy Davis Jr. to leap out of one of the Naugahyde booths and start tap-dancing. It's right in the middle of First Hill, within walking distance of most city government buildings, so my old man and his cronies used to hang out there in the late afternoons. They got too drunk to walk, they'd toddle across the street to the Sorrento Hotel and take a little siesta.

Over the years the place got progressively seedier and more run-down, until, back in 2008, somebody walked in and blew another customer's head off while he was sitting on a bar stool. They closed for renovations, presumably to scrape the poor guy's brains off the ceiling. When it reopened a couple of years later, it looked exactly like it had back when my old man hung out there. Sorta like an oldovation, instead of a renovation.

Eagen was waiting for me. He was sitting at the close end of the bar with his back to the door. I slid onto the stool next to him and ordered an iced tea. The bartender barely managed to suppress a sneer.

"I think you may have missed the craft cocktail movement," Eagen said.

"Always figured booze was the one vice I could do without," I said. "Besides, man, I was making a living as a private eye. Just too much of a cliché for me."

"You've got a point," he conceded. "But it's my day off." He toasted me.

"Things must have calmed down a bit, if you wanted to meet here," I said.

"Woodward's moving heaven and earth to get this thing swept under the rug as soon as possible. They're all sitting around city hall on the edge of their seats, waiting to see how much Rebecca's gonna sue them for."

"You hear anything about that van they towed from up by the golf course?"

"It's for sure the one from the Durka hit-and-run. I'm hearing they found a couple pounds of Mr. Durka wedged up in the frame." I winced. He went on. "According to DMV, the van was crushed and scrapped four years ago, so it don't look like that line of inquiry is going anywhere either."

"I went out to see Patricia Harrington today."

He looked up from his drink. His brow wrinkled. "Don't fuck with those people, Leo. One word from her and Seattle ain't a place you can live anymore. I don't care who your father was."

"I know. I know."

He took a sip of his drink. "So?"

"You know anything about her son Charles?"

He thought for a minute. "Disabled, as I recall. That same night the daughter died, Patricia Harrington's husband . . . what's his name . . ."

"Sidney Crossfield."

"Yeah . . . supposedly he overheard the girl calling her brother for drug money, followed him up to Volunteer Park, and found them together on the ground. She was dead. The brother was in some sort of drug-induced coma. Did some sort of permanent damage to his brain, from what I hear."

"I'm gonna bop out to Issaquah and have a word with him."

"Kid gloves, man. Kid gloves."

"The very soul of discretion and tact."

He laughed. "That'd be a first."

"Hey, and while I'm at it . . ."

"What?"

I told him what I'd found out about Willard and the whorehouse. "They're tellin' me it's kids, man. Kids. The idea of a kid . . ." I let it go. Not for his sake, but for mine.

Eagen took another sip of his drink and shrugged. "I could run it by vice, but you know as well as I do what's gonna happen. If this Asian humpathon has been going for as long as you think it has, then somebody's running interference for them. Somebody savvy enough to know that anything going on after two A.M. is going to draw attention, the way shit draws flies. Somebody on third-shift patrol for sure. Somebody with buddies on the second shift too. That way, they've got it covered from both ends. So vice is going to refer this thing down the line, where it's going to land in the lap of the same people who are running interference for them. At which point, they'll pack up and move the operation someplace else, and we'll be even further from doing anything about it than we are now."

"Ain't life grand," I said. I downed the rest of my tea and hopped off the stool. "If I'm not back in three days, send out the dogs."

▪ ▪ ▪

Back before Columbus, they used to think there was an "end of the world." Someplace where you were just sailing along and then suddenly dropped off into nothing. They had it right. They just didn't know it was located in Issaquah.

Seattle isn't one of those places where urban life slowly peters out and gives way to farmland. Nope. You drive fifteen miles east to Issaquah, and one minute you're in the trendy burbs, and the next minute you're about as far out in the woods as you care to be. And it stays that way until you get all the way over east of the Cascades, at which point there's nothing but wheat and high desert for the next thousand miles or so.

I pulled off I-90 at the second Issaquah exit and wheeled past the obligatory collection of car dealerships and into downtown Issaquah, which looked a lot like something out of *Leave It to Beaver*. I stopped at a Shell gas station and asked for directions. The kid working the register didn't know where he was, let alone where I was going, so after I filled up, I wandered over to an antique shop two doors down from the station and found a nice elderly woman who actually knew where she was standing.

Took me twenty minutes to find the gate and another ten to negotiate the long paved driveway. The Tiger Mountain Lodge looked, for all the world, like some sort of trendy vacation spa. All fieldstone and stained wood, backed up against the looming bulk of Tiger Mountain.

I followed the signs to the visitor's parking lot, got out, and headed for the administration building. Cute African American girl personing the desk. Nametag read **LaTeisha**. Gave me a big, bright smile as I walked up. "Can I help you, sir?" she asked.

"I'd like to see Charles Harrington," I said.

She was shaking her head before the words were out of my mouth. She came out from behind the desk, took me by the elbow, and led me back through the entrance. The mountain air was filled with the sounds of wind and rushing water. She pointed at a separate stone building way over on the far side of the parking lot.

"Mr. Harrington . . . he's separate," she said.

"What's that mean?"

"That's Mr. Harrington's part of the facility over there. He's not technically a patient of the Lodge. He has his own private caregivers and doctors. The only thing the staff does for him is clean the building on Thursdays." She leaned in close. "I heard his family owns the whole place."

"They do," I said.

"As far as I know, Mr. Harrington doesn't take visitors."

"Well then, you probably better go back inside, honey, because he's about to get one whether he likes it or not."

She put a hand on my arm. "His caregivers . . . they . . ."

"They what?"

"They're not very nice," she said.

"Me neither," I said, and started across the lot. When I looked back over my shoulder, she was still standing there watching me go.

The closer I got, the bigger the building looked. Same stained wood and stone. Must have been four thousand square feet, all on one floor. There was a door on this side that looked like nobody used it much. The three windows evenly spaced across the back of the building were dark and unblinking. I was guessing that the house was designed to face out toward the forest, so I walked around to the south until I found the driveway. Two vehicles were parked side by side in the paved yard next to the building. A black Chevy SUV about a year newer than mine and an oversize white Mercedes van with a rack on top, something like a plumber would use.

No matter who you are, keeping out of the rain is high on the list of Pacific Northwest priorities, and that meant that the entrance to Casa Charles was likely to be as close to where they parked the cars as possible. I walked between the cars and proved myself right.

Charles Malcolm Harrington himself was sitting in a redwood Adirondack chair, reading what looked to be a comic book, when I tiptoed around the corner of the house.

He was a mousey-looking little thing. Maybe five-eight, a hundred fifty pounds or so. The tight curls clinging to his skull didn't look natural to me. Like maybe he'd had a perm or something. Unlike his sister the professor, he didn't look a bit like Patricia Harrington. Much narrower face and a pair of close-set, expressionless eyes. And most interesting of all, he was wearing a GPS ankle monitor. I know because a year or so back I'd worn one for a couple of weeks, when the cops thought I might have offed one of my neighbors because I was sleeping with his wife. Turned out to be the wife who did the offing.

He looked over at me and folded the magazine in his lap. "You're not allowed to be here," he said.

I shrugged. "But I am."

I could hear his ragged breathing from where I was standing. "You have to go now."

"I'd like to talk to you about—"

"I didn't mean it. Please. You can't be here. They'll . . . I don't want to go to jail. Please . . . if I . . . I didn't . . ." I watched his thoughts scatter like windblown leaves as one of the huge glass panels that made up the front of the house slid back and two men dressed in blue scrubs filed out. You want to talk about a Maalox moment. You could almost hear the roulette balls of recognition clicking into place. It was the fake UPS guys. Both of them. I knew for sure. And they knew that I knew. Worse yet, I knew that they knew that I knew.

I was still at the stammering stage when the second guy out the door stepped around his friend, pulled a chrome automatic from behind his back, and pointed it at my forehead. The gun was rock steady. Parts of me contracted like a dying star.

The guy with the gun motioned me toward him.

"Over here," he grunted in an accent thicker than a brick.

Wasn't going to happen. Every instinct in my body told me that putting myself in their hands would be the last thing I ever did.

The other guy started for me. I let him get close, feinted a right to his head, and then buried a left hook into his solar plexus. He huffed out a great burst of air, bent double, and staggered two steps backward, sucking air like a broken bilge pump.

Charles Harrington was on his feet now, his face the color of an eggplant. "Oh please . . . oh please," he whispered. He was hopping from foot to foot. I'd seen the look in his eyes before. Equal parts fear and longing. Fear of what tomorrow brings and a deep longing for whatever peace they'd once known.

The guy with the gun took two steps forward. His black eyes were telling me my time had come. I held my breath.

"Sir." The voice rose above the rushing in my ears.

The barrel of the gun looked to be the size of a bowling ball. I tore my eyes from it and threw history's quickest glance over my shoulder. LaTeisha. The receptionist. When I turned back, the guy had the gun hidden behind his back. With his free hand, he reached down and hauled his partner to his feet.

I didn't hesitate. I kept my hands in sight and started backing up, moving as quickly as I dared toward LaTeisha and the driveway. My heart felt as if it were going to beat its way out of my chest and fly off up the mountain. There was enough blood rushing in my head to float a kayak.

The second we backed around the corner of the house, I took her elbow and broke us into a run. I could hear my pulse slamming in my ears as we bounded across the parking lot like woodland creatures running before a forest fire.

Her eyes were the size of hubcaps. I fished around in my wallet, found an ancient business card, and handed it to her. "You see anything out of the ordinary going on out here, you give me a call, okay?"

She nodded and took off running.

■ ■ ■

"They're antipsychotics," Rebecca said. "Clozapine is kind of old, but it's still the drug of choice for treatment-resistant schizophrenia." She pointed at the list. "Olanzapine, quetiapine, and ziprasidone. All of them are serious-ass schizophrenia meds."

"He didn't seem psychotic to me. Confused, scared, not able to hold a thought for very long, sure, but nothing like crazy."

"And you're certain those were the same two guys you saw at my house on the night that . . ."

"The UPS brothers. One hundred percent."

"And you're telling me Charles Harrington graduated from Lakeside?"

"Two thousand twelve. Top quarter of his class."

"Way out of my mom's tuition league," Rebecca mused.

"They wouldn't take my ass" passed my lips before it passed my brain. The aggrieved sound of my voice told me, beyond doubt, that I'd been pissed off about the rejection for the past twenty-five years or so, and had never realized it until right then.

"Somebody points a gun at you, you can always go to the cops," Gabe said with a smirk. "Trust me. It's illegal as hell."

I shook my head. "He said, she said. I say they did. They say they didn't."

"Which leaves us where?" Gabe asked. "'Cause, you know, nice as it is to hang out with you two . . . I wasn't planning on making it a career."

"Yeah," I said. "We're just treading water here. We're no closer to knowing what in hell is going on than we were before."

Gabe bumped off the kitchen wall. "We're also no closer to eliminating the threat. According to you, the same two hitters are still around."

"We need to shake something loose," Rebecca said.

I thought about it for a long while. Then walked over to the fridge and got myself a glass full of ice and a San Pellegrino Limonata, most of which I swallowed in one pull.

I stifled a belch and looked over at Gabe. "You up for a little late-night adventure?"

Gabe grinned. "Ready Freddy. Whatcha got in mind?"

"What a guy I know referred to as an Asian humpathon."

"Wouldn't that be considered cultural appropriation?" Gabe teased.

"No . . . I don't believe it would. The humpathon part's completely universal."

"Nothing's completely universal," Gabe chided.

"Close enough for government work."

▪ ▪ ▪

The growl of the city gets deeper after the bars close. You can hear the streets heave a sigh of relief after the last drunk loses his lunch and staggers home. When the chairs are banged up onto the tables and the floors get swept, things quiet down for a few hours as the city checks the mirror, runs a hand through its hair, and gets ready for another day in Jet City.

The door on Jackson Street eased open at 2:37. Willard Frost poked his head out the door and said something into his phone. Half a minute later a big white Access van rolled around the corner. Twenty-seater they must have bought used from Metro. I could see where the **METRO** logos had been crudely painted over.

Gabe and I watched silently as eleven girls marched out the door and into the van. I tried to block it out and just stay professional, but my sense of moral outrage was screaming in my ears like an air raid siren. For me, that's never a good sign. Some of the most dumb-shit things I've ever done in my life have come at times when I was feeling self-righteous and didn't think something all the way through because my blood was up.

They kept the girls stored in a boarded-up three-story house in Little Saigon, half a block off Jackson. As the crow flew, it couldn't have been more than a mile from the building on South Main. Doing their part for the commute, they were.

Gabe and I watched from a block away as the van parked in the driveway, the door popped open, and the girls trooped up the front stairs and into the house, with the driver bringing up the rear. He checked the street before closing the door.

"The old Metro van's a nice touch," Gabe said, just as the porch light went out. "Last thing on earth the heat's gonna pull over late at night."

We waited about fifteen minutes. "You ready?" I asked.

"How many times do I gotta tell you? We're always ready," Gabe said.

I eased the car forward. Stopped right in front of the house. Both of us put on blue latex gloves, got out, and walked around to the back of the car. I'd borrowed a couple of armloads of firewood from Rebecca, some of which I'd split into nice, dry kindling. I grabbed an armload of wood and some newspaper from the back of the car and walked it over to the sidewalk directly in front of the house, where I crumpled up the paper, threw the kindling on top, and then added the bigger pieces.

When I looked up, Gabe had muscled one of the wooden pallets we'd stolen from Dunn Lumber about an hour ago off the Tahoe's roof rack and laid it on the pile. I went back to the car and fetched a new can of charcoal lighter and was dumping the stuff all over everything when Gabe added the second pallet to the pile.

By the time I got the car turned around and had rolled it back out onto Jackson Street, the flames were twenty feet tall and I could hear the dry wooden pallets popping and crackling from a block away. No-tech mayhem at its finest.

I pulled over, grabbed one of the throwaway phones from the glove box, and dialed 911. I reported a fire and gave them the address. Told 'em to send the cops because the joint was filled with undocumented aliens, then got out, put the phone in front of the tire. Made a nice solid crunch as I pulled back into the street.

Must have been a slow night for emergencies, because a fire engine, a police cruiser, and an aid car all screamed past going in the opposite direction before we'd covered the mile or so back to Pioneer Square.

I pulled the car to the curb on South Main and shut it off. George appeared from a darkened doorway and stumbled over to the passenger window. Gabe slid the window down. "He ain't come out this side," George said. "And Judy says nobody but the workin' girls ever comes out over on Jackson."

"Okay," I said. "Good job." I handed him a fifty. "You guys get your asses out of here. Things are about to get interesting." Didn't have to tell him twice. I'd gotten him shot at a while back. The speed with which he crossed the street and disappeared down the alley suggested that, as I'd suspected, he hadn't been too crazy about the experience.

Gabe had that big automatic out again. Going over everything. Checking the slide and pair of extra clips from the coat pocket.

"Let's go."

Gabe bopped me on the arm. "Never too old to rock and roll."

I pulled a rusty four-foot crowbar out from under the seat. The thing had been hanging from the wall in my garage for as long as I could remember. Who bought it, why, and when were a complete mystery to me, but, having seen this particular door close up the other day, I intuitively knew the garage mystery bar would be just the ticket.

We waited for a garbage truck to pass, then sauntered across the street, jammed the business end of the crowbar into the doorjamb, and both of us gave it all we had.

Sucker snicked open with no more noise than a pop-top.

Gabe pointed up the stairs and whispered in my ear, "Hall goes off to the left. Stay way over on the right. Leave me a clean line of fire."

I nodded and started creeping up the stairs. I had my Smith & Wesson massaging the small of my back but was hoping like hell we wouldn't need it. Downtown gunfights were considered extremely poor form, and I wasn't looking forward to spending a night in jail before Rebecca could bail me out the next day. Again.

I climbed slowly. One tread at a time. Straining my ears as I moved up, trying to catch any hint of movement or sense of alarm. A car passed in the street outside, and then another. I thought maybe I heard faraway voices but couldn't be sure. I took another step. The old wooden stairs groaned. I stood still and listened. A dog barked. I kept moving up. Gabe was two stairs behind me as I stepped up onto the landing and peeped around the corner.

Long hallway. A single bug-stained lightbulb hanging from the ceiling. Looked like it used to be an old hotel. Probably from back at the Alaska Gold Rush period, when Seattle had been the jumping-off point for the Klondike. They'd slapped up any number of low-rent shitholes intended to accommodate the hordes of would-be gold miners. They'd stacked 'em in like cordwood, at five bucks a day, while they literally and figuratively waited for their ships to come in.

I moved my feet carefully. These old buildings could be deathtraps. Back in the eighties, at the height of the Peruvian Marching Powder Period, coke dealers regularly cut holes in the floor as a way to discourage unwanted guests. A guy George and I both knew had met his death over on Yesler when he'd stepped in a hole, dropped four stories, and kebabed himself on a pile of hundred-year-old construction rubble.

The dog barked again. Weird-sounding dog, like it had laryngitis or something. Coming from somewhere down at the end of the hall. I shuffled in that direction.

I was standing directly on the other side of the door when the barking started again. Room 104. Gabe tiptoed past me and set up on the other side. We caught our collective breaths and made eye contact. I stepped away from the wall, raised one of my boots, and gave the door the full Monty.

Gabe rushed in. I grabbed the Smith & Wesson from my belt and followed along. I knew immediately that the scene wasn't something I was ever going to forget. Red velvet walls, big red velvet chesterfield couch, upon which an Asian woman in a leather garter belt lounged. Looked like a Victorian brothel, except maybe for the steel cage sitting on the floor in front of the couch. And the fact that Willard Frost was languishing, on all fours, stark naked, inside the cage. Willard and a big chrome doggy dish. **FIDO** in big green letters.

The woman on the couch started to jump to her feet. Gabe took three quick steps forward and pressed the gun barrel to her forehead.

"Don't" was all it took to sit her back down. On a doilied side table, a cell phone began to ring. Gabe reached over and picked it up and lobbed it my way.

I caught it on the fly. Even upside down, I could see the screen read Blocked. I had a feeling the caller was probably someone with news of what was going on over at the Little Saigon house. I walked over to the nearest window, bench-pressed the old-fashioned casement up a few tough inches, and dropped the phone out the window. There was just enough light for me to see it shatter on the cobblestones below. Evidently the phone wasn't alleyproof.

I closed the window and turned back toward the room. Apparently, phone loss was simply more than the Asian woman could bear. She came off the cushions like a rocket, long red fingers extended, looking to scrape my face off onto the floor. Gabe reached out and grabbed her by the hair.

The black wig came off in Gabe's hand. I ducked low and threw a shoulder into the woman's onrushing chest. The force of the impact drove her backward. Wasn't until she finished stumbling back onto the couch that I noticed the obvious. I was still at the staring-and-stammering stage when Gabe pointed and then said it out loud.

"She's got a dick," Gabe said.

"Aw . . . Jesus" came rolling out of my mouth.

Willard was shaking the cage like a mad mastiff, trying to break out, but the door had a little silver padlock and was holding fast.

I pointed at the person on the couch and said to Gabe, "Take care of that one while I have a few words with Willard here." I walked closer to the pair.

"Where's the key to the cage?" I asked.

Madame Woo reached down into his bodice, if that's what one calls it, and fished out a chain that held two silver keys. "You assholes have no idea who you're fuckin with here," Suzie said. "I make a couple calls . . ."

Gabe ground the barrel into Suzie's forehead. The noise stopped.

Woo opened his painted mouth again, only to have Gabe stuff it with the gun barrel. About the time Gabe jacked a round into the chamber, Madame Woo's eyes got to be the size of pie plates. His red lips quivered around the black steel.

Gabe threw an angry glance down. "And if you don't get rid of that boner, I'm gonna blow the back of your head off."

Thing disappeared like it had hydraulics. Now ya see it, now ya don't.

I dropped to a knee in front of the cage. One key was bigger than the other. Looked to be about right for the lock on the cage. I slipped the Smith & Wesson back into my belt, figuring I was probably going to need both hands.

Like I thought, he came out swinging. Tried to paw me in the nuts as soon as I pulled the door back, but I turned sideways and took it off the hip. He was about halfway out when I kneed him full in the face. No sense busting knuckles. The force of the knee toppled him back onto his haunches. Over to my left, Gabe broke out laughing. Willard was wearing plastic dog paws on his hands and feet and a pair of friggin' doggy ears. And a horsey tail, one end of which seemed to be stuck up his ass. And a pink rhinestone collar . . . and . . . a little stainless-steel cage that was locked around his gonad package. I groaned.

"What's wrong with you assholes?" Willard wanted to know.

I held up a restraining hand. "Lemme see if I've got this straight," I said. "You're inside a steel cage, wearing plastic paws, a dog collar, and dog ears, with a butt plug stuck up your ass so you can't get it out, and you're wanting to know what's wrong with *us*."

"It's just cosplay, man. Just cosplay. You got no right to—"

"He's my dog," Suzie said.

I pointed at Willard's crotch hardware. "What the fuck is that?"

"A chastity cage," he said.

"You're shitting me."

"It's a fetish, man," Willard said, from the squatting position. "You know, man . . . pet play. Power transfer. It's real big in San Francisco. It's trending," he said hopefully.

He started to get to his feet. I pulled the Smith & Wesson back out of my belt and pointed it at his head. He sunk back into a deep squat. That's when I realized he couldn't sit all the way down because of the plug in his ass. I involuntarily smiled.

"Here's what we're gonna do here, Rover. I'm going to ask you some questions. You're going to answer me truthfully, or my friend and I are going to fuck you up so bad you'll wish you'd gone to the great boneyard in the sky. You understand?"

He nodded.

"Lamar Hudson," I said.

He looked at the floor. I popped him on the head with the gun. He got the message. "Okay . . . okay . . . I was just tryin' to make a little money."

"From who?"

"Charlie's folks."

"The Harringtons?"

"Yeah."

"Money for what?"

"Keepin' my mouth shut."

"About?"

"About Lamar."

I bopped him between the ears with the gun. He sat down, instantly regretted the hell out of it, and used his paws to push himself back into doggy-squat position. He had that same embarrassed look on his face that dogs get when they notice you're watching them take a dump.

"About where Lamar really was when that Charlie kid's sister got killed."

"So . . . where was he?"

"He was in juvie with the rest of us."

"Who's the rest of us?"

"Me and a guy named Terry, and some Latin guy named Gilbert something, and the Okie . . . that Lamar guy. Cops caught me rolling fags up in Volunteer Park. I was on probation at the time, so they threw me in the can for a week or so." He doggy shrugged. "'Cept for that Charlie kid—he came in later. I heard they found him wid the dead girl." He shook his head. "That motherfucker was fucked up. Rollin' around on the jailhouse floor. Foamin' at the mouth. Eyes rolling around in his head like a pinball machine. Soon as the cops figured out who he was, it started raining doctors and lawyers. That motherfucker was gone in a heartbeat."

I thought about it for a while. "So you're telling me that at the time Tracy Harrington was killed, Lamar Hudson was in jail."

"Yep. You could check it out."

"What jail?"

"Juvie. Like I told you. The kid jail, over by Seattle U."

"So . . . you make any money?" I asked.

"Five grand."

"Who paid you?"

"Charlie's people. Coupla guys didn't speak English so good brought me the dough. That's when the whole thing . . . you know . . . that's when the shit came down. That's when we—"

Suddenly car doors were slamming out in the street. The downstairs door banged open. I grabbed Willard by the hair and jerked him to his feet.

"You're gonna show us how to get out on the Jackson Street side. Let's go."

I frog-walked him down the hall, with Gabe covering our backs, figuring that as long as he was out front, he wouldn't be leading us into any deadfalls. We'd turned about three corners when the sound of shouts and feet pounding up the stairs began to ricochet off the walls. Two more corners and a long flight of rickety stairs and we were at the Jackson Street door. I pulled it open and pushed Willard out into the street.

The door closed behind us with a thump.

"Aw, Jeees . . . ," Willard moaned. "I can't get back in, man."

I grinned. "Should be an interesting trip home," I offered.

The final image my brain stored was that of Willard Frost clopping naked down South Jackson Street on plastic paws, with his horsey tail bobbing in the breeze.

■ ■ ■

"You seen this?" Eagen threw the *Seattle Times* onto my kitchen table. I finished chewing my Eggos and then flipped the paper open with a sticky finger. Gabe and I hadn't rolled in till just after three thirty and were still sleeping it off when Eagen started hammering the gate buzzer about twenty minutes ago.

Gabe fished four more waffles out of the toaster and slid them onto a paper plate. Eagen picked them up from the counter and sat down across from me, grabbed the butter and the maple syrup, and went to work.

The headline read:

Police Break Large-Scale Prostitution Ring

"To protect and serve," I said around a mouthful.

Eagen picked up the newspaper and began to read out loud.

> "Twelve men and one woman have been charged with promoting prostitution following a wide-ranging investigation that resulted in the shutdown of twelve brothels in Bellevue and the seizure of two sex-trafficking sites in downtown Seattle, according to police and prosecutors. Information provided by the sex workers led authorities to Bellevue brothels that were operated out of high-end apartment complexes, where prostituted underage women from South Korea were forced to work often for twelve hours a day, seven days a week, to pay off debts, according to Bellevue police chief Steve Mylett."

Eagen looked up from the paper. He nodded in Gabe's direction. "Sounds a lot like something you and Goldilocks here might have pulled off."

"Makes it sounds like they'd been workin' on it for months."

"Official spin."

"See . . . sometimes the good guys win," I said.

"They'll be back in business in a month."

"One does what one can."

"They picked up sixty-three women and girls."

I grinned. Gabe slapped the table. Scared the hell out of both of us.

"So what now? Cinderella here bodyguarding *your* ass now?"

I shrugged. "Can't imagine why Rebecca would need a watchdog now," I said. "That ship done sailed. I was just about to take my friend Gabe here back to wherever it is Gabe wants to go."

"So . . . what now? You packin' it in? Gonna let sleeping dogs lie?"

We both knew better, so I told him about my trip out to Issaquah. About Charles Harrington and the Croatian UPS caretakers.

"You're sure it was the same two guys?"

"One hundred percent."

He unhanded the waffles and leaned back in his chair.

"Shouldn't be hard to check," he said.

"If I hadn't gotten real lucky, those Croatians would have offed my ass, right then and there, and buried me up on Tiger Mountain." I caught his gaze and held up a scout's honor hand. "Guy had eyes like charcoal briquettes."

He took my word for it. "How do you know they're Croatians?"

"Carl said the names were Croatian."

Eagen didn't say anything. Just went back to cutting his waffles up. We both knew Carl's history with the Bosnian War. If he said the names were Croatian, they were Croatian. End o' story.

Gabe joined us at the table.

"Exactly where does one go to hire a pair of Croatian thugs anyway?" I asked.

"Probably not on craigslist," Gabe offered.

Eagen shrugged. "Love to see those juvie records . . . but that ain't gonna happen."

I just smiled. He picked up on it. "Don't tell me."

I stuffed my mouth full of Eggos and chewed like a contented cow.

"So?" Eagen pressed.

Took me a while to chew and swallow. "So . . . I'm gonna go and visit Charlie's sister. She's a prof at Seattle U. Seemed to me there was a hell of a lot of tension between her and her mother when the subject of Tracy came up. Thought maybe I'd see if I couldn't shed a little light on why that was."

"Losing a child, even a stepchild, is big-time traumatic, no matter how screwed up the kid is."

"This was way more than that. Crossfield's got Charlie squirrelled away out in Issaquah and Mrs. Harrington don't like the arrangement one bit."

I watched as Eagen geometrically dissected his waffles, moving the knife strictly in line with the little squares. Like he was performing brain surgery.

"You can cut across them, you know," I threw in. "You know . . . like diagonally."

He looked horrified. "But then they don't hold the syrup."

I looked over at Gabe, who obviously agreed.

"Even if he *is* a cop. He's got a point," Gabe said.

■ ■ ■

Gabe dropped the Gladstone bag onto the floor mat and climbed in. "Gonna take the passenger ferry out to Vashon," Gabe said. "Got a friend who'll pick me up at the other end. Gonna take a few days of R and R."

We'd spent the rest of the morning and early afternoon doing just that. Cleaning ourselves up and doing a bit of laundry. Trying vainly to get the smell of charcoal lighter off me and my clothes. I'd settled up with Joey through the miracle of direct deposit, and was beginning to feel that my life was regaining some sense of order.

"Pier Fifty?" I asked.

"Yep. Leaves at four thirty."

I checked the dashboard clock. 2:17. "We've got time to burn; what say we do lunch?" I said as I started the car.

The weather had taken its usual turn for the worse. What had started as a balmy morning had gone steadily downhill as the day had progressed. The wind was roaring through the tops of the trees, swaying the dark branches like skeleton fingers. A whirlwind of leaves swirled around the pavement as I rolled down the hill toward Interbay.

"Soon as I get a few days off, the weather goes to shit," Gabe groused.

"Assuming it wasn't already shit," I countered.

As we rolled down the face of the hill, intermittent rain began to splat on the windshield. By the time I pulled to a stop in front of Red Mill for a spot of lunch, it had worked its way up to a full, wiper-thumping deluge. We sprinted from the car to the front door, arriving at the counter in a full drip.

Gabe went for the Red Mill burger. Six solid inches of steaming cholesterol on a sesame seed bun. Being a man of great restraint, I ordered a plain bacon cheeseburger. In deference to our girlish figures, we decided to split an order of onion rings.

"You know, Leo . . . most of the time my job is like what they say about sailing. Hours and hours of boredom punctuated here and there by moments of extreme terror." Gabe waved a half-eaten onion ring in the air. "But this one . . . this was about as screwy an assignment as I've ever been on." The rest of the onion ring disappeared. "Usually, it's just simple shit. Somebody owes Joey money. Somebody's gonna pay up. Somebody's bothering one of the girls. I convince them that's an unhealthy thing to do. Shit like that. Wham, bam, thank you, ma'am."

I took a sip of iced tea, swallowed. "You know, I had a feeling we were just about to get something useful out of Willard when the cops showed up last night."

Gabe nodded. "Me too. Fido was gonna spill something. I could feel it."

I swallowed the last of the burger. "Maybe we should go ask him what it was he was gonna tell us," I suggested.

Gabe cocked an eyebrow at me. "You serious?"

"I know where he lives." I nodded out toward the car. "Still got the crowbar under the seat too."

"Unless the cops picked him up last night."

"Didn't see anything in the news about them arresting anybody dressed like a puppy dog."

"If Eagen had heard about it, he'd have said something, for sure. He's the type."

"Absolutely."

"We've got some time to kill."

"Nicely put."

"Yeah . . . I'm quite the wag."

■ ■ ■

The door on 407 Walter Street was a piece of cake. One crowbar, one bump, one squeak, and we were in. Georgie's friend said Willard lived on the third floor in the rear, so we didn't have to waste time knocking on doors and then dealing with the denizens of the dark who answered the doors.

A young Goth couple passed us on the stairs. Black all over. Ripped and torn, studded everything. More tattoos than teeth. The walking dead of The Walking Dead.

Halfway down the third-floor hallway, an old woman in a flowered kimono pulled open a door and lurched out into the corridor. She looked from me to Gabe and back. "You don't belong here," she gummed.

"You best go back inside, Mama," Gabe told her.

She was still grumbling when she pulled the door closed behind herself. Gabe pushed past me and started toward the door at the end of the hall. That's when I noticed the CC camera up high in the corner. The door flew open before I could get my mouth in gear. I was in midshout when Gabe's head jerked violently backward in the doorway. I watched openmouthed as Gabe tumbled backward onto the floor—twitching like a nerve, unconscious for sure.

I thrust the crowbar into the open doorway. Something hit the metal bar hard enough to tear it from my hand. Before I could decide what to do next, Willard Frost came bouncing out into the hallway. Swinging from his right hand was an evil-looking spring-loaded sap. Looked like a piece of lead about the size of a hen's egg, covered in leather and attached to a spring that let it wobble around like a skull-seeking missile.

He looked at Gabe lying unconscious on the floor and sneered.

"Not so fucking tough now, huh, bitch?"

I took a step back. The sap wasn't big, but I knew from painful past experience that it was going to break anything it came into contact with, so I had best keep out of range if I wanted to stay in one piece.

Willard bent over and screamed in Gabe's unconscious face. "Fuckin' dyke," he screamed. "You ain't shit." He raised the sap like he was going to flatten Gabe's skull with it.

What happened next wasn't something I thought about; it just happened. I took two quick steps in his direction and then dove at him. Superman-style. And friggin' missed. He skittered right and then raised the sap to cave in my skull. I saw it coming and rolled the other way; I hunched my shoulders and took the sap between the shoulder blades. A groan escaped from my throat unbidden. Felt as if I'd been shot in the back.

For about two seconds, I thought I might be paralyzed. Felt like my body had suddenly turned to concrete. Pain and terror gave me the strength to keep rolling. I heard the lead ball smash into the floorboards about an inch from my left ear as I pinwheeled over to the back wall and climbed to my feet.

Willard was shuffling my way, waving the sap out in front of him like it was the dangling dong of destiny. Gabe had managed hands and knees behind him, and the hall was suddenly full of gawkers, when Willard made his first mistake. If he'd kept trying to take my head off, the law of averages says he'd have eventually made contact, but for reasons known only to Willard, he decided he wanted to take out one of my knees.

He dropped low and swung the sap at my left knee in a vicious arc. I jumped backward. The sap's momentum sent it crashing through the ancient plaster, where it stuck for just long enough for me to launch a dropkick at Willard's head.

He rolled left and took three tries to yank the sap from the wall. I stepped in belly to belly, leaving him no room to wind up and bash me. He swung anyway. It looped around my body and crashed into my sternum. I grunted and head-butted him in the face. I heard his nose break like a Popsicle stick. He let out a yowl and stumbled backward, broken-nose blind, trying to backhand me with the sap and not coming close.

I bull-rushed him, driving the top of my head into his already broken nose. He screamed like a mezzo-soprano. I kept coming, using my bulk to slam him into the wall and keep him there, while I groped for the hand with the sap. He managed one more weak blow to my right shoulder before I grabbed his hand and dragged him to the floor, where I used my weight to pin him down.

On my left, Gabe was sitting now, back against the wall, open-mouthed, forehead sprouting a purple knot the size of a golf ball. I put everything I had into a couple of major elbows to Willard's face, the impact of which seemed to make serious inroads into his desire for further fisticuffs.

Took me half a minute and a couple more elbows to get the sap away from him.

I dropped it into my coat pocket, grabbed him by the hair, dragged him back into his room, and kicked the door closed after us. The place looked like he hadn't taken out the trash in about eleven years. Shit was piled everywhere. Whatever he had for furniture wasn't even visible anymore.

"Jew busted my dose," he blubbered.

I pulled the sap out of my pocket and gave him a little love tap on the shin. He whinnied like a horse.

"We're gonna finish our little chat from last night," I told him.

"I tole you before . . . we was all in juvie when Tracy got killed."

I raised the sap. He tried to extrude himself through the carpet. "Okay okay okay," he chanted. "I went back . . . tried to get a little more . . . tole 'em about the DNA thing. That's right when things went to shit, man." He waved his free hand. "Had guys coming around looking for me, all of a sudden." He pointed toward the front of the building. "Guy in the front left come out and wanted to know what in hell they were doing in the hall. They said they was looking for me and then beat the fuck out of him. That's why I ain't been coming back here. Been staying over on South Main with Rico, but Rico and everybody else got busted last night, so there ain't shit goin' on till things cool down."

"What DNA thing?"

"In juvie."

I raised the sap again.

"Okay okay. You remember. That was like right back at the time when the cops decided to take a DNA sample from everybody who got arrested."

"Yeah . . ."

"So we're all sittin' in the holding cell when this fat-ass comes in and calls out for Gilbert the Greaser to come on out so they can take a sample from him . . . and Terry gets up and makes like he's this Gilbert guy."

"And?"

"And then Gilbert gets up and makes like he's somebody else. The fat-ass cops don't know nothing. This DNA shit was all new to them. They didn't have a clue." He shrugged. "We all did it. Everybody got tested under somebody else's name. Except for that Charlie asshole and the guy who was passed out on the floor. They stuck a Q-tip in his mouth right there and wiggled it around. We just thought it was funny, man. You know, a little ha ha on the fucking cops."

"Lamar Hudson too?"

"The Okie? Yeah, him too."

The only reason I was inclined to believe his story was because the whole damn testing program *had* turned out to be a little ha ha on the cops. While the notion of genetically testing everybody they pinched had seemed like a natural to law enforcement, it turned out to be big-time unconstitutional because it didn't account for people who were wrongly accused or those who were acquitted. Everybody who didn't get convicted of a felony wanted their DNA profile removed from the system. Cops said no. They had the DNA profiles and they were keeping them. After a hail of class-action lawsuits, the courts agreed with the citizens. If I recalled correctly, the whole mandatory testing thing lasted less than a year.

"So you're telling me that the DNA profile they have as Lamar Hudson wasn't really his?"

"Uh-huh."

He started to crawl to his feet. I wobbled the sap in his face. "Just stay on the floor, Beavis," I told him. "So whose DNA was it?"

He shook his head. "Dunno, man. All I remember is Terry pretending to be this Gilbert guy. After that . . . I don't remember who pretended to be who."

I took a threatening step forward. He wrapped his arms around his head. "I was higher than shit, man. We was just havin' fun. And then next thing I heard, the Charlie kid fried his brain, somebody offed Gilbert in the joint, and that Okie Lamar was doin' hard time . . . there was guys lookin' for my ass, man, it . . . it was like the whole fucking world came apart."

"What else?"

"Ain't nothin' else."

I had the feeling I'd wrung everything out of him that I was gonna, so I lobbed the sap over into the far corner of the room and then put my face right up in his. "I'm gonna collect my friend and get out of here. If I were you, if, at any time in the rest of your miserable life, you see my friend Gabe there—I'd run like hell."

He didn't say anything. Just sat there on his ass, bleeding onto the orange shag carpet as I backed over to the door.

Gabe had managed to get upright but was the color of old oatmeal. I got a shoulder under and began to half walk, half drag us down the hallway. Gawkers scattered like chickens as we shuffled down the corridor cheek to cheek.

The stairs were tough. One at a time, almost like Gabe had never seen stairs before. The fresh air massaged my sweaty face as we stepped into the street.

We shuffled up to First Avenue like slow-dancing drunks and kept going for another block until we got to South Washington Street. As we turned the corner, the deep rumble of engines rose above the din of the city. Half a dozen tandem dump trucks were lined up end to end along the westbound curb, engines running, spewing diesel smoke into the air, each waiting for its turn to dump its load into the new seawall before making a run down to the barges at Harbor Island for a refill. A tight knot of truck drivers was assembled on the sidewalk, waiting their turns, smoking cigarettes and telling lies until they got the call.

Gabe seemed to come around for a second. "The ferry," Gabe said. "Gotta get the Vashon ferry."

I kept us moving. "Tell you what, partner. I'm gonna run us by the Harborview ER so they can have a look at your head," I said as we shuffled along.

"No . . . no . . . I'm okay . . . the ferry . . ."

Half a block up, my car sat in the shadows of the viaduct. I adjusted Gabe's arm over my shoulder and picked up the pace a bit.

From the corner of my eye, a movement on the opposite sidewalk jerked at my attention. I couldn't be sure, but it seemed like somebody was shadowing us from the other side of the street. The back of my neck began to tingle. Two guys. Dark hoodies. Before I could get a better read on them, they disappeared behind a dump truck. I kept watching as the two sets of feet motored along the sidewalk. And then they stopped walking, up by the front of the big rig, as if they wanted to keep the truck between us. That's when Gabe's legs gave out, nearly pulling me to the pavement.

The only thing I kept from crashing into the pavement was Gabe's head. The rest of the two hundred pounds went down like a stone.

I was still deciding what to do next when Gabe's eyes popped open and then looked around. "Huh? How . . ."

I stood up and held out both hands. Had to put my back into it, but I got Gabe back up. I checked the other side of the street. No feet in sight.

The forty yards to my car seemed more like a mile and a half, but, with a couple of fits and starts, we made it. I muscled Gabe into the passenger seat, fastened the seat belt, and walked around to the other side of the car, which was parked close up to one of the hundreds of concrete road dividers the crews were using to keep traffic at bay during seawall construction.

I was still fumbling with my own seat belt when I heard the shout and looked up. It was one of those times when seeing something about to happen was way worse than being totally taken by surprise.

A trio of dump truck drivers were sprinting down the sidewalk in our direction, waving their arms and screaming like their hair was on fire. I was staring at them, trying to figure out what the problem was, when I realized the nearest dump truck was roaring in our direction. Headlights ablaze. Big chrome grill. INTERNATIONAL across the front. I waited for the wheels to turn, for it to drive off up Alaskan Way to deliver its load, but that didn't happen. It kept coming right at us.

Any doubts I had as to what was going on evaporated the moment the driver shifted the big rig into second gear. I watched as the cab door flew open and whoever was behind the wheel leaped headlong from the cab. The last thing I remember seeing was a white Mercedes van skid to a halt next to the rolling dump truck driver.

At that point, the big rig roared across the southbound lane and hit us broadside. It wasn't going very fast. Twenty-five miles an hour, tops. But it was thirty tons of International steel and the forty-eight tons of gravel that were about to crush us like June bugs.

Every window in the car exploded simultaneously. I was awash in safety glass. I could feel the Tahoe's frame begin to collapse. Steel struts were coming up through the floorboards. I pulled up my feet. Gabe was moving my way inch by inch as the passenger compartment began to fold in half. It was like we were in a car crusher. Gabe's shoulder touched mine. I bent forward to make more room. The dump truck's tires chattered on the pavement as the engine kept forcing it forward.

The screech of tearing metal assaulted my ears. I was pawing at my door handle when I felt the concrete road barrier begin to move. I threw a glance to my left. The chain-link fence had disappeared into Puget Sound. I watched in horror as the road barrier followed the fence into the inky water below.

The roar of the engine, the popping of plastic, and the sound of metal being torn asunder became everything in the universe. I felt the car begin to tilt in the second before gravity threw me against the driver's door. The Chevy rolled up on two wheels, balanced like a ballerina for the briefest of moments, then toppled over onto its side.

The driverless truck kept pushing. In fits and starts, the Chevy began to skid across the pavement on its side. And then I felt the cold air on my ear, right before the pitted asphalt disappeared and there was nothing in my peripheral vision but the obsidian waters of Puget Sound.

And then we were airborne. For about two seconds. The weight of the engine spun the Chevy a quarter turn. We hit the water pretty much nose first. With all the windows blown out, we bobbed on the surface for only an instant before the black water folded around us, and we headed for the bottom like a cobblestone.

Wasn't till I floated up to the headliner that I realized I'd never gotten my seat belt fastened. I took a couple of swimming strokes and reached for Gabe's seat belt. Missed. The water was arctic. My muscles felt like I'd been flash frozen. I reached again and found the buckle. Pushed. Pushed again. And then Gabe floated free of the seat.

The Tahoe plowed into the bottom with a muted thud, and even in the deep-space dark, I could see a mushroom cloud of mud roiling around the car. I fought my feet and then the rest of me out through the driver's window, then reached back in, grabbed Gabe by the shoulders, and started to pull.

Hypothermia was starting to kick in. My lungs were on fire. My vision was getting screwy. I could barely force my muscles to move. I had Gabe's head and shoulders out of the car when a flash of light streaked across my field of vision. I looked up, saw the dump truck's headlights, and nearly screamed in terror. The truck was still coming. The cab was now hanging over the edge of the seawall, tumbling down through the water to crush us.

I heaved Gabe with all I had, pulling on the coat collar until we were both outside the car, floating free, and then I started swimming blind, flailing for all I was worth, pulling Gabe along beside me. I had no idea what direction I was swimming in. All I knew for sure was that I didn't want to be underneath when that friggin' dump truck hit the bottom.

That's when my lungs decided they'd had enough abuse for today. Wasn't like I intended to take a breath of salt water. It just happened, and it paralyzed me. I'd like to be able to tell you that I had the presence of mind to relax and let our natural buoyancy take us to the surface.

Truth was, I couldn't move. Matter of fact, I thought I might be dead. For some odd reason, I found the notion comforting.

I arrived at the surface as a choking, puking pile of shit. My lungs were spasming in my chest. Felt like my eyes were going to pop out of the sockets. I gulped air, barfed salt water all over the front of myself, and gulped some more air. My hand hit something solid. In desperation, I groped for it. A seaweed-and-barnacle-encrusted piling met my flailing fingers. I hugged the piling like a long-lost brother, then used my other hand to pull Gabe to my side. Same deal. Gabe gasped and coughed up enough to water to float a canoe. The forehead knot had begun to seep blood.

Five feet behind us, the dump truck hit the water. Three seconds later, the rest of the load arrived. The wake from seventy tons washed both Gabe and I off the pole like sand fleas. Gabe went under. I waited. Still gone.

I sucked in a deep breath and went under. Groping around, finding nothing. Had to go back up for air. Gabe was back up when I surfaced, clinging to the piling. Gabe's eyes were focused now. Amazing what a little brush with eternity will do.

"Don't let go of that pole," I shouted. "People saw what happened. They'll be on their way to get us. Just hang in there."

Gabe nodded and hugged the pole like it was Santa. Above the lapping of waves and the rumble of traffic, I could hear Gabe's teeth chattering like castanets. My body began to shake uncontrollably. I wrapped my legs around the pole. The barnacles were tearing my hands. Every time a piece of kelp brushed against my legs, I'd hear snippets of Robert Shaw's *Indianapolis* speech from *Jaws*, about how seven hundred souls had gone into the water when the ship went down and how the sharks had methodically torn them to shreds. I made a serious effort not to whimper.

I don't know exactly how long it took the water cops to get to us. Seemed like an hour but probably wasn't. I had to boost Gabe back onto the piling a couple of times. All I recall is seeing the pulsing blue light from the police boat bouncing around on the surface of the water, and then the spotlight shining in my eyes. I willed myself to reach for the light, but my muscles wouldn't work. After that, it's pretty much a blank slate until I opened my eyes again in the Harborview Emergency Room and saw the Virgin Mary staring down at me. Turned out to be Rebecca.

▪ ▪ ▪

"What are you going to tell the cops?" Rebecca asked.

"With the SPD, it's more of a matter of what they want to hear."

"Are you certain about what you saw?"

I thought about it. "No," I said. "Things were really out of hand at the time. And even if I was right, the cops don't seem to believe anything I tell them, and I can't think of a single reason they're gonna to believe this either."

"I heard a couple cops talking," she said. "The truck drivers are saying somebody tried to hijack one of their trucks and that you and Gabe were just in the wrong place at the wrong time."

"Seems to be happening to me with an alarming frequency."

"Always has."

I pretended not to hear. "How's Gabe?"

"Semicompressed skull fracture. Non-life-threatening. But Gabe's not going anywhere for a few days, while they run the concussion protocol."

I lifted my head and looked down along my body. "And me?"

"You lost about a half inch off your left elbow, which is why they put that arm in a splint. They say it's going to be real sore for a while." She took a deep breath. "They spent about an hour picking safety glass out of you, and then gave you a dose of antibiotics big enough for a rhino with the clap, in case the water you swallowed contains anything toxic, which everybody around here with a triple-digit IQ knows it does. Other than that, I'm free to take you back to your place whenever you feel good enough to go."

"I'm not even gonna ask about my car."

"From what I understand, it's under the dump truck, forty feet under the surface of Elliott Bay. Tomorrow, they're calling in a Matson barge crane to raise the truck."

"My insurance company is gonna go ratshit."

"How many wrecked cars is this?"

I pretended I needed to think about it. "Three total losses in the past four years."

"I think maybe you should expect a significant rate hike."

"I want to see Gabe."

"Not going to happen."

I fell into a full sulk, before Rebecca piped up and ruined my pity party. She leaned in close. "What were you guys doing down there, anyway?"

"Having a little chat with Willard Frost," I whispered.

"Chat about what?"

I told her, at length, after which she lassoed her lower lip and stepped back from the bed. "You gotta be kidding me."

"That's what he told me."

"So this new piece of evidence that supposedly links Lamar Hudson to Tracy Harrington's murder, assuming it's DNA—it . . . theoretically . . . it could belong to any of them."

"Yeah. And since Lamar was actually convicted of her murder, they're probably still using that original DNA sample for comparison."

"No reason to take another," Rebecca said.

"How we gonna figure out who it really belongs to?" I asked.

She took a minute to answer. "We'd have to retest all of them."

"One of them's dead. One of them's crazy. Another likes to pretend he's a Pekingese." She looked blank. "Puppy play," I said.

"What's that?"

"You don't want to know, honey. Trust me."

"Any of them been convicted of a felony since that time?"

"A real good bet."

"Then their DNA profiles will be on file with the state. All convicted felons give up a sample. It's part of the state sentencing document."

"Can you check?"

She shrugged.

"Under the radar," I added. "Way under the radar."

She gave me a brief, nearly imperceptible nod. "It can't show up in the departmental budget," she said. "I'll have to work that part out—but yes, unless any of it's sealed for some reason or other." She held up a finger. "We'll need another sample from Lamar too. The more verified profiles, the closer we get to a simple process of elimination."

"I'll talk to his lawyers."

She looked around disgustedly. "Why do we always wind up here?"

"Send in the cops," I said. "Then we'll get the hell out of here."

■ ■ ■

Took four days before I started feeling human again. Rebecca was still trying to clear the body bag backlog created by her suspension and hadn't had a chance to locate anybody's DNA. So, assuming you could still call it a case . . . the case was going nowhere.

She called me a couple of times a day but was up to her elbows in entrails, working double shifts, trying to get back to the normal level of carnage, so our communication was all very *love ya, love ya, see ya later.*

Late in the morning of the fourth day, I took an Uber downtown and rented myself a car. Another silver Tahoe, just like the one at the bottom of the bay. Consistency is my middle name.

After I drove home, I called Angela St. Jean at the Innocence Project.

"Can you get a fresh DNA sample from Lamar Hudson?" I asked.

"Who is this?"

"Leo Waterman. You remember . . . you came to my—"

"Of course I remember, Mr. Waterman. New profiles are always one of the first things we ask for when we take on a case . . . and most often the first thing they turn down. Always citing fiscal responsibility, of course."

"What if Lamar volunteers and pays for it himself?"

"Then they'll have to comply, but they'll make it take as long as they possibly can."

"Why would they do that?"

"Because in cases such as this, people in power have their careers and egos tied up in Mr. Hudson being guilty of what they convicted him of and are loath to do anything that might suggest they made a mistake. Convicting innocent people is bad for the résumé."

"Start the process."

"Why would I do that?"

I told her.

"Are you sure?"

"Sure enough to pay for a new DNA profile myself, if I have to."

"Done," she said. "And we'll pick up the tab. It'll look better that way."

I hung up and wandered out into the front parlor. I was standing there, trying to make sense of things, spacing out and looking out over the lawn toward the front gate, when I saw a yellow cab pull up and Gabe get out.

I walked over to the front closet, pushed the gate button, and then pulled open the front door. A black-and-white SPD SUV drove by. Gabe was halfway to the front door and the gate was mostly closed when another police cruiser rolled by the opening.

Gabe had found a knit watch cap and had it pulled way down over the ears. I walked down the front steps and met Gabe out in the driveway.

"Good to see you up and around," I said.

We embraced as ardently as somebody with a severe concussion and a guy with one arm in a splint could manage.

"That little bastard made a dent in my skull," Gabe said.

Another police car crept by. Gabe jerked a thumb toward the road. "Assholes on parade. The heat's been up my butt from the second I walked out of Harborview. Two or three cars switching off, all the way up here."

"You punch anybody?"

"Nope."

"Shoot anybody?"

"Nope."

"Fuck 'em, then," I said with a grin, as I threw an arm around Gabe's shoulders and kicked the front door closed. We started down the hall toward the kitchen.

"You know, Leo," Gabe said, "color me with a curious crayon, but getting my head stove in just naturally makes me wonder what the fuck is going on here, even more than I did before. You find out anything useful from that little shit?"

"Oh yeah." I told Gabe what Willard had told me about the DNA switching.

"No shit," Gabe said. "So . . . you know . . . is there a next?"

"Coffee. I just made a pot."

"Hell of an idea," Gabe said.

We got three steps closer to the kitchen when the gate speaker went off.

"THIS IS THE SEATTLE POLICE DEPARTMENT. OPEN THE GATE OR WE WILL BREAK IT DOWN. OPEN THE GATE NOW."

I walked back to the front of the house, pushed the button, and then pulled the door open. Like Yogi said, it was like déjà vu all over again. The storm troopers of the status quo were coming down the driveway at a lope. Black visors, helmets, and assault weapons. Four of them. Couple of plainclothes and K-9 unit guys bringing up the rear.

"PUT YOUR HANDS ON TOP OF YOUR HEAD," one of the storm troopers yelled.

I did. The dog was straining at the lead and barking his brains out, slobbering all over my asphalt.

"GET DOWN ON YOUR KNEES. NOW!"

Seemed excessive, so I didn't. The dog seemed to take offense and redoubled his barking and snarling efforts.

"You want to tell me what's going on?" I said, without moving a muscle.

Apparently, they didn't. They rushed me instead. Washed over me like a wave. Next thing I knew, both Gabe and I were handcuffed, lying facedown on the floor.

"Get 'em up," somebody said.

A pair of beefy cops grabbed each of us by the elbows and sat us down on the big brocade couch in the front room.

The dog was hot to trot. I could hear his feet scratching on the stone floor of the entranceway.

"Get that flea-bitten drool factory out of my house," I yelled at the cops.

One of the plainclothes guys stepped forward with a fistful of paperwork. "Leo Waterman, Gabriella Funicello, you are under arrest for aggravated murder." Needless to say, I was a mite nonplussed. Took me a minute to process.

"Who is it exactly we're supposed to have murdered?" I asked.

"Willard Stephen Frost," the cop said.

■ ■ ■

She slapped the crime scene photos down onto the table one at a time, like she was dealing blackjack. Somebody had beaten on Willard Frost to the point where I was having trouble deciding which way was up in the photographs because whatever was lying on the floor bore such scant resemblance to anything human.

I pointed at the one on the left. "A bit out of focus," I said.

Detective Andrea Feeney was not amused. "They told me you thought you were a funny guy. A real card, they said."

"Always nice to be appreciated by the fan base."

"You still claiming you don't know anything about this?"

"I'm not claiming anything except that I want to speak to an attorney."

"Your playmate is giving you up, Waterman. Funicello's in there singing the Mouseketeer theme song." She slapped a hand down on the table. "First birdie sings gets a deal. The other gets to spend the rest of his days inside."

I laughed out loud. "Gabe wouldn't give you the friggin' time of day."

She went for the throat, pulling out an evidence bag and dropping it on the table. "And I suppose you're going to tell me that you've never seen *this* before."

It was the spring-loaded sap I'd taken away from Willard Frost. From the look of the stains on it, this was the blunt object that somebody used to reduce Willard's head to the consistency of refried beans.

"I'm not going to tell you anything," I said. "I want to call my lawyer."

Detective Feeney was in a quandary. They were sure as hell taping the interview—that's what they did—and I'd now asked her twice for a lawyer. If she kept after me, I was going to have big-time grounds for an appeal. She knew it, and I knew it, and I knew she knew. 'Nuff said.

"Your creepo lawyer's waiting outside," she sneered.

Which was amazing because I hadn't made any phone calls yet. Hadn't had the chance. Not even to the Creepo Lawyer Line. They'd stuffed us into separate holding cells and let us cool our heels for an hour or so before moving us into separate interview rooms. I'd asked the jailers to let me make my phone call a couple of times, but they'd ignored me, and now, all of a sudden, I had a creepo lawyer I hadn't even called. Do tell.

"I'd like to speak to my attorney," I repeated.

Third time was the charm. Feeney disgustedly scooped up the photos and the brain-encrusted sap and bustled back out the door. Thirty seconds later the door opened again. In walked a guy I'd never seen before. Forty or so, bald, five-ten, and at that stage where guys begin to lose sight of their belt buckle. When he knew without being told that the chairs were bolted to the floor and simply slipped into the seat across the table from me, my confidence took wings.

"You mind if I ask who in hell you are?" I said.

He stuck out a hand; I gave it a shake or two. "Ricardo Dupuis," he said. "I'm on permanent retainer from Entertainment Associates."

Entertainment Associates was Joey Ortega. The strip clubs, the dance clubs, the massage parlors, the casino—all of it was run under the innocuous umbrella of Entertainment Associates. The kind of entertainment businesses Joey ran had a tendency to require twenty-four-hour access to legal help. He probably had a couple dozen shysters on retainer at all times. Seemed a good bet that Gabe had managed a phone call and Joey had immediately sent the cavalry.

"If you'll excuse me for a moment," Dupuis said.

I watched as he got up and walked over to the door. It was locked. He pounded on it until somebody on the other side of the one-way panel pulled it open. "Just so we're clear here," the lawyer said. "I'm officially invoking attorney-client privilege. There will be no recording of any kind of my conversation with Mr. Waterman." At which point, he slammed the door in somebody's face and sat back down across from me.

"So . . . what happened?"

I told him the whole story. He interrupted only once.

"Pet play?"

I explained it to him the best I could. Left him shaking his head.

"Willard Frost was sitting on the carpet trying to stop a nosebleed when I left," I finished up.

"And how did Mr. Frost come to have a nosebleed?"

"I head-butted him."

"And Miss Funicello can attest to this?"

"Miss Funicello was pretty much unconscious at the time," I said. "You can check with Harborview as to the extent of Gabe's injuries."

He took some notes. Read some note, and then looked up. "That's consistent with Miss Funicello's statement," he announced. "And with the preliminary results of our own investigation."

"What investigation is that?"

"My firm sent several adjusters down to Mr. Frost's building. Seems there's an old woman who claims to have seen Mr. Frost in the hall after you and Miss Funicello left. Said he had a rag pressed to his face when she saw him. My associates are taking her deposition as we speak. She says he threatened her." He made a dismissive gesture with his hand. "Of course, the police, as is their habit, discounted her version so they could clear the case as quickly as possible."

"Anybody check the CC camera?" I asked.

"What CC camera?"

"Up high in the corner, over Frost's door."

He excused himself again, went over and stood in the corner of the interview room, whispering into his phone for a full five minutes before he broke the connection and sat back down. "No CC camera. My associate says he can see where it was ripped from the wall. No recorder or monitor in the apartment either."

"Somebody was careful."

"Apparently," Dupuis agreed.

He got up again, walked over to the one-way window. "I'll need jumpsuits for both Mr. Waterman and Miss Funicello. I want their clothes tested for the presence of organic material."

"Orange is not my color," I whined.

He ignored me, collected his stuff, and got back to his feet. "I've seen the crime scene photos," he said. "There was brain matter on an eleven-foot ceiling. Whoever killed Mr. Frost surely must have parts of him all over their clothes."

"I might have a little of his blood on me."

"The perpetrator of this crime must have breaded himself like a veal cutlet," Dupuis said. "A little blood isn't going to be enough."

"What now?" I asked.

"Aggravated murder is not a bailable offense in this state, so you and Miss Funicello are going to have to hang tight until I can petition for a hearing in the morning. By that time we'll have a formal deposition from the woman in the building and at least some preliminary results from the tests on your clothes." He almost smiled. "I'm given to understand that you've had some previous experience with jails."

"More than I'd be willing to admit," I said.

The smile finally got the best of him. "Well . . . then I don't have to tell you not to say anything to anybody, do I?"

■ ■ ■

Took three days. Three days of plastic coveralls, mystery meat, powdered eggs, and cherry Kool-Aid. Just like Jesus in the desert. Except, in this case, the Devil was a bunch of pathetic souls who really should have been in a psychiatric ward somewhere, getting help with their problems. But, since that costs a whole bunch of money, nowadays we just lock their crazy asses up in jail, with the real criminals. Cheaper that way.

Holding cells are segregated. Not by the jailers, but by the inmates. First thing I do when they put me in a holding cell is join the Caucasian section. I don't give a shit whether they're Aryan Nation skinheads, slackers, skaters. Don't care if they're inside for murder, mopery, or a bad mullet, just as long as they're white. Whatever progress our society has made in race relations goes right down the toilet in jail. There's a white-guy section, a black-guy section, and a Hispanic-guy section. That's just the way it is. If you've got half a brain, you find like-looking creatures and make some friends. I'm pretty sure Charlie Darwin would tell you it's a matter of survival.

The plan worked for about a day and a half. The holding cell crowd had thinned a bit by then, so I had a bench to myself. I had my feet pulled up and was dozing when somebody kicked my feet off the bench.

"Move your ass, cracker."

New arrival. Big black man with a red do-rag covering the top of his bald head. Under normal circumstances, I would have made a serious effort to defuse the situation. Tried to reason with the guy or something. Made a joke. Who knows? But I'd been in jail eating roadkill for thirty hours or so: a situation more or less guaranteed to make me a bit testy. And then there was the matter of the splint on my left arm.

This was a big ol' boy hassling me here. I like to think I'm as fanciful as the next guy, but even in my most vivid imaginations, I couldn't see myself whipping this monster with one hand. Wasn't gonna happen. Definitely time for plan B.

"You gonna move your cracker ass, or am I gonna kick it for you?" he yelled again. Over his shoulder, I could see several of his homeboys from the ghetto section milling around, waiting for the show to start.

I unwound myself slowly. Putting both feet on the floor, then surreptitiously slipping my right foot down under the bench until it came into contact with the wall. I levered myself off the seat in slow motion. About halfway up, I jammed my foot against the wall for traction, made like I was losing my balance, scoped out a spot on his solar plexus, put all my weight behind my right fist, and tried to punch my way through to his backbone. Damn near made it too.

The air burst out of him in a single groaning blast. He staggered backward, wide eyed, hiccuping, gasping for breath, and sat down on the filthy floor. Several of his buddies started shuffling my way. Cautious, now that their champeen couldn't get his lungs to work. That's when the guy with the Charlie Manson swastikas tattooed on his cheeks came off the far end of the white-guy bench like a missile.

"Fuckin' niggers," he bellowed as he hurled himself into the fray.

Not very PC, but an effective rallying cry, nonetheless. Both benches emptied in a flash, and a full-scale melee began. All assholes and elbows. Took a dozen jailers nearly ten minutes to get things under control.

That's how come I was in an isolation cell the next morning when Ricardo Dupuis showed up with my release papers. I could tell the news was positive when the jailer left the door open and walked away.

"Nice to see you've been making friends and influencing people," Dupuis said.

"Tell me you're gonna get me out of here," I said.

"We got lucky," he said. "There wasn't enough forensic material on either you or Miss Funicello to prove gerbil battering. And, about the time you and Miss Funicello were going into the water, the guy running the coffee shop across the street from Mr. Frost's apartment building came outside to see what all the yelling was about. Swears he saw two guys in hoodies going into Frost's building. Signed a deposition to that effect." He lifted a disgusted hand. "They wanted to stick you with an aggravated assault rap for the jail fight, but even they're not dumb enough to think that was going to float, so they'll drag their feet for a few more hours, long enough that the state will have to reimburse them for another day of your incarceration. Soon as they get paid, you'll be out of here."

"Thank Joey for me," I said.

■ ■ ■

As usual, the docs were right. The elbow hurt like hell. I'd thrown the splint in the garbage about five minutes after I got home from jail but still couldn't use the arm worth a damn. Had to use the good hand to lift the bad one up, but at least I could cut my own meat, which, unlike King County jail food, was readily identifiable as to species.

Usually you have to pick up a ringing phone to find out who's on the other end. I didn't have that problem with my landline. I don't know how my old man managed it, but the house had what he'd referred to as a secure line. A phantom phone line. Not in all the years I'd lived in the house since his death had I ever received a bill. I'd inquired once, years ago, and discovered that, as far as the phone company was concerned, the number didn't exist. One of those rare instances where I decided to let well enough alone.

In the nearly fifteen years since he'd popped a heart valve, nearly all his old cronies had joined him, leaving only three people with the phantom phone number. George had it, Rebecca had it, and Carl had it. That was it. The damn thing didn't even get computer-generated sales calls, so when it started to ring, I had a pretty good idea who was on the other end.

Carl wasn't much for pleasantries. "Where the fuck have you been?" he immediately demanded.

"Eating powdered eggs on the county," I said.

"Our friend Mr. Frost?" He waited. "I saw it in the papers."

"So . . . to what do I owe the honor?"

"Charity got those juvie records for you."

I winced. Driving had turned out to be tough. No place to put my damaged elbow, except to keep it pressed to my chest, which, I gotta tell you, is a real awkward way to drive a car. "I'm a little under the weather," I said. "Howsabout I send an Uber car over to your place, and you seal up the info and have him bring it back here to me."

"Oh . . . Mr. Valet Parking," Carl mocked.

"Gimme a break, asshole. Just send the stuff over."

"Aye aye, Captain Commerce," he said, and hung up.

■ ■ ■

"They've all been arrested since," Rebecca said. "Multiple times. Except for Charles Harrington, and we know where he's been."

"Then we should be able to get DNA profiles on the rest of them."

"Yes . . . *we* should."

"But we don't have a profile for Charlie," I said.

"Nope."

"And you've still got the Tracy Harrington crime scene material?"

"Sure do."

"How long will it take to get the profiles?"

"A week, maybe. Terrence Poole is in prison down in Salem, Oregon. That one may take an extra day or two. The others have all been tested in Washington. They should be easy. These kinds of requests are very much business as usual."

She flicked her fingers at the pile of papers Carl had sent over. "Funny thing is with our friend Mr. Frost, I don't see anything in here that deserved to be sealed. It's all the same petty criminal stuff he'd been arrested for before . . . and since. Theft, burglary, breaking and entering, trespassing, simple assault, theft of services, arson on abandoned houses . . . nineteen kinds of drug charges." She looked up at me. "Nothing that needed to be sealed. Nothing sensitive or sexual."

"What the Harringtons want, the Harringtons get, and I'm betting they wanted Lakeside Charlie's record cleaned up and figured the best way to make that happen was to expunge the whole crew so nobody had any reason to drop a dime on anybody else."

"Except, from what you tell me, the late Mr. Frost saw an opportunity to extort some money from the Harringtons."

"Twice. Said they paid him the first time but that everything came apart when he went back and tried to sell them the info about the mix-up with the jailhouse DNA samples."

She thought it over.

"I'll request the DNA profiles first thing in the morning."

"This is gonna get interesting," I said.

"How so?"

"What if none of the profiles matches the genetic material you've got stored from the Tracy Harrington rape kit?"

"Then we're back where we started."

"Or it's Charlie."

"Or an unknown perpetrator. Process of elimination isn't going to work here. At the time, I ran the rape kit profile through CODIS and came up empty, but who knows? CODIS is up over ten million profiles now. I'll run it again and see what happens."

"And what if this new evidence isn't a match for Lamar Hudson? What if whoever put this together didn't know which profile belonged to which guy either, and was just trying to match what the SPD had on file as his profile? If that's the case, then there's no telling who did what to who."

"Whom."

"Yeah, yeah."

"Then Mr. Hudson goes home."

"Which, of course, automatically reopens the Tracy Harrington case."

Neither of us said anything for a good while.

"First thing I did when I got back in the office was to check that I had Tracy Harrington's evidence file. As soon as I got the notice from the Innocence Project, I did what I always do with capital cases. I pulled it and put it in a storage area that I'm the only one with access to. My seal is still on it. It hasn't been tampered with."

My turn to ponder. "All I can think of is that whoever bribed Ibrahim must know who *really* killed Tracy Harrington and doesn't want that to come to light."

"Who would know that, other than someone who was there?"

"No one."

She folded her arms across her chest and leaned back in the chair. "So . . . we wait."

■ ■ ■

I'm not a good waiter. Never have been. Put me on hold and this voice starts to whisper in my ear that I'm never gonna see these minutes again, which probably explains why, a day and a half later, I was sitting in Seattle U's Garmen Hall, waiting for Jessica Harrington to finish up with her office hours. Sitting around was killing me. I just had to do something.

It was ten to four when her office door opened and she stepped outside, wearing a white silk blouse and a coral-colored pencil skirt. Looked a whole lot more like a fashion model than a political scientist. Not that I was complaining. I'm still gonna be a sucker for a pencil skirt when they put me under the sod.

"Ah . . . Mr. Waterman," she said. She checked her watch. "I have an administrative meeting in forty minutes."

I stood up. "Shouldn't take that long," I said.

She gestured me inside with a long, bare arm. For an academic, her office was neat. Usually they have to move a pile of something so visitors can sit down, but her office was as orderly as could be. Lots of books, couple of plaster busts of people I didn't recognize, and an enormous jade plant filling up the two-story window.

"Mother said you'd come to see her about Tracy."

"Yes," I said. "Your sister was—"

"Stepsister. Tracy and Charlie are Sidney's children. Charlie by . . . I think his third marriage. Tracy by his second."

"Ah . . ." was the best I could do.

"They'd always lived in Geneva with Charlie's mother. When she died a while back, they didn't have any place to go except to their father, who, I'd like to mention, was adamantly opposed to the idea of them moving in with him. Mother said he went completely off the handle. Offered to buy them a house in Europe. It was my mother who insisted they come to Seattle. She and Sidney had quite a row over it. Mother gave them the family name because . . . as I'm sure you're aware, there are certain advantages to being a Harrington." Her eyes clouded a bit. "As you also probably know, I had a younger brother, Robert, who died in a boating accident when he was quite young. I've often thought she was just trying to fill the gap that losing Robert left in her life and maybe that was why she insisted the kids come to live with Sidney . . . despite his vehement objections."

"Tell me about Tracy," I prompted.

Her brow furrowed, as if my questions had dragged her back to a land she no longer wished to inhabit. "What's any of this to you?" she wanted to know.

"A case I was working on . . . it keeps coming back to the period of time when Tracy was killed. I can't tell you what's going on, because I don't know. I'm just out here kicking over rocks—you know, seeing if anything metaphorically crawls out."

"You do realize, don't you, Mr. Waterman, what a difficult and painful subject this is for my family?"

"I assure you, I wouldn't be dredging all this up if I didn't think I had a good reason."

"Which is?"

"The Innocence Project thinks Lamar Hudson is almost surely about to be granted a new trial," I said, "which, of course, will reopen your stepsister's murder investigation."

"I thought new evidence of his guilt had come to light."

"Maybe . . . maybe not."

She gave it some thought.

"Young women don't get more troubled than poor Tracy," she said after a pause. "I don't think in all my life I've ever met anybody with quite the set of issues Tracy was walking around with."

"Such as?"

"It all started with the drugs. It was like she was born with a heroin habit." She looked at me hard. "Have you ever spent time with a junkie, Mr. Waterman?" She didn't wait for me to respond. "Nothing in the universe matters to them except getting their next high. They'll lie, cheat, steal . . . anything so they don't get sick. They lie when there's no need to lie. You can't believe a single word they say. It makes them nearly impossible to deal with on a day-to-day basis."

"There's an epidemic of it going around."

"Tracy was our own personal epidemic." She closed her eyes for a moment, going back in time. "She'd been with us for about six months when things started to go missing around the house. Small, expensive things. Money. Prescription drugs. Anything that wasn't nailed down." She heaved a sigh. "It was one of those situations where, after a while, we all knew what was going on, but nobody wanted to say it out loud . . . almost like it would go away if we didn't verbalize it."

"And nobody—not the former wife, not Sidney, none of them—bothered to mention that this girl had a heroin habit?"

"No," she said. "It came as a bolt out of the blue."

"How'd it come to light?"

"The Zieglers."

"What's a Ziegler?"

"Eustace Ziegler. He's a famous Alaskan painter. He and my great-grandfather were chums back in the forties. We had half a dozen of his paintings hanging around the house. You know, the kind of thing that had been on the wall for so long that nobody noticed them anymore—until a couple of them turned up missing."

"And?"

"And . . . as I said, it wasn't like, on some level, we didn't know what was going on. Tracy would stay out for days at a time and then come home looking like death warmed over. Lock herself in her room, not eat . . . sleep for days on end." She made a disgusted face. "On some level, we all knew what the problem was."

"What happened when the paintings turned up missing?"

"The art dealer—he has a gallery in one of the downtown hotels—specializes in Northwest painters. He took one look at the paintings and immediately knew who they belonged to. He called Mother."

"And?"

"Mother had finally had enough. Told Sidney to do something or she'd call the police. Sidney went crazy. Tracy ran off." She threw a disgusted hand in the air. "Then she ran back home and things just got worse, to the point where Mother finally made Sidney throw her out of the house. Told the gate not to let her in anymore. Cut off her trust fund. Tried to get her into a halfway house . . . everything . . . .the whole nine yards . . . all for nothing. Every time Sidney found her a new treatment facility, she'd run away." She paused and took a deep breath. "The amazing thing . . . what was truly extraordinary was that she always managed to get drugs somehow. No money. No place to live. Not a coat on her back. It didn't matter. She always managed to keep herself in drugs."

Kinda made me wonder if Tracy hadn't maybe taken up being a working girl in order to support her habit. That's why most of the hustlers are out on the streets these days. Supporting a jones of some kind, or a boyfriend with a jones, or a kid with a jones. Far as I'd seen, you don't start selling your ass for money until things are about as bad as they can get. Not that I was about to make any such suggestion to a

Harrington family member, mind you. Mercifully, Jessica Harrington went on.

"When they finally threw her out of the house that time, she started telling anybody who would listen that she'd been a victim of sexual abuse. That Sidney had been abusing her since she was five. That the house phones were bugged. That my *mother* had tried to kill her, for pity's sake. It was beyond ridiculous."

She checked the time again.

"What happened to Charlie?" I segued.

Her face morphed from anger to sadness in an instant. "Poor Charlie. The sweetest kid. Smart. Just naturally kind and considerate. Everything you could want a kid to be, and now . . ." She let it trail off.

I waited.

"All he ever wanted was for his big sister to be well."

"They don't get well," I said. "The smart ones just stop using."

"I'm convinced Charlie went out that night to help his sister. I think she called and talked Charlie into bringing her some money. You know what he got for his trouble?"

"What?"

"She stabbed him with him some kind of speedball. The needle broke off in his chest. He had some sort of drug-induced aneurism or stroke of some kind . . . the doctors aren't sure. Eventually, she managed to drag him down into the hole she was in."

"I thought I detected quite a bit of friction between your mother and Sidney on the subject of Charlie's medical treatment."

She glared at me. "You do have a knack for putting your finger on the sore spot, don't you, Mr. Waterman?"

"It's a gift," I said. "Who's Dr. Thorpe?"

She huffed out a huge sigh. "After Tracy's death, Charlie was a complete mess. Barely conscious. Couldn't do anything for himself. He was being cared for in a treatment center Dr. Thorpe runs downtown. My mother knew Dr. Thorpe from somewhere. He runs Homewood

Recovery Center. Dr. Thorpe thought the worst was behind us. He thought Charlie was making progress."

"And?" I pressed.

"Then all of a sudden Sidney insists on moving him out to Issaquah. Mother was adamantly opposed. They've been arguing about it ever since. Mother's had Thompson drive her out there half a dozen times. Charlie's always asleep. Every time. Mother wants a second opinion, but Charlie is, after all, Sidney's son, so she defers to Sidney on the matter."

"What do you know about Charlie's caregivers?"

"Sidney found them," she said. "I believe he knew them from his last posting."

"What's a posting?"

"Sidney was in the diplomatic corps. Third assistant secretary to the cultural affairs secretary, something of that nature. All very midlevel."

"Where was this?"

"The Balkans somewhere. He pretends the details are classified so he can't talk about them, but my uncle Harry—who was with the State Department since the Nixon administration—told me Sidney left the service under some sort of very serious cloud. All very hush-hush. Things he wasn't allowed to be specific about. Harry made a concerted effort to talk Mother out of getting involved with him, but when my mother doesn't want to hear something, she doesn't." She shrugged. "She'd been alone for nearly twenty years at that point. He's charming. She was smitten."

She leaned forward across the desk. "Sidney's mostly a professional board member these days. Whereas Mother will lend her name to charity, she's not inclined to actually attend the board meetings. She sends Sidney instead. He loves it. Makes him feel like he's still involved and important."

She anticipated my next question.

"Mother met him at some sort of embassy charity function in New York. He swept her off her feet. He makes witty cocktail party chitchat.

He looks good in a tuxedo. Just between you and me, I'm with Uncle Harry: Sidney's always seemed more than a bit dodgy to me. He's always so circumspect. Never answers a question directly. But he makes Mother happy, so I guess that's enough."

"Your mom was quite a catch for a defrocked diplomat," I commented.

"Actually—not that he admits to it—but Sidney seems to have his own money. He claims to be living on his pension and some family bequests, but any time he needs to come up with some cash, he seems to be able to."

"And you don't worry that he's in line for the Harrington gravy train?"

"First of all, Sidney's only in line for my mother's money. The Harrington money is a whole different matter. My mother and I share power of attorney for the Harrington money. Anything Sidney might have in mind, over and above community property, would require both of our signatures, and that, I can assure you, isn't going to happen."

Third glance at the watch. She got to her feet.

"Afraid I've got to go," she said.

"Thank you for your time," I said, getting to my feet.

"Hope I was of some help. Lord knows we'd love to put this awful tragedy behind us for good."

Yeah, I thought to myself. *You and everybody else.*

▪ ▪ ▪

Two days later, I got a musical message from Eagen—Al Green singing "Take Me to the River." And, for the first time ever, Eagen was waiting for me when I got there. The air was still, so I could smell the river. There are no words, lyrical or otherwise, to describe the odor of that tidal sludge.

"Clerical error," he sneered.

"So Lamar Hudson *was* in jail at the time of Tracy Harrington's murder."

"John Doe Number Three, on September eleventh. I watched the interview tape. It's him. They ask him who he is. He asks them why he's been arrested. That goes on for twenty minutes. They figure him for a moron, give up, and throw him back in holding. Next day they find out his real name because his prints are in the system. They also find out he's nineteen years old and transfer him over to the county jail, where they log him in by his real name as being arrested on the twelfth. And since they caught him choking his Chihuahua on a bench in Volunteer Park on the night of the eleventh, the Tracy Harrington investigation team drops by—you know, just covering their bases, see if maybe he didn't see something. Never for a minute imagining he's a suspect. They show him a few crime scene pictures and he fucking confesses."

"Your bosses know about this?"

"Not yet."

"How we gonna do this?"

He slashed the still air with his hand. "Sure as hell can't be either one of us."

I nodded. He was right. No way he could be poking the departmental bear. That would surely be the end of his career. And if it came from me, they'd have a pretty good idea where I got it from.

"I've got an idea."

"Better be damn good. "

"I know just the folks for the job."

■ ■ ■

"Innocence Project. Angela St. Jean."

"I need you guys to discover something."

"What?"

I told her. At considerable length.

Long silence to follow. "Are you serious? Can this possibly be true?"

"It's real important that you guys discover it on your own."

"Why's that?"

I told her that too, without using Eagen's name.

"There's an actual interview tape?"

"The juvenile facility on Twelfth Avenue. John Doe Number Three on the night of September eleventh, twenty twelve, according to my source. They signed him at the county jail the next day, when they figured out who he was and how old he was."

"Do you have a copy of the tape?"

"You guys will have to do that on your own," I said. "And I'm guessing that, if you give the SPD much notice, the tape will suddenly cease to exist."

She laughed. "We have quite a bit of experience dealing with matters such as disappearing evidence," she assured me. "Thank you. And I'm sure Mr. Hudson thanks you too."

"How you doing with that sample from Mr. Hudson?"

"It's being sequenced as we speak."

"Good, because they're dropping like flies. Of the four guys who were in that cell with Lamar Hudson that night, two of them are dead. You tell me one is in prison in Oregon, and the other one had some sort of stroke and is not taking visitors. The other guy was unconscious on the floor. That means Poole and Harrington are our only—"

She cut me off. "Mr. Poole is completely off the board. He's doing life without the possibility of parole and is thus disinclined to be of any help. We've approached him on several occasions, to no avail. We have nothing we can offer him. He won't see us anymore, and, by the way, we're now being told that the new evidence isn't forensic. It's Tracy Harrington's driver's license. Supposedly found on Lamar Hudson at the time of his arrest."

"Which leaves us with Charles Harrington."

I had an *or*, but I kept it to myself.

Chapter 4

Uncle Harry turned out to be Harriman Francis Standish III, Patricia Harrington's older brother, who had, until his recent retirement, been in the diplomatic corps for nearly thirty-five years, according to LinkedIn. Western Europe mostly. I'd like to be able to tell you that if he hadn't called me back, I'd have just given up and gotten on with my life, but truth was, this thing was gnawing at my insides like a bulimic beaver.

When Harriman Standish returned my call about twenty minutes after I'd left him a short voicemail message, suffice it to say I was surprised.

"Leo Waterman, please."

"Speaking."

"This is Harry Standish. Your message said you have something you'd like to discuss with me."

"Sidney Crossfield," I said quickly. You know, what the hell, may as well cut to the chase.

Thirty seconds of agonizing silence followed. I thought maybe he'd hung up on me and was about to open my mouth when he broke the spell.

"My brother-in-law." He said the words in much the same tone of voice people used when discussing lingering sinus infections.

"Yes, sir."

"What would your interest in Sidney be?"

I gave him the whole load, figuring if his niece Jessica was right and he'd been seriously opposed to his sister's relationship with Sidney

Crossfield, maybe he'd see this as a chance to finally do something about it. Old grudges die hard.

He listened to the whole gory story without interrupting. I'd always operated on the assumption that Mark Twain was on the mark when he'd noted that for many people the only thing better than hearing something good about themselves was hearing something bad about somebody else. Back when schadenfreude was known as nasty.

"You'll have to come here," he said, about two seconds after I stopped talking. "This isn't something for the phone."

"Where's here?" I asked.

"Hat Island."

I stifled a groan. If The Highlands, with its fortified guard gate, was too public for you, you moved to someplace like Hat Island. Not only was it a ferry ride, but, if I recalled correctly, it was a ride on a passenger-only ferry that ran from Everett to Hat Island on a highly irregular schedule. Once off the ferry, your ass was on foot.

"Take the ten o'clock tomorrow. I'll pick you up at the dock."

▪ ▪ ▪

Turned out he knew the ferry schedule. Not that it was hard to remember. The Hat Island ferry ran from the Everett Yacht Club on Wednesdays, Fridays, and weekends only. Took your ass out there at ten in the morning, picked your ass up at one that afternoon. You didn't want to stay that long, you best break out the water wings.

As promised, he was waiting for me at the end of the ramp. Sitting at the side of the road in an immaculately restored Chevy pickup truck. Beautiful turquoise paint job. Gleaming wooden side rails. Shiny as hope. Late fifties, I was thinking, as I pulled open the door and slid up onto the tuck and roll bench seat.

We introduced ourselves and shook hands. He was a big man, with small features gathered in the center of his face, like they were having a meeting. The effect gave his face a pensive quality. Like he was working on a math problem he couldn't quite get a handle on.

"Fifty-nine?" I asked as he dropped the truck into gear.

"Fifty-seven," he said, as we rolled around in a circle and started up the hill.

"Always wanted one of these," I admitted, as we rolled along.

He'd done a bit of homework on me. "Your old man certainly had the price," he commented. "He cut quite a rather wide swath."

"My old man also had very definite ideas about what he was and wasn't going to spend his money on. And believe me when I tell you, sir, my hormonal yearnings were not high on his fiduciary agenda."

"He was right," Harrison Standish said. "Sentimentality is that which we fall back upon when true emotions fail."

Knowing I had a few hours before chugging back over to Everett, he decided to give me the grand tour. It didn't take long. The whole damn island was just slightly under five hundred acres. Last time the United States census came around, in 2010, there were forty-one residents.

He said there were a dozen or so cars on the island. All of them barged out from the mainland. Couple of which belonged to the island community association and were for public use, the rest of them in private hands.

He told me how the island's real name was Gedney Island, probably named after the first dumb shit who rowed a skiff out here, and how the island's only tourist rental was an apartment at the marina owned by the community association.

Like most folks who live in odd places, he'd worked up a tour and spiel for visitors. Kinda like, if your South Dakota relatives show up in Seattle, you pretty much gotta take 'em to the Pike Place Market so they can watch the guys lob salmon around. It's simply de rigueur. No gettin' out of it.

The whole thing took about forty minutes. Mostly we made small talk and drove around. I was trying to be patient and let him bring up

Sidney Crossfield, so it wasn't until he braked to a stop that I bothered to look around.

Interestingly, we were back where we'd started—at the ferry dock. He turned off the engine. I could hear the rhythmic tick tick tick as the engine began to cool. That's the moment when I realized the fifty-cent tour wasn't going to, as I'd imagined, end up back at Villa Standish, where we'd sip tea and nibble at scones. No . . . this was as close as I was going to get. The old *you can't know my address* thing was apparently genetic.

He pinned me with a gaze. "Do you imagine that Sidney was in some way responsible for what happened to his children?"

I gave it some thought. "It's possible," I said. "What I *am* sure of is that somehow this all relates back to the night his daughter Tracy was killed."

"In what way?"

"I don't know. All I know for sure is that a girl ended up dead. A young man's life nearly came to an end and the only witness is their father."

He looked away, out the driver's side window, at the dark, rippled water of Possession Sound. "Charles was such a sweet boy." He swallowed hard and ran a hand over his face. "He deserved a better fate."

"And Tracy?"

His face lost a little more color. "God knows nobody deserves to be murdered . . . but that poor thing was a walking disaster." He shrugged. "While I certainly won't say she deserved her fate, I can hardly say it was totally unexpected either." He looked my way. "I mean, that's the cliché, isn't it? If you live that lifestyle, that's precisely what will happen to you."

I had to agree. Tweakers don't generally come to good ends, that's for sure.

"How come Sidney left the diplomatic corps?" I segued.

He took a minute to answer. "You do realize, I hope, that whatever I tell you here is strictly confidential. If necessary, I'll deny having told you this." He paused for a beat. "First of all, you must understand that no one is ever publicly fired from the diplomatic service. That would mean they'd made a hiring miscue to begin with, which, of course, would serve to undermine public confidence in the corps, and thus the country. So what happens is that you're simply not promoted. Everyone involved knows the drill. If you're not promoted, it's time to polish your résumé." He made a resigned face. "If you don't take the hint, you get a new posting to some garden spot like Kabul, where one can't go out to lunch without an armored division in attendance." He showed the truck's headliner a palm. "Then, of course, for the truly pigheaded, there's always East Africa."

"Is that what happened to Sidney?" I pressed.

He thought it over. "More or less . . . except that Sidney was an old, experienced hand and saw it coming well in advance, and . . . he went into business for himself."

"What business was that?"

"Selling identity papers and American visas to Bosnian war criminals."

"To who?" Yeah, yeah, I know it should be *whom*, but the word creeps me out.

"War criminals. My sources seem to think he managed to get something like twenty of them out of the country and into the USA over a span of nine months or so, before somebody at the embassy caught wind of what he was doing and blew the whistle on him." I was trying to come up with another question when he went on. "At something like half a million dollars apiece, I'm given to understand."

"And then?"

"He took the money and ran." He frowned. "I tried to talk Patricia out of getting involved with him, but she was beyond obdurate, and my position didn't allow for me to be specific. I told her what a piece of unprincipled scum he'd turned out to be, but she wouldn't listen. She hasn't spoken to me since. She won't even take my calls," he said bitterly.

That was the moment when I knew I'd been correct in assuming he was still holding a serious grudge. He blamed Sidney Crossfield for alienating him from his sister.

"You ever met Charles's caregivers?"

"No. I have not."

"Couple Croatian guys."

He made a rude noise with his lips. "Draw your own conclusions."

"I met Charlie very briefly and, you know, he didn't seem to me as if he needed watchdogs. A little scattered and confused, maybe, but not like somebody who needed full-time care."

"Nothing would surprise me. Sidney will do whatever is necessary to protect himself. He has no ethical foundation other than that of self-preservation."

"His daughter—" I began.

He held up a restraining hand. "I won't speak any more ill of the dead. I've already said more than I should have."

"Thank you," I said.

He leaned closer to me. "You should be careful, Mr. Waterman. Life is cheap in the Balkans. Their primary problem-solving technique involved killing anyone who got in their way. There were a myriad of rumors regarding Sidney's bodyguards. Murderous Croatian thugs, I'm told. Worked directly for Sidney, not the embassy. I've also been told there was an undersecretary who confronted Sidney privately about some of the visas he was approving. Seems Sidney sent him into the city on an errand, and he mysteriously disappeared. Never been seen since." He gave it a chance to sink in, before adding, "A word to the wise."

I assured him that caution was my middle name.

He started the truck. I took the hint and got out.

Before I could close the door, Standish shot me a glance and said, "Bring him to bay, Mr. Waterman. I don't know if the world will be a better place without the likes of Sidney Crossfield, but I'm quite certain it will be for my sister."

I never did shut the door. When he dropped the truck in gear and started off, the door closed itself. I wandered over to the concrete bench, sat down, and watched his dust float up toward the steel wool clouds and disappear.

■ ■ ■

Rebecca hadn't said anything for forty minutes, while she sat at her kitchen table and went over the DNA test results. She'd stopped reading only for long enough to jot down a few notes now and then, and then was right back at it.

I was on my second cup of coffee by the time she pushed herself back from the table and heaved a massive sigh. "All these tell us is who it's *not*."

"Do tell."

"Terrence Poole's DNA profile from the night of September eleventh, twenty twelve, is actually the DNA profile of Gilberto Duran. Lamar Hudson's sample was actually the late Mr. Frost's. And Willard Frost's DNA profile, by process of elimination, was probably recorded as Charlie's, although we can't be certain without a sample from Charlie. Kevin Delaney, who I'm given to understand was unconscious at the time the samples were taken . . . his profile is consistent with his own sample, and unequivocally proves him guilty of the crime with which he was charged, so it's safe to assume he wasn't part of their little charade."

"How can we not have a genetic profile for Charlie?" I groused.

She slowly shook her head. "Probably disappeared along with his juvenile file for the night of Tracy's death. What Patricia Harrington wants, Patricia Harrington gets."

"So we're right back where we started."

"Not quite," she said. "What I can tell you is that none of their profiles—not Poole's, not Duran's, not Frost's or Delaney's—none of them is consistent with the genetic material found in Tracy

Harrington's rape kit. Doesn't matter who was pretending to be whom. The tests eliminate all of them from being the donor of that genetic material, regardless of how the swab is labeled."

"So none of them was the donor." Conversation by repetition was the best I could manage at that moment.

"Right."

"You know . . . Jessica Harrington said Tracy had an amazing ability to get drugs no matter how broke or destitute she was at the time. Got me to wondering if maybe she wasn't . . . you know . . . giving it up for money."

"If that was the case, the profile could belong to anyone. Except . . ."

She had her smug face on. Same look she used to get when she was the only one in the class who knew the answer to the algebra problem.

"Except what?" I prodded.

"Reading these things has become quite the scientific specialty, and I'm by no means an expert, but if I'm reading these at all correctly, Tracy Harrington's DNA profile is about a thirty percent match to her attacker's."

I started to open my mouth, but she cut me off. "Understand . . . a thirty percent match isn't in the same area code as a successful prosecution. Not even close. They're looking for a less than one percent of one percent of a one percent chance of it being somebody else. We're talking about truly astronomical figures here."

She took a deep breath. "It's not my field, but whoever left that genetic material, specifically the saliva, shares at least one common ancestor with Tracy Harrington. Somewhere in the past two generations. Which brings us back to Charlie."

"Or Sidney Crossfield," I said. "He's their father by different mothers."

"That's too horrible to think about."

"What if . . . ," I said.

"We need a sample from Charlie."

"I'm drawing a blank on how that might be possible. He's on private property owned by his stepmother. He's supposedly being cared for because he's not capable of caring for himself. It's posted no trespassing. Virtually anything we tried to do would result in a kidnapping charge. Worse yet, those Croatian croakers of his would be within their rights to shoot us if we tried to interfere."

The pin-drop silence suggested I wasn't alone in my frustration.

"What if . . . ," I said again after a minute.

"What if what?" she snapped.

"You said you attended an insurance company board meeting in support of Ibrahim's claim when he was trying to get the company to pay for Nikka's treatment."

"Twice. What about it?"

"Can you look up and see which board members were in attendance?"

"Why would I want to do that?"

"Humor me. Can you do it?"

"The meetings are a matter of public record."

"Then there should be minutes . . . no?"

"Theoretically." She reached out and pulled the MacBook Pro closer. "Who are you looking for?"

"Patricia Harrington."

"She wasn't there. I'd remember if she'd been in attendance."

"What about Sidney Crossfield? Jessica Harrington told me that her mother sits on all these charity and public service boards but doesn't actually attend the meetings. She said that Sidney always goes in her place. She said he likes it. Makes him feel important."

"I'm not sure I've ever seen Sidney Crossfield."

"They're crème de la crème of the Seattle social set. There's bound to be a picture of him swallowing a canapé somewhere online."

Took her ten minutes of pecking before she sat back in the chair.

"That asshole," she said.

"Was he there? At the board meeting?"

"Oh yes . . . what a patrician son of a bitch. Sat up there and said people had no God-given right to experimental medicine or, for that matter, to any medicine they couldn't afford to pay for. He and I got into a major shouting match. Things got rather heated, on both occasions."

"You know . . . yesterday when I was waiting for the Hat Island ferry to come and pick me up, I had an hour with nobody around and nothing to do. So I was sitting there running every possible scenario I could think of, trying to come up with some kind of story that made sense, and the only thing I could think of was almost too crazy to talk about."

She laughed out loud. "You've never let that stop you before."

I took a minute to gather my thoughts. "Suppose everything Tracy Harrington told people was more or less true. What if Sidney *had* been molesting her since childhood? Her stepsister told me that every time Tracy started going into withdrawal, she'd start telling anybody who'd listen that she was a victim of abuse, that the house phones were bugged. That Patricia Harrington had assaulted her. That would explain why she always had money for drugs: Sidney gave it to her to keep her quiet. When she was wasted, she was less of a problem than when she wasn't, so he kept her wasted."

"And as long as she was a junkie, nobody would believe a word she said."

"Exactly."

"So it was in Sidney's best interest to keep her addicted."

"Which also explains why Sidney was so adamantly opposed to having his children move to Seattle, even when they didn't have any other place to go."

"So . . . somebody murders Tracy Harrington. Somebody who's a partial genetic match to her. Crossfield says he found Charlie passed out on the grass next to her body—out of his mind, foaming at the mouth.

I mean, it doesn't take a genius to see that the most likely scenario is that Charlie killed his sister and then tried to kill himself. And, crazy as it sounds, I think Crossfield was prepared to let his son take the rap for it. Except that"—I held up a stiff finger—"crazy ol' Lamar Hudson confesses to the crime, and the cops, predictably, take the line of least resistance. Not only don't they have to prosecute a Harrington or face a battalion of high-priced lawyers in a lengthy and expensive trial, but they've got a ready-made patsy volunteering to go down for the crime. Sidney breathes a huge sigh of relief and goes back to trying to figure out how to get some of the Harrington fortune to fall in his lap."

"That's awful."

"Sidney's a first-class scumbag . . . and unlike Ibrahim, Sidney's children weren't his weakest link. He really didn't give a shit about either of them, one way or the other, as long as they didn't get in the way of the gazillion-dollar gravy train he'd stumbled onto."

"Jesus," Rebecca whispered.

"Everybody's been working on the assumption that on the night she died, Tracy called her brother for drug money. So if I'm right, she called Sidney. What if she always called Sidney? What if what she said about the house phones being bugged was true? Crossfield claims he overheard Charlie on the phone with Tracy. I mean . . . that place is the size of a department store. What's the chance of anybody overhearing anybody else? More likely the place *was* wired for sound, if you ask me. The guy spent twenty-five years in the cloak-and-dagger business. Wiring up the house phones couldn't have been too hard for a guy like that. What if Charlie overheard what was going on between his sister and father and followed Crossfield up to the park that night, instead of the other way around?"

"And then what?"

"One of them injects him with some deadly drug cocktail that permanently screws up his brain. Which one we're probably never gonna know for sure. And then Sidney gets rid of Charlie by privately institutionalizing him, and everything quiets down for a while."

"Until the Innocence Project starts talking about reopening the case, and Sidney gets real nervous."

"And then, to make matters worse, Willard Frost hits him up for money."

"Yeah. Hush money to keep his mouth shut about Lamar being in jail when the murder was committed."

"Exactly."

"Crossfield pays him but goes looking for a way, short of killing him, to make sure he can't come back for more. He remembers Ibrahim from the board meeting. Remembers getting into it with you. Approaches Ibrahim . . . or I'm betting gets somebody to do it for him. Probably one of those two gorillas posing as caregivers. They cut a deal with a desperate man. He steals Lamar's file for them, along with the four others as a smokescreen, just in case somebody clicks to the theft. Which is just what happens when Kevin Delaney files an appeal. They can't find the Delaney file, so they start to investigate. Find out there's a bunch of files missing, and because of the slipshod way deliveries to and from the precincts are handled, they suspend all four of you."

"Then why kill Ibrahim?"

"I'm thinking that at about that point, Willard Frost comes back trying to hit him up again, this time about the DNA samples being all mixed up. This gets Willard pureed by the Croatian goons but gives Sidney something new to worry about. He decides it's time for those files to magically reappear, so that the driver's license can be found and hopefully stop the investigation of Tracy Harrington's death from being reopened. He's hoping that the license will put the squash on the Innocence Project's effort to get Lamar Hudson a new trial, because he knows a new trial is going to dredge everything up all over again, and his position is so tenuous, he can't take any chances. That's what the whole thing was about. Not stealing the files, not trying to get somebody out of jail, but adding that driver's license to the mix, so it could be found later, ensuring they'd keep Lamar Hudson behind bars."

"But Ibrahim couldn't put the files back because he'd been suspended, which was not part of the original plan."

"Exactly. They tell him to find the files. It doesn't happen. They come to his house and threaten him. Maybe he tries to explain. So Sidney decides the best way to put this whole thing to rest is to kill you and make it look like suicide—that way you'll take the blame, and Ibrahim can be reinstated and finish what he started. Which almost surely would have worked. But then when you didn't die, I think maybe Ibrahim got a case of conscience and couldn't bring himself to go through with it. Who knows? What we know for sure is that he doesn't finish the job and return the files, so they kill him."

"What makes you think they threatened him?"

"Nikka told me that some men had come to see her papa. Said Ibrahim told her not to say anything to them about the storage unit."

"So . . . they were pressing Ibrahim to make the files reappear . . . and when he can't or won't, they run him down."

I nodded. "It all goes back to all four of you getting suspended. Then their failure to kill you. If you'd died that first night, the whole stupid-ass scheme would have worked to perfection. Putting the files back would have been easy. All eyes would have been focused on your untimely disgrace and demise. Nobody else would have been suspended. Ibrahim could have just gone back to work, put everything back in its place, and waited for the DA's investigators to find them; or he could have miraculously found them himself. Whatever Ibrahim had in mind for getting the files back went to the grave with him, so all we can do is guess."

"So what now? You going to storm The Highlands and drag Sidney out of his castle by the heels?"

"Nope," I said. "You know that line 'just because you're paranoid doesn't mean they're *not* out to get you'? Sidney's paranoid as hell. And rightly so. He should be. His position is dicey. He's walking a tightrope, and he knows it. He can feel the whole house of cards beginning to sway in the breeze, and it makes him nervous as can be."

"This sounds more and more like a mystery story."

"Yeah," I admitted, "it does. It's the old story of someone's past coming back to haunt them. Our boy Sidney gets caught screwing the pooch in his banishment posting, but by the time the shit starts to shake down, he's married to one of the wealthiest women in the country, who probably wouldn't believe why the diplomatic service fired him even if they'd admitted it. Things are looking good for Sidney. And then what happens? His two kids from previous marriages suddenly show up on his doorstep, one of who's a junkie he's been molesting since childhood. He volunteers to buy them a house in Europe—anything they want—just as long as they stay missing from his life. But Patricia Harrington isn't having it. She insists they take them in, and all of a sudden, everything he's put together is big-time at risk." I paused for effect. "And he overreacts," I said. "He's so accustomed to getting what he wants, he believes he can fix anything. Why not? He's got a whole collection of escaped war criminals to do his bidding. He knows who they really are and probably where to find most of them. He wants something done, they don't have much choice except to do it for him. Things start to go to hell. Ibrahim either can't or won't make the files reappear. They kill him, and when I start snooping around, sticking my nose in things, Sidney really starts to sweat, so he decides Gabe and I've gotta go too. What the hell, it's worked before, no reason it shouldn't work again, right? He's got his own little army."

"You better have eight-by-ten glossies of him holding a bloody ax in one hand and a bowling bag with a severed head in the other."

She was right. This wasn't one of those places where I could go off half-cocked. Which was a pity, because I'd pretty much mastered that move. No . . . unfounded accusations weren't gonna cut it here. Way too much sympathy for the Harringtons in this neck of the woods.

No matter what, I had no intention of being the one who visited yet another tragedy on their regal heads. No way.

"When you look back on the whole thing," I said, "what Sidney should have done when Willard Frost came to him the first time was . . . nothing. He should have thrown Frost out on his ass and sat tight. I mean, the guys in that juvie cell that night weren't in the same area code as credible witnesses. Murderers, a lifetime petty criminal, a moron, and a passed-out drunk, who later also turned out to be a murderer too. I mean, who was going to believe anything any of them said? First-year law students could have proved all of them unreliable witnesses with any five seconds they had to spare."

"The publicity was what he was afraid of," Rebecca said. "Nothing Patricia Harrington likes less than her name in the paper. Except the society column, of course."

"Of course."

Again . . . she had a point. Sidney couldn't afford the faintest whiff of scandal. Patricia Harrington's refusal to believe unfounded rumors about her hubby was one thing. Finding the family smut plastered all over the front page again would be something else entirely. That was exactly the kind of thing that would get Sidney Crossfield thrown out on his ass. And with the kind of clout she had, community property or no community property, there was an excellent chance Patricia Harrington would end up pocketing Sidney's secret money, rather than the other way around.

"He just might get away with it," Rebecca mused. "He can just sit up there in The Highlands and simply wait this thing out, hiding behind his wife and her billions. It's like he's on another planet, as far as the law is concerned. What he knows for sure is that absolutely nobody, and I mean nobody, in any position of authority is going to be knocking on his door anytime in the foreseeable future."

"Then we'll have to get him to come out and play, won't we?"

Her expression suggested she had serious doubts. "Like how?"

"Let's give him the chance to do something stupid."

"How are we going to do that?"

"I don't know quite yet," I said. "But I'll figure something out. Like you said, I've had quite a bit of practice in that area."

■ ■ ■

Gabe leaned forward in the chair. "You know I'm on board here, Leo—you dent my skull and I'm a prime-time player—but there's a serious fly in this ointment of yours," Gabe said. "The kid. Charlie. If *any* of this shit you been running by me is true, then the only living link to what happened that night is Charlie. Somebody threatened me, like we been doing to Crossfield, I'd off that fucking kid in a heartbeat." Gabe shrugged. "If you're right, he already offed his own daughter. One more dead kid shouldn't be any problem for an asshole like that."

"Yeah," I said. "I'm thinking that as far as Sidney's concerned, Charlie's pretty much *always* had a 'use by' date on him. I'd bet money that, once things cool down sufficiently, when everybody's forgotten about Tracy, Charlie is going to have some sort of fatal accident or is going to escape from his keepers and never be seen again, and the whole thing will be written off as yet another unfortunate chapter in the Harrington family tragedy."

"And we gotta make sure that shit don't happen," Gabe growled. "We're the ones been making our friend Crossfield nervous. Anything happens to that kid, at this point, I'll feel like it's our fault."

■ ■ ■

Gabe left to pick up Joey. I was still procrastinating, trying to work out what to do next, when the phone rang.

"Leo," I said.

"I'm hearing they picked up a pair of assholes and got 'em dead to rights for the Willard Frost murder." It was Eagen. No Robby the Robot this time, just Tim Eagen. "Got 'em on CCTV from a kite store up on Second Ave, which also got the license plate of the rental car they were driving. Traced 'em to a hotel down by Sea-Tac. Willard Frost's CC camera and recorder were still in the trunk. They flew into town from Milwaukee day before yesterday. One of them left fingerprints all over the sap he used to puree Willard Frost's frontal lobe. And get this—the other one of 'em's got a case of road rash you wouldn't believe."

"The flying dump truck driver," I muttered.

"Problem is, they lawyered up and ain't saying a thing. Not who they are, not nothin', and neither of their prints are in the system either."

"Try Interpol," I said.

"In process."

I almost laughed out loud. "This is why Crossfield is so damn sure of himself. These guys don't have any choice but to do what he wants. And he doesn't have to worry about them rolling on him either, if something goes wrong, because no matter what, they're not gonna admit to a damn thing," I said. "Whatever happens to them here in the United States doesn't begin to approach what would happen if they got sent home to face war criminal charges. I'm bettin' they'll take their chances with the American justice system."

"Sure as hell's what I'd do," Eagen said, and broke the connection.

Before I could pocket the phone, it rang again.

"Mr. Waterman?"

"Speaking."

"This is LaTeisha."

I drew a blank. Pins dropped.

"Tiger Mountain Lodge. Remember? You gave me your card."

"Sure I remember."

"They're leaving."

Took me a second to process. "Charles Harrington?"

"Yes," she said. "Mr. Stocker, the GM, told me to call the cleaning company for Monday. Said they're going to vacate the building this weekend."

My stomach took a dive toward my ankles.

"When was this?" I asked.

"Right after lunch today. I had to wait until I got home to call you. We're not allowed to make personal calls."

"Well . . . ," I stammered. "Thanks."

"Is Mr. Harrington okay?"

"Yeah," I lied. "I'm sure he's fine."

■ ■ ■

It had been twenty-seven minutes since the gate guard had patched me through to the Harrington house and Thompson had connected me to Jessica. I was sitting in the driver's seat of the rental car. Gabe was seated directly behind me. The guard had never taken his eyes off us the whole time we'd been sitting there.

I was starting to get pessimistic. Thinking maybe what I'd told her hadn't been enough to bring her around. Wishing I could have told her what her uncle Harry told me, but he'd made it clear that was confidential.

I watched as Jessica Harrington walked up the private road and past the guard gate.

The glow from the guard shack lit her way over to the passenger door. She climbed in. I introduced her to Gabe. They shook hands over the seat as I backed the car into a little alcove among the trees, away from the prying eyes of the guard.

"You called Dr. Thorpe," she said. "I told you about him in confidence."

I ignored her complaint. "He was dubious as hell but said he'd take Charlie back as long as the legal ducks were all in a row."

She closed her eyes and leaned back in the seat.

"I don't understand what you think *I* can do," she said.

"You said you had your mother's power of attorney."

She slowly leaned forward, looked over at me.

"But Charlie's Sidney's child . . ."

"Your mother adopted him. That means she's got the same legal rights regarding Charlie as Sidney does, and since you have her power of attorney, that makes you one of his legal guardians too."

"And you expect me to go against my mother's wishes?"

"From what I saw, it's not against her wishes. She's the one who first mentioned Dr. Thorpe's name to me. Seemed to me she was in favor of the idea."

She rolled her eyes. "They've been arguing about it ever since your last visit."

"Look at it as an intervention."

"And you need me to keep it legal."

"Thorpe checked with his legal department. He won't do it without a signature from either you or your mother . . ."

"Kidnapping's twenty-five to life," Gabe said from the back seat. "I feel bad about what's happened with Charlie, but not *that* bad."

She thought it over. "Those two . . . nurses of his, or whatever you call them," she said finally. "They're not going to step aside and let you take Charlie."

"We'll take care of the hired help."

She looked from Gabe to me and then back out the side window, as if trying to decide whether we were up to the task. "Shouldn't you have an ambulance on hand for Charlie?"

"He's not ambulatory?" I said. "When I saw him, he was up and around."

"My mother is very old-fashioned. The man of the family and all that. The idea of her defying Sidney . . ."

"Charlie's the only loose end," Gabe added. "He's the only thing between Sidney and getting away clean. If you ask me, Charlie's not long for this world."

The car got quiet.

"Thorpe says they'll be waiting for us," I said, "prepared to do a complete psychiatric evaluation."

A long minute passed. She slowly shook her head.

"No. No. No. I can't do this," Jessica Harrington announced. "This is just not possible. Mother would never forgive me." She reached for the door handle.

I was still working on how to keep her in the car when a pair of halogen headlights lit up the access road heading out of The Highlands. The guard barely got the gate open in time. The car rocketed through the opening, passing no more than six feet from my front bumper as it raced by.

"Fancy ride," Gabe offered.

"Aston Martin," Jessica said, through clenched teeth. "That's Sidney's car."

"Sits on the road like a tiger," Gabe said.

"When he brought it home, I looked it up on the Internet. A bit over a million and a half."

Gabe whistled.

"You better get out," I said to her. "Things are about to get ugly."

She took a deep breath, folded her arms across her chest. "No," she said. "In for a penny, in for a pound. Let's go."

I started the car, dropped it into gear, and eased out of the leafy bower. By the time I got to the light at Greenwood, Sidney was two cars in front of me. I followed him up 145th, over Aurora, and through the woods to the I-5 freeway entrance.

In the movies, once we got to the freeway, the Aston Martin would put the pedal to the metal and leave the Tahoe in the dust. In reality, Seattle traffic was way too thick for any of that Hollywood crap. Even the HOV lane was bumper-to-bumper with Friday-night revelers. We were both tooling along at a fast and furious fifty-five.

I moved over into the center lane and followed at a respectful distance. Nobody said a word until Sidney took the on-ramp for the I-90 bridge.

"I'll be damned," Jessica said. "He's going to Issaquah." She clamped her arms over her chest. "I was telling myself you were wrong. That maybe he was going someplace else. That Sidney couldn't possibly be as much of a shit as you claimed he was . . . but . . ." She stopped herself. "That son of a bitch," she mumbled.

Traffic began to thin out after we rolled past Factoria. Sidney kept his rocket ship at a stolid sixty until we hit the Snoqualmie Falls exit, at which point he put his foot into it and shot away from us.

I fed the Tahoe some gas, got her up to a cheek-flapping eighty-five or so, but couldn't begin to keep pace with Sidney's million and a half bucks. So I stifled a curse, took it back down to the speed limit, and watched his taillights fade to pinpoints.

Six minutes later, we were at the exit. Another four and we pulled into the Tiger Mountain Lodge parking lot. I wheeled left and turned off the headlights. No sense giving them any advance warning. Jessica was the first to notice.

"Where's Sidney?" she asked.

No Aston Martin. No Sidney. Thinking he may have stealth-parked elsewhere in the parking lot, I crimped the wheel and took a full lap of the parking facilities. Half a dozen beater cars in the staff section, but otherwise nothing but unoccupied asphalt.

"We better get on with what we came here to do," Gabe said.

I swung the car left and then right, looping around curbs and islands, until we'd covered every nook and cranny in the lot and were back at the rear of Charlie's house.

I don't think Jessica Harrington fully appreciated the gravity of what was about to come down until I reached under my seat, pulled up the Smith & Wesson, and began to check it one last time. Her eyelids quivered at the sight of the gun. She looked over the seat as if hoping for a soothing word from Gabe, only to find Gabe checking the slide on that big, shiny automatic of theirs.

I looked up from my gun to find her staring at me in disbelief.

"You're not going to shoot anybody, are you?" she asked.

"Sure hope not."

"Don't plan on gettin' shot, though, neither," Gabe said from the back seat.

Gabe and I popped open our doors and stepped out into the night. The air was colder up here, and it had begun to spit rain. Beneath a thick ribbon of clouds, Tiger Mountain loomed above the lodge like an ogre.

Jessica Harrington hadn't budged. She was staring out through the windshield with a thousand-yard stare. A muscle in her cheek twitched rhythmically. I leaned back into the car. "Might be best if you stayed in the car," I said, holding out the keys to her. "Things get dicey, I don't want to have to keep track of what's going on with you."

She looked over at me as if she'd awakened on an alien planet and was trying to figure out where in the galaxy she was. She shook her head, like she was having an argument with herself. "Oh God," she huffed finally, as she grabbed the door handle and stepped out of the car.

I slid the Smith & Wesson into my belt at the small of my back, reached under the seat again, and found a crowbar I'd stashed earlier in the day.

"New crowbar?" Gabe inquired.

"Yeah," I said. "True Value Hardware. Cops got the other one."

"Shall we?"

"Indeed," I said.

We covered the forty yards to the back door on tiptoes. The rain had picked up, coming down now in a steady rush as we approached the back of the building, the hiss of falling water covering the sound of our advance as we slogged along.

Having had quite a bit of practice jimmying doors lately, I made short, silent work of the back door. I shifted the bar into my left hand and found the Smith & Wesson with my right. I leaned in close to Jessica. "Just stay out here until Gabe and I have things under control. One of us will come back and get you." I pressed the car keys into her hand. "Just in case things get hairy, you get the hell out of here."

She nodded.

"And if Sidney shows up, you better come inside and get one of us," I added.

She nodded again.

Since the door wasn't wide enough to accommodate both of us at once, Gabe gave me a big grin and stepped aside. "You first this time, big guy. I already had my annual melon mashing."

I pulled open the door and stepped inside of what was like an old-fashioned mudroom. Coats hanging on hooks. Shoes on the floor. Nobody home. Light glowing through a thick set of curtains. Gabe was glued to my back now as we shuffled forward in unison, parting the curtains with our shoulders as we soft-shoed into the next room.

Big modern kitchen. Lots of stainless steel and granite. Twenty feet across. Dark-haired guy, back to us, rinsing his hairy hands in the sink. He must have had some sort of Central European radar, because I didn't get more than three silent shuffles in his direction before he spun around and started reaching for his belt. There was no doubt. It was the shorter of the UPS guys.

I rushed him. I was close enough to smell his breath mints by the time he got the gun out, but not close enough to stop him from raising it. I lashed out with the crowbar, caught him flush on the wrist, heard the bone snap like a dry twig, and watched as the gun went bouncing across on the floor.

He let out a groan and cradled his arm, which was now hanging at an angle unknown to Mother Nature. Gabe stepped quickly around me and pressed the barrel of the big automatic into his forehead. Something about cold steel boring into your skull surmounts the need for verbal communication. A freeze-tag moment ensued. I kicked the Croatian's gun toward the far corner of the room.

The guy leaned back against the sink, rocking on the balls of his feet as he fondled his mangled arm and moaned. Gabe reached in a coat pocket, pulled out a handful of black plastic zip ties. "Get down," Gabe growled into the guy's ear. The guy began doing as he was told, dropping, one at a time, to his knees in front of the sink.

The noise the guy made when Gabe pulled his hands behind his back and fastened his broken arm to the other was truly piteous. His ebony eyes filmed over when Gabe pushed him over on his side.

Gabe rolled him onto his belly with his foot and then, keeping one knee planted in the middle of his back, fastened his ankles together. Then he zip-tied his ankles to his hands, leaving the guy trussed up like a calf in a rodeo roping contest. I grabbed a dish towel off the kitchen counter and stuffed it in his mouth. He started flopping around like a trout on a riverbank. I leaned down in his face.

"I hear any noise from you, I'm gonna come back in here and make you wish you'd shut the fuck up," I told him. He turned his face away from me and brought the noise down to a low moan.

"He's not going anywhere," Gabe assured.

I poked my head through the double swinging doors and looked around. What, these days, they call the great room. Big stone fireplace and a bunch of overstuffed leather furniture. Nothing whatsoever on the walls. No people. I could hear water running somewhere and took two tentative steps into the room. Above my head, a wide mezzanine ran the length of the space, with a freestanding metal staircase at either end. I was about to head for the set of stairs at the far end when the trussed-up guy's phone began to ring in his pocket. Gabe made a dive for him.

I eased the doors closed and watched as Gabe rifled his pockets, rolling him over and patting him down until the phone was located. Gabe's thick finger stabbed hard at the phone. The ringing stopped.

And then it started ringing again five seconds later. Gabe hung up again and hustled over to the only other door in the kitchen and pulled it open. A bathroom. From the doorway, Gabe lobbed the phone at the toilet and swished it, getting a satisfying plop as it hit the water and sank to the bottom of the commode.

Gabe had just turned a grin my way when the damn phone began to ring from underwater. Muted and a bit bubbly, but ringing nonetheless.

"Takes a flingin' and keeps on ringin'," Gabe stage-whispered.

I motioned out toward the great room with my head. Gabe got the message. We went through the doors together. I tiptoed the length of the room and then looked back at Gabe. We started up the stairs at opposite ends of the mezzanine.

Sounded like somebody was filling a bathtub upstairs. I kept moving up. At the other end of the room, one of the stairs objected and emitted a loud squeak. Gabe and I stopped. So did the running water. I heard the snick of a door latch opening, ducked down, and held my breath. The second UPS guy leaned out over the railing.

He saw me at the same moment I saw him and immediately pulled his head back from the bannister. With the element of surprise gone for good, both Gabe and I abandoned stealth and rushed up the stairs at flank speed. No sign of the guy, so I started kicking open doors, looking for Charlie.

I found him behind door number two. He was lying on his back in bed, his eyelids fluttering like hummingbirds. Out cold. I pulled up one of his sleeves. His arm had more holes than the Albert Hall. I reached down and put a couple of fingers on his carotid artery. His pulse was slow but steady. I was betting they kept him doped up most of the time so he was easier to deal with.

That was as far as I got with the speculating. The scrape of shoes behind me jerked my head around in time to catch sight of the second UPS brother working the slide on a nasty-looking 9 mm. He got it about up to knee level before Gabe piled into him from behind, sending him lurching forward, right up into my face. I hit him in the head with the crowbar. I watched his eyes roll in his head like a slot machine. The 9 mm went off when it hit the floor, plowing a jagged hole in the hardwood about six inches from my right foot. UPS went down in a heap and stayed there, his left foot twitching to some faraway music. Took us less than a minute to find the gun, pat him down, and truss him up.

I pointed down at the GPS monitor on Charlie's leg. "We've gotta get rid of that thing, or we could take him to the moon and they'd find us." I dropped the crowbar to the floor and hurried over to the bedside.

We hauled Charlie out of bed by the armpits, threw our shoulders under him, and waltzed him out of the room. The stairs were harder. The three of us were mashed together on the narrow stairway like an alcoholic tango troupe.

We one-stepped it to the ground floor. I've gotta admit that, at that point, I was feeling pretty good about things. The Croatians were under control. We had possession of Charlie. Things had gone about as well as we could have hoped.

As we backed through the swinging doors, dragging Charlie, I was preoccupied, still patting myself on the back for how easily things had gone and thinking about what kitchen utensil I could use to remove the GPS tracker from Charlie's ankle. So when the gun went off I damn near baked a load of brownies in my shorts.

Within the confines of the kitchen, the roar of the gun sounded like a howitzer. And then the operatic screaming started. A moment passed before another shot screamed through the swinging door, and the air was suddenly full of splintered wood. Gabe and I dropped Charlie and dove for the corners.

The impact of the round pushed the door all the way open. Croatian number one had somehow gotten his hands loose and managed to worm around the floor and find the gun. I cursed myself for not picking it up when I had the chance.

He raised the weapon and pointed it in our direction. I ducked my head back around the corner. Another round ripped through the doorway. I could hear his ragged breathing as he crawled around on the floor. The phone in the toilet began to ring again.

Bluuuuuurb. Bluuuuuurb. Bluuuuuurb. Bluuuuuurb.

"Pssst."

I looked over at Gabe. The big automatic was cocked and ready to go. "He's shootin' with his left hand," Gabe said. "You busted his gun hand. Give him something to shoot at. He gets up on his knees again, I'll put him out of his misery."

I shook my head. I wanted to come out of this without a corpse to explain away. I used my foot to push the door open again. Another round whistled through the doorway, smashing into the stone fireplace on the far side of the room. And then another, sending a spray of pulverized river rock into the air.

Much as I hated to admit it, Gabe was right. Something had to give. We couldn't afford to be pinned down for very long. Much as I didn't want to have to shoot the guy, everything else I could think of was worse.

"Okay," I whispered to Gabe. "But try not to kill him, if you can."

"Better him than one of us."

I nodded, stuck the Smith & Wesson back in my belt, got my feet under me, and then popped sideways into the open doorway, like one of those mechanical bears in an arcade shooting gallery. UPS number one was sitting on the floor clawing at the zip tie around his ankles. He caught sight of me in his peripheral vision, snatched the gun from the floor, humped up onto his knees, and pointed it my way. I pulled myself back behind the door frame a nanosecond before both guns went off at the same instant. The fireplace took another hit.

Gabe's round took him just below the left elbow, painting the far wall with a mist of blood and bone. UPS went all operatic again. The gun fell from his hand.

I was on him before he stopped screaming. Something about profanity transcends language. I didn't understand the words he was spewing into the air, but I was pretty certain it wasn't scripture. This time, first thing I did was pocket his 9 mm.

Gabe used the same dish towel I'd stuffed into UPS's mouth to bind the gaping hole in his arm, then looked over at me. "That's the best we can do for now. We can call 911 once we get out on the road."

"Let's went," I said.

Gabe and I were quick-stepping across the kitchen carrying Charlie when I looked up and caught sight of Jessica Harrington. And the gun pressed to the back of her head.

And Sidney Crossfield holding the gun.

"Put your weapons on the kitchen counter," Sidney said.

When neither of us complied, he threw Jessica to the floor and pointed the gun at her head. "Guns on the counter."

"No." When I looked over, Gabe was grinning at him.

"I'll kill her," Sidney snarled.

"Have at it, motherfucker," Gabe said, grinning wider. "You'll be dead before she hits the floor."

The disbelieving look on Jessica Harrington's face was priceless. If she'd had a dialogue bubble over her head, it would have read: "Hey, this isn't the way it's supposed to go."

It'll be quite a while before I stop asking myself what might have happened next, had things played out a little further. Whether we would have actually let him shoot her, rather than give up our weapons. I'd like to think not, but violent moments have a way of working out in strange, unanticipated ways. It's like Mike Tyson said: "Everybody has a plan until they get punched in the mouth."

Didn't really matter, though, because right at that life-defining moment, a large-caliber lead projectile hit Sidney Crossfield in the back of the head and then shattered the microwave oven a couple of feet to the right of Gabe.

When I looked up, the right upper quarter of Sidney's skull had gone missing. He staggered one step forward and began to drop. Even with his right eye and most of his medulla oblongata vaporized, his left eye managed to register surprise on its way to the floor.

Jessica Harrington looked like she was going into shock. Gabe and I each had Charlie in one hand and a gun in the other when Patricia Harrington stepped into the kitchen, with her driver, Thompson, in close attendance. In her bejeweled right hand was an enormous old British service revolver. A Webley, I thought.

She lifted the gun above her shoulder, pointing it straight up at the ceiling. Thompson took it from her hand, wiped it clean with an old-fashioned pocket handkerchief, and then refurbished the bulge under his left arm with it.

"We should call the cops," I said to nobody in particular.

"Thompson," was what she said.

He stepped around his employer and lifted Jessica from the floor. I guess after forty-seven years with somebody, you sort of automatically know what they want. We watched in silence as Thompson, with Jessica cradled in his arms, pushed his way through the curtains and disappeared.

Patricia Harrington started to leave. Stopped and turned around.

"I'll send an ambulance for Charles," she said.

I told her about the Homewood clinic and what we'd arranged for Charlie.

She set her jaw and nodded. "I'll instruct them to take him there," she said.

The phone in the toilet began to ring again. Nobody said a word until it stopped.

She raised her chin and fixed me with those blue eyes. "He was going to shoot my daughter," she said. "I had no choice." She thought for a moment. "And . . . yes, you should call the authorities. If they have any questions, they know where to find me."

The second Croat began to groan. The toilet phone started ringing again.

Patricia Harrington turned and walked away.

Gabe looked over at me. "Well . . . that went well, don't you think?"

I pulled out my phone and dialed 911.

■ ■ ■

When the announcement arrived in the mail I thought it was a joke. Then I realized it had to be Patricia Harrington. I mean, who else was gonna treat me and up to twenty guests to a night at the most expensive restaurant in the Pacific Northwest? The note said that all I had to do was call Canlis a week or so in advance, tell 'em when and how many, and they'd close the joint for the night and give us the royal treatment. Gratis, of course.

It undoubtedly says something about me that when it came time to sit down and make a list of who I was going to invite, I couldn't come up with anything like nineteen other people I wanted to have dinner with. That's when it came to me.

So you won't be thinking I'm completely nuts, I want you to know I did the best I could on my end. I rented a ten-seater van and took 'em all out and got 'em coiffed at HairMasters. Then dropped 'em off at the Y for showers before hauling them all down to K&D in Renton for some new duds. Rebecca had done much the same for the girls, so by the time we arrived at the restaurant that night, we didn't look half-bad. George, Ralph, Harold, Billy Bob Fung, Red Lopez, Heavy Duty

Judy, Large Marge, Frenchie, and Nearly Normal Norman marched into the joint like they were old, valued customers. Lots of brand-new shirts and ties and dresses that rustled like the wind. Rebecca and I and Eagen and Gabriella made up the rest of the guest list. I invited Joey Ortega, but like I figured he would, he begged off, so I invited the van driver to join us.

And I've got to admit, the restaurant staff was marvelous. Never batted an eye when we came marching in, and I assure you that, despite my best efforts, nobody was ever going to mistake this group for an itinerant accounting firm.

Life on the streets takes its toll. Baths, haircuts, soft lights, and a new suit of clothes can do only so much. Every form of refuge has its price.

Ralph wanted to start out with the oysters in a red-wine mignonette. George favored the Dungeness crab with bok choy and fermented ajoblanco. It went on and on. They were like gypsies in the palace. Perusing the wine list with the sommelier. Hooting and hollering, throwing napkins at one another. Everybody having something to say about what everybody else ordered. It was a sight to behold.

Wasn't till we were damn near two hours in that I noticed glances being pitched back and forth by the waiters. I'm pretty sure they'd never seen a group who could put booze down quite like these folks, but, to their credit, they swallowed hard and kept on pouring. I was betting they were gonna need an emergency liquor delivery first thing in the morning.

Dinner had been cleared away and dessert had just showed up when I leaned over and said to Eagen, "What are you hearing about Patricia Harrington and our late friend Sidney Crossfield?"

He wiped his mouth with his napkin and said, "Absolutely nothin'."

"Me neither. I checked the papers. The Internet. Not a peep."

"Story disappeared like Jimmy Hoffa," Gabe said around a mouthful of Japanese cheesecake.

Eagen chuckled. "We asked the court for a search warrant to go through Harrington Hall. You know . . . see if maybe the place wasn't wired for sound. They laughed in our faces. Her attorneys have got this thing cinched up tighter than a frog's ass."

Rebecca leaned in. "Sidney's remains didn't come through us either. I got a note from the attorney general to the effect that the family had made private arrangements. A very carefully worded butt-out message, if you read between the lines. Nobody's filed a death certificate either, at least nothing that can be found in public records."

"How long did the county mounties hold you and Cinderella for?" Eagen asked.

"Less than an hour," I said. "Never put either of us in a cell."

"With your history and Gabriella's rap sheet, I think it's safe to say you've got friends in high places." He took a sip of coffee. "What's going on with the kid?"

"The story that Charlie was autistic was just what Crossfield told people. He's got some brain damage from whatever he was injected with, but nothing to the extent that Crossfield claimed he had. They're saying he might be okay to go back home fairly soon."

"But nothing about who injected who and why or who killed the girl."

"They won't let us talk directly to the kid." Eagen made a disgusted face. "According to his attorneys, anyway, he doesn't remember anything before waking up in jail that night. Doesn't remember going up to the park. Doesn't know who injected him. Doesn't know a damn thing."

"You think that's true?" Rebecca asked.

Eagen shrugged. "We're never gonna know, is what I think. Whatever happened in the park that night went to the grave with Tracy Harrington. Looks to me like all we're gonna know is what Patricia Harrington and her lawyers want us to know."

"This thing's got more loose ends than a macramé project," Rebecca groused.

Eagen reached inside his suit jacket and came out with a folded piece of paper. He used his palms to flatten it on the tabletop and then handed it to me.

"What's this?" I asked before I looked down.

"A speeding ticket," he said. "Same night as your little adventure in Issaquah. Issued seventeen minutes before you called 911. Techs found it in Sidney's car. I spoke to the state trooper. He says Crossfield took a real long time to pull over, drove all over hill and dale before he complied, and then got real mouthy with him, threatened to get him fired . . . You know, the usual rich-guy shit . . . so the trooper took his sweet-ass time issuing the citation. Said Crossfield went completely red ass over how long it was taking."

I was way over my monthly cliché quota, so I didn't say anything about how I'd rather be lucky than good.

ABOUT THE AUTHOR

G.M. Ford is the author of nine other novels in the Leo Waterman series: *Who in Hell Is Wanda Fuca?*, *Cast in Stone*, *The Bum's Rush*, *Slow Burn*, *Last Ditch*, *The Deader the Better*, *Thicker Than Water*, *Chump Change*, and *Salvation Lake*. He has also penned the Frank Corso mystery series and the stand-alone thrillers *Threshold* and *Nameless Night*. He has been nominated for the Shamus, Anthony, and Lefty Awards, among others. He lives and writes in Seattle, Washington.